BORDERLESS

ALSO BY ELIOT PEPER

"True Blue" (A Short Story)
Neon Fever Dream
Cumulus

The Analog Series

Bandwidth

The Uncommon Series

Uncommon Stock: Exit Strategy
Uncommon Stock: Power Play
Uncommon Stock: Version 1.0

BORDERLESS

an Analog Novel by
ELIOT PEPER

47NORTH

Text copyright © 2018 by Eliot Peper
All rights reserved.

Published by 47North, Seattle

www.apub.com

Amazon, the Amazon logo, and 47North are trademarks of Amazon.com, Inc., or its affiliates.

ISBN-13: 9781503904729 (hardcover)
ISBN-10: 1503904725 (hardcover)
ISBN-13: 9781503904736 (paperback)
ISBN-10: 1503904733 (paperback)

Cover design by The Frontispiece

Printed in the United States of America

First edition

BORDERLESS

CHAPTER 1

Our secrets *define* us. Diana felt the truth of that in her gut. Secrets were the dark matter whose mysterious pull shaped people's grandest dreams, deepest fears, and sense of self. Unspoken truths inspired visceral passion and brought down entire nations. They were the crux upon which the world turned. Diana knew that the only material worth reading lay between the lines.

That was the reason there was no future for her and Dag. Or *a* reason anyway.

"Breakfast is served." He padded toward her with a lopsided grin, bare feet slapping on the bright tiles of the mosaic path that curled from the back door of the cottage to where she sat at the center of the greenhouse. She curled her own toes against the tile, remembering how her back had ached for days after laying the path under the hot sun of a Berkeley summer.

She had built the entire greenhouse herself, constructing the roof and walls to extend the lines of the cottage into a single rectangular structure that housed humans in the front and plants in the back. Spiraling tendrils of vine hung from the ceiling, rough trunks supported a verdant canopy, and dozens of blooming flowers formed islands of vibrant purple, saffron, and periwinkle against an ocean of green. Many specimens were souvenirs from clandestine missions, calling to mind dead drops under rattling metro tracks, games of cat-and-mouse with countersurveillance along Dutch canals, and that time she'd exfiltrated a blown agent out of the jungles of Mindanao—and later watched with quiet pride as he opened a small croissant bakery in Minneapolis. The humid air, filtered light, and sweet smell of freshly watered *Michelia champaca* grounded her, reminded her that this small corner of the universe was her domain.

Dag unloaded the heaping tray onto the table and sat across from her. The feast featured a steaming stack of buttermilk pancakes prepared with fresh milled grain, a small cask of grade A maple syrup, a French press brimming with fragrant coffee, a plate piled high with crispy bacon, and a bowl of seaside strawberries.

Diana sighed theatrically. "Monsieur, I'm walking a knife's edge between hungry and hangry. You know, outside the bedroom, it does pay to finish fast."

"My sincerest apologies, madame. Is discipline in order?"

"A flogging at the very least."

"Someone woke up in fine form."

"Did you just roll your eyes at me?"

"Never!"

She snorted and served them both, buttering up the pancakes and drizzling a generous amount of maple syrup on top. Dag might not be able to cook much else, but she couldn't deny that his pancakes were mouthwatering.

"Thank you," she said. "This looks delicious."

As they both tucked in, she studied the man who had somehow managed to sidle into her life. Since his abrupt retirement from high-stakes political lobbying a few years ago, Dag had let a short beard grow out to complement his floppy dark hair. A loose linen shirt hung across his shoulders. And there was something about his face, the lines around his eyes, that had softened. The desperation that had hovered just below the surface of his every move had faded to a chic worldliness. There was less of an edge to his gaze, fewer moments when the armor of ambition snapped into place.

His contentment drove her crazy.

Cynicism she could do. Fatalism, even. Her grandmother had lived that one to the fullest. But contentment? It was too assured, too passive. It left the scratch unitched, the question unanswered. For someone like Diana, who hunted, kept, and traded secrets for a living, it was anathema.

Couldn't she just be happy he was happy? She was. Of course she was. At the very least, he deserved a welcome respite after what he'd gone through. But then again, she wasn't. Her annoyance burned brighter because it was so patently unjustifiable. She resented herself for resenting him. It was a vicious cycle that she didn't know how to reverse.

As the stack of pancakes dwindled and the food coma set in, their conversation waned. Dag told her about the new series of drawings he was working on, sketches capturing the multiyear fire that had consumed all of Southern California. His enthusiasm for the project was ardent, fueled by guilt over how he'd helped others profit from the historic disaster. But Diana put her side of the conversation on practiced autopilot and surreptitiously scanned headlines on her feed.

Seasteaders were buying up distressed oil and gas assets, converting abandoned offshore drilling platforms into tiny sovereign communities. The acerbity of their overlong manifestos suggested that actually trying to live the libertarian ideal wasn't much fun after all. Disney was holding a press conference at their Singaporean headquarters, announcing a Star Wars reboot that would extend the franchise into a new trilogy of immersive feed dramas. Foreign policy forums still bristled with debate over the questionable legal basis for Commonwealth's terms of service update that had implemented a global carbon tax three years prior. Leading scientists pointed out that it was the first international regulatory effort that had actually resulted in declining emissions, enforcement guaranteed by the threat of losing access to the feed. But President

Lopez had harshly criticized the move in a recent interview, sparking renewed speculation that the US was preparing to take a firmer hand with the tech conglomerate that ran the feed.

In Diana's own feed, Lopez leaned forward in his chair to deliver a talking point, earnest and intense. The squat man with his conservative suit and thick gray hair invoked a host of conflicting memories for Diana. He was one of the few politicians who genuinely strived to make people's lives better rather than boost his own polling numbers. Sure, he had a healthy ego. That was guaranteed in every candidate who had ever stood for election. But Lopez had been steadfast in supporting evidence-based policy even when the tide of public opinion turned against him. If the ultimate judge of character was action taken under duress, Lopez wasn't all bad. He had served as vice president under Freeman until the heart attack that had resulted in the mother of all promotions. Years later, Lopez had campaigned and won a second term. He was the kind of leader Diana would have been proud to serve during her tenure at the CIA.

Too bad she knew more than she cared to admit about his ascent to power.

Diana couldn't see Lopez without thinking about Helen. Helen, who would have so much to say about Diana's present predicament. *Espionage requires sacrifice.* Her Southern accent had garnished the words like powdered sugar. *We are the shield that guards the innocent, the shadow passing in the night that allows others to sleep in peace. Within these walls, America is our only soul mate. Fuck who you like as long as it doesn't endanger the mission. Love if you can't help it. But trust? Never.* Helen, with her ready maxims and unflinching confidence. Helen, who had taken Diana under her wing when she emerged green and eager from covert-action training. Helen, who was the mistress of a secret history Diana could never quite escape.

Diana's stomach turned, the remains of the rich meal suddenly nauseating.

"Who knows? Maybe we could go off-grid, start over," Dag was saying. "Find a little beach town somewhere."

Diana grunted noncommittally.

"In the meantime, I was thinking we could drop by the nursery together today," said Dag, fingering the fiddlehead tip of a fern frond. "We can pick up some seeds and you can coach me. I've killed every plant I've ever tried to grow." He shrugged wryly. "I'm not going to earn a green thumb cooking pancakes."

"What? No." The words came out harsher than she had intended. She backpedaled. "I mean, don't you need to get back to your project? You said the La Jolla piece is almost done."

He had already taken her to bed, moved into her home, invaded her life. Wasn't that enough? The greenhouse, the garden, the plants, they were hers.

Hers.

Instinctively she summoned her feed to check soil humidity, pest density, nitrogen levels, temperature, and environmental stressors. Nothing out of the ordinary range. Her wards were thriving.

"Sure, but we've still got time this morning." Dag grinned. "Wouldn't you like to have an assistant for the yard work? Like a sous chef but with dirty fingernails?"

She stood abruptly, the chair legs scraping against tile.

"I have to go," she said, fighting to keep the strain out of her voice.

"Is everything okay?" His concern was as sweet and sickening as the syrup-smeared plates.

Before she could say something she'd later regret, Diana strode up the path and through the back door into the cottage. The kitchen was covered in the evidence of Dag's industry, cast-iron pan filled with bacon grease, griddle speckled with little blobs of batter, sink full of dirty dishes. Her handsome and generous boyfriend had prepared her a beautiful brunch. The least she could do was help tidy things up. But she kept moving, self-reproach at abandoning the mess quickening her stride. She pulled on boots and headed for the front door, passing Dag's drafting table on which a half-finished sketch was mounted.

This was her home. Her sanctuary. There was a good reason she had never brought clients here, or anybody aside from the occasional plumber. Now there wasn't an inch of the place that wasn't contaminated by Dag's presence.

Stupid. Spies didn't have real relationships. Spies didn't deserve real relationships.

Closing the front door behind her, she set off along the sidewalk at a brisk pace. The fresh air and sunshine began to calm her frayed nerves. Oaks, redwoods, and craggy outcrops of igneous, metamorphic, and sedimentary rock peppered the yards of her North Berkeley neighbors. Tectonic uplift, volcanic activity, and the Hayward Fault combined to make the East Bay a geological melting pot, and the dramatic features helped it earn a reputation as a gardeners' paradise. She could glimpse the bay through gaps between the picturesque period houses. Onshore wind kicked up tufts of white on the swell. Across the water, a complex system of marine walls and levies protected the soaring graphene skyscrapers of Commonwealth's headquarters in San Francisco from rising sea levels.

Exile from DC had its perks.

Diana took a deep breath. It wasn't Dag's fault. She was being unfair to him, displacing aggression, lashing out. Worse, losing control like that was *unprofessional*. Helen would have chewed her out to hell and back. But fuck Helen. Diana hadn't had a real puzzle to sink her teeth into for too long. That was it. She was wound up tight, energy fizzing and sparking inside her. She needed an outlet.

She needed a *mission*.

Summoning her feed, she began cycling through her secure caches. It was hopeless. Her current stable of clients was always trying to buy her time, but there were only so many mistresses she could unveil, cryptographic keys she could pilfer, disinformation campaigns she could execute, and competitive negotiations she could penetrate before Diana wound up stuck in a rut. During her most recent gig, the assigned intermediary in Santiago hadn't even attempted a surveillance detection route before their meeting in Parque Forestal. She shook her head. Once you ran Langley's gamut, freelancing was a demotion to the minor leagues. Busywork, no matter how lucrative, wasn't going to cut it. She wanted something really interesting, or at least something new.

Once you acquired a taste for secrets, nothing else could satisfy.

Ping.

An inbound meeting request surfaced in one of her caches. New client, claiming referral from a Bogotá-based financial investigator she'd met a few years prior while working a money-laundering case. They wanted to brief her ASAP. If people got to the point of approaching her with a project, the schedule was always ASAP.

But what the hell, it was new blood. And if her instincts hadn't entirely deserted her, some of it might already be in the water.

CHAPTER 2

Diana had always liked the way Analog stood apart from the surrounding buildings. Unlike the glistening superstructures or meticulously maintained Victorians that defined the San Francisco aesthetic, the club was the kind of postindustrial stronghold a Viking might build if transported to the present. The hulking black building seemed to absorb all the light unlucky enough to touch it. Bouncers blocked the massive wooden doors, arms crossed and suits straining to contain overdeveloped biceps and deltoids. The name was spelled out in wrought iron above their shaved heads. The place glowered out at the city with self-conscious insolence.

The fact that Haruki wanted to meet here meant one of two things. Either this was such a sensitive mandate that it required a high level of paranoid tradecraft, or he was so enamored with the prospect of a covert operation that he had mined obscure forums, geeked out on espionage dramas, and couldn't wait to play the part. Either way, she wasn't going to take any chances.

It hadn't been hard to trace the supposedly anonymous address from which he'd posted in her secure cache. Once she'd cracked it, it was even easier to link it to Haruki's public identity on the feed. Then it was just a matter of connecting the dots to his employer, interests, and associations. She aggregated, indexed, and cross-referenced his public data. Pictures of Haruki danced around her field of vision alongside his résumé, tagged posts, group affiliations, demographic profile, music preferences, social graph, and some indiscreet footage indicating a penchant for experimenting with psychedelics. This guy lived on-grid, which could mean a lot or a little. Truth was always the best cover.

"Gerald, Sam, you're looking sufficiently intimidating today." Lightning quick, Diana poked both bouncers in their bellies as she stepped between their bulky frames.

The men guffawed, and Sam leaned over to open the door for her.

"Aww, come on, D," said Gerald. "You're ruining the effect."

"Even mighty warriors have to relax sometimes," she said. "Stop taking yourselves so seriously."

"People taking us seriously is our entire job."

"Then you need to do a better one, cuz I don't."

"I could toss you out of this joint with my pinkie."

"Oho, I'd like to see you try." She balled her fists and hopped around like a boxer as she backed through the doorway. "Show me what you got." Despite their opaque aviator sunglasses, she knew their eyes were rolling as the heavy door swung shut.

"Harassing the staff again?" said a cool voice.

Diana turned. "Nell," she said. "What the fuck? How is it that you look so damn stunning every single time I see you? It's like you have no regard for us regular humans who have mediocre genes, appalling style, and wake up with bedhead. Really it's just rude how gorgeous you are."

"Always with the sweet talk." Nell shook her head, but her pale-gray eyes twinkled, and the corner of her mouth quirked to reveal perfect white teeth. With her pageboy haircut, smooth dark skin, and impeccably cut black dress, she could be the envy of any feed fashion star. A small pin featuring a retro air force insignia was fastened over her heart, and knee-high suede boots completed an aesthetic that was sophisticated and idiosyncratic. "It's good to see you."

Nell stood behind a polished wooden podium that was the anteroom's main feature. A slim vase held a bouquet of lilies of the valley, their delicate white blossoms hanging like tiny bells off bright-green stems. Behind Nell, plush red satin curtains separated them from the club proper.

"Likewise," said Diana. "How are the girls?"

"Jorani's going through a bit of a manga phase, but they're good otherwise."

"Can't blame her. Manga's the shit. I knew she had good taste."

Nell harrumphed. "Want me to show you in?"

"Nah," said Diana. "I can handle the disconnect."

"Go on then, lovely."

Diana slipped through the curtains and into the room beyond, savoring the rich texture of the fabric. Analog was enormous. Bow-tied bartenders tossed cocktail shakers behind a wide wooden bar that ran along the entire left wall, countless rare liquors filling the shelves that rose behind them. Booths lined the opposite wall, which was covered in medieval tapestries depicting epic battles, fabulous monsters, and scenes of royal grandeur. In a far corner, a jazz trio worked their way through the standards, the vocalist riffing up and down scales in a haunting series of nonsense syllables. It smelled of honey, leather, and paraffin, the latter emanating from the oil lamps hanging from the high ceiling on slender chains, filling the space with warm, flickering light.

Despite her nonchalance with Nell, Diana knew she needed to give herself a moment to adjust. No matter how many times she visited, it was still disorienting.

Silence.

Profound, disturbing silence that the music did nothing to dispel. No more photos of Haruki. No more neatly correlated logs. No more analytical overlays. Her entire dossier on the man, every digital breadcrumb of his personal history, had vanished.

But that was only the beginning.

Diana's feed had disappeared. It was the umbilical cord linking her to the buzzing global hive mind, the forum for every strand of cultural conversation, the source of all knowledge, the venue for endless entertainment, the information infrastructure upon which the world was built. Gone. Gone so completely that it might never have existed. She couldn't access the refractive index of her greenhouse panels, the contents of her secure caches, the Bulgarian folk playlist she'd assembled, the messages in her queue, or the local weather forecast. She was beyond the reach of the familiar cascade of updates and notifications. The steady hum of chatter that dissected every possible angle of any topic or story was abruptly cut off. The inevitable raging controversy over the twice-delayed release of Malignant Kernel's new album was as inaccessible as the pundits sparring over President Lopez's next move.

The world was both naked and obscure, shorn of the layers of metadata that made its mysteries legible. She was banished from the digital universe, its ever-present symphony of data reduced to a pervasive and unsettling quiet. The severed connection was a phantom limb, its absence leaving her aching for access.

Diana took a breath. Then another one, letting the jazz, muted laughter, and clinking of glasses wash over her. This respite from the feed was what Analog veterans treasured above all else, while virgins often needed Nell's guiding hand on their arm just to make it to their seats.

Trying to embrace the information drought, Diana threaded through the tables that filled the space. As always, Analog was busy. Patrons ate, drank, and gabbed. She overheard an entrepreneur pitching a venture capitalist on a new synthetic biology pathway, a pair of old women arguing over a game of go, and a small group of stand-up comedians regaling each other with rough-cut jokes.

This was a place you came to get away from the public eye. That made it a magnet for the rich and powerful as well as those whose intentions were especially sensitive. Over the decades, the club's reputation had acquired the sheen of mythology. Diana had heard through the grapevine that Ting-Ting Kuo, the legendary Taiwanese National Security Bureau chief of US operations, had run agents from here while sipping on rhum agricole, running FBI countersurveillance teams in circles. Gossip columnists claimed Lewis Parfit had announced his intention to divorce Sebastian Knight in one of these booths, setting off a socialite quake that had shaken celebrity culture to its foundations from Addis Ababa to Seoul. It was here that Huian Li had been struck with the inspiration to found Cumulus. William Gibson had spent three weeks holed up in a corner working on a novel, refusing to leave until he completed the rough draft of what would become the defining masterpiece of his literary career. Entrepreneurs, poets, technologists, politicians, scientists, builders, and dreamers flocked like starlings. The rumor mill never stopped churning. Famously, only a single person had ever made it in and out of Analog with an electronic recording device intact. Lynn Chevalier, the legendary investigative reporter, had used the incendiary audio to expose Vince Lepardis.

Diana thought about Chevalier every time she visited Analog. How had the woman done it? Even with the benefit of hindsight, nobody could figure it out. Journalism and espionage were sister professions. The only difference was that when they got their hands on something juicy, reporters ran wild like exhibitionists at the Folsom Street Fair while spies filed it away as leverage. When had appealing to the public interest really changed anything? Diana held pros like Chevalier in the highest esteem, right up to the point of publication.

Finally Diana reached the far side of the long hall where a magnificent fire roared in a hearth the size of an ox. She took care not to look too deeply into the heart of the dancing flames. They could conjure dark memories far too easily. Instead, she knelt to greet the three vizslas curled up on the thick Persian rug. The regal dogs lifted their heads, their golden eyes clear and intense.

"Hey, guys, it's been a while."

Waves of heat poured over her as she took turns scratching the dogs behind the ears. Up close she could see the strands of gray in their copper coats. One lifted a leg so she could rub his soft pink belly.

"I brought you something."

They perked up with surprisingly human expressions of anticipation as she slid three pieces of bison jerky from a pocket.

"Don't tell anyone, okay?" she stage-whispered as she fed them.

They responded with rough licks and wagging tails, which she took as confirmation.

"All right, fellas, enjoy your fire."

Rising, she made her way to her favorite booth. It was the last one against the wall in the corner closest to the fire. From here she could see the entire club and keep an eye on anyone coming in or out.

No surprises.

An enormous scarlet cocktail topped with a mountain of garnishes sat sweating in the middle of the table. A Caesar. Diana blew a kiss to Virginia, who saluted her from behind the bar. Sliding in, she took a sip and savored the powerful mix of house-distilled gin and Clamato. There were hints of basil and even a touch of passion fruit.

That was the beauty of disconnection. Without the feed, everything was more sensual, more *real*. Analog should rent rooms by the hour. Sex here would be better than even the best pharmaceutically enhanced orgy.

But Diana wasn't here for fun.

Across the club, the red satin curtains parted, and Nell led in a newcomer by the arm. The pair paused, giving the man time to adjust. Nell shot Diana a look, telling her what she already knew.

Haruki.

It was time to find out what this job was really about.

CHAPTER 3

"We need you to look into Commonwealth," said Haruki, dark eyes intent.

With his tailored suit, intelligent face, coiffed hair, and air of supreme confidence, there was something about Haruki that reminded Diana of Dag. Or Dag before his initiation at commando camp in Namibia. Before she and the other instructors ground him and his fellow participants down until their egos fell away like chaff from wheat.

Dag. All of a sudden, she realized she hadn't spared him so much as a thought since getting called to this meeting. Instead, she'd spent the intervening two days tracking down the anonymous sender who'd posted to her cache. Dag was probably consumed in one of his epic illustration sessions right now, totally immersed in the act of conjuring new worlds with nothing but graphite and paper. A fresh sense of affection surfaced within her. The avocado sapling in the front yard had benefited from a certain amount of benign neglect. Fussing over it too much yielded nothing but wilting foliage. Only when she left it alone for a while had it perked up. Maybe relationships could be the same way.

Speaking of relationships, she needed to make sense of Haruki.

"Okay," she said.

He looked nonplussed, then rallied.

"Yes, well," he said, "we need to dig deeper than the public data that analysts have access to. What's really going on inside the boardroom? What initiatives are they considering that haven't been announced yet? What's the political hierarchy within the executive team? How are they going to respond to President Lopez's comments? Do they have plans to make additional changes to their terms of service? Why are they doing what they're doing, and what are they going to do next? That kind of thing."

Her ploy had worked. Like so many elite strivers, he was the kind of person who wanted to fill silence. Diana loved people like that.

"I see," she said, keeping her expression neutral.

He tried not to squirm.

"So that's why we're here, you know?" he said, raising his chin to indicate Analog. "Outside the feed. Off-grid."

"Are you concerned about feed infosec? Do you have reason to suspect Commonwealth might be tapping our communications?"

"No, no, no." He shook his head. "Of course not. We just want to do things right. I'm sure you understand."

"Why?" she asked.

"What?"

"Why? Why are you trying to get inside info on Commonwealth? Are you a competitor?"

Some of the confidence returned, and he smiled tightly.

"Look," he said conspiratorially. "Obviously this is sensitive stuff, and we'd like to keep everything confidential. The less you know, the better, right?"

Diana slid out of the booth and stood.

"It's been a pleasure, Mr. Abe," she said, reaching down to slug the dregs of her Caesar. "Actually it's been rather dull. But you can't win 'em all, right? I'd say see you around, but I don't believe in coincidences."

"Wait." He looked around, incredulous. "What are you doing? Are you leaving?"

"Mr. Abe." Diana splayed both palms on the table and leaned down so that her nose was inches away from his. "I flew over from an op in Nay Pyi Taw specifically for this meeting." She hadn't, of course, but he didn't know that. "I did that because Jorge apparently thinks highly enough of you to direct you to one of my caches and let you drop his name. Based on this meeting, I plan to delete that particular cache and stop taking referrals from Jorge." With these hot-shit types, you needed to put them in their place. If you didn't, they'd get cranky later. Client work was all about up-management. When she left the CIA, Diana had hoped that the private sector would live up to its rhetoric of relentless efficiency and innovative leadership. It turned out to simply favor a perkier flavor of bullcrap. "I ought to thank you. You wasted my time, but you're simplifying my life."

"Stop. Look, I'm sorry." The words were tumbling out. "Just sit back down, okay? I'll give you all the background you want, all right? Listen."

She could see the gears turning in his head, could imagine the boss who was going to harangue him for dropping the ball, the bonus that suddenly looked a lot less like a sure thing. People could be so predictable.

She straightened up, not breaking eye contact.

"We'll double your fee," he said, quieter this time, almost plaintive.

"I'm a professional," she said. "And professionals need better reasons than money."

"Okay, I get it," he said. "We'll triple the fee. Not to sweeten the pot, just to pay it forward. Lay the groundwork for a constructive working relationship. And I'll explain our reasons. Just sit. Please."

He still hadn't noticed that she'd dropped his last name, which he hadn't used when introducing himself. She glanced over at the dogs. They'd noticed when he joined her in the booth but had returned to intermittent napping immediately. It was hard to beat canine judgment for first impressions. Another reason she always took the table nearest the fire.

Enough. She slid back into the booth.

"You ordered a martini." She nodded at his glass. "A *martini*. This isn't an old-timey James Bond movie. That kind of shit makes you look like a fool."

At least he had the decency to blush. Not a bad kid, just a little overexcited. Well, she had her answer as to why they were here. Aspirational espionage. She could imagine Helen's sneer. Maybe Diana should have brought an explosive pen just to spice things up.

"Now," she said, "explain."

"Okay, listen," he said. "I work for Hoffman and Associates. We're a global private-investigation firm. We worked a corruption case down in Colombia a while back. That's how I know Jorge."

All of which she already knew, of course. But it was good to hear him say it. The easiest way to catch someone cheating was by knowing what cards they held. The fact that he worked for Hoffman fit. Folks who joined PI firms often had bad cases of spy-envy, especially when they discovered that asset tracing, litigation, and due diligence often consisted of little more than doing other people's homework for them.

At least her little scene had greased the wheels on this conversation. She spun an index finger in the air.

"Go on," she said.

CHAPTER 4

Blood pounded in Diana's ears as she ducked under a low-hanging manzanita branch to follow Sofia's bouncing ponytail up the trail. Blinking away sweat, Diana tried to ignore the steady burn in her thighs and focused on regulating her breath. Apparently she wasn't in as good shape as she had thought she was. On the other hand, Sofia was a maniac, running marathon after marathon in her spare time as if being a rockstar network engineer wasn't enough. No wonder Diana was struggling to keep up.

Ahead, Sofia cleared a root and emerged onto a wider section of trail. The view opened up too, meadows falling away toward the Pacific Ocean on their left. Purple needlegrass, Idaho fescue, blue wild rye, and numerous other perennial grasses carpeted slopes that were scattered with glassy green outcrops of serpentine.

Diana loved it here. The greenhouse was a way for her to capture and cultivate a tiny sliver of wilderness, bring nature into her home, into her life. But these hills inspired an altogether different sense of wonder. There weren't many areas left with the deep root systems necessary to support these wide swaths of native grasslands. The onslaught of climate change, farming, development, and invasive species had taken its toll. But with its diverse microclimates and decades of careful stewardship,

Mount Tam was a bastion of biodiversity in what sometimes felt like a dying world.

Diana accelerated so they could run abreast.

"It's been a while since we ran together," said Sofia. Her Italian accent immediately marked her as a refugee, but Diana thought that the long vowels and singsong rhythm of her words turned English into a husky lullaby.

Diana puffed up her cheeks and opened her eyes wide in exaggerated distress. "And it'll be even longer until the next time, if I manage to survive this Navy SEAL attrition exercise. Are you joining the Olympic team or something?"

Sofia's laugh started as a bark and ended as a tinkle. "Not quite," she said. "But I'm signed up for an ultra up in British Columbia later this year."

"You're a masochist! Is there a zombie apocalypse coming that you haven't told me about? What on earth are you running from?"

Sofia shot her a look. She was smirking, but there were shadows behind her large eyes. Reflected in them, Diana could see the streets of Rome burning, the infamous sacking of the Vatican, and the shattered families of her hometown near the French border. Sofia would never again taste the white truffles, hazelnuts, and Barbaresco once consumed in such quantities at the annual *Fiera Internazionale del Tartufo Bianco d'Alba*. Today Alba was just another line item in the curriculum of high school history classes, one of thousands of towns destroyed in the slow-motion collapse of the European Union.

It reminded Diana of her own grandmother's potent silences, stand-ins for untold atrocities and acts of desperate heroism. Diana's confused, disturbing memories from early childhood were little better than a cheap kaleidoscope. Looking up at the crumbling stone walls of the ancient Tsarevets fortress, the sweet-and-sour taste of *kiselo mlyako*, the incomprehensible but palpable fear shimmering off the adults around her as they boarded a smuggler's boat in the early hours of the morning. Bulgaria had fallen years before Italy, but the tragedies of war were universal.

It was that hard kernel of loss that had kept Diana and Sofia connected over the years since they first met in a dusty, crowded refugee camp outside of Marseille. That shared sense of being uprooted, of yearning for something fading into the mists of time, of needing to escape the inescapable.

What was Sofia running from? The same thing Diana was.

The trail turned in toward the mountain, adjacent ridges wrapping them in a tight embrace. Majestic redwoods stood guard over the creek that had carved out this wash. As Sofia and Diana crossed into the shade, the temperature dropped ten degrees. It was as if they had been transported into a new world. Rare Methuselah's beard lichen hung from branches in wispy, ghostlike tufts. The rough auburn bark and soft forest floor muffled the sounds of their footfalls. This was a place where spirits might reside, where secrets could be confided.

Neither the grove nor the timing of Diana's seemingly innocuous question had been accidents. In the quest for human intelligence, anything and everything could be a tool.

"So how are things at work?" asked Diana.

"Oh, I'm sure you can guess," said Sofia. "It's crazy, as always. Herding cats."

"Yeah? What's the current flavor of crisis? They seem to have you moving from one to the next."

And because Sofia was smart and had the honed instincts of a survivor, she shot Diana another, sharper, look.

"You know what Commonwealth is like," said Sofia. "Ironclad NDAs and all that. My lips are sealed with the nastiest draconian terms our lawyers can dream up. Slipups earn an eternity of fire and brimstone. They're worse than the pope. It's irritating not being able to talk about projects with people. But what can I do?"

"I guess that's the price you pay for providing the world's information infrastructure, right?"

Sofia had landed a job at Commonwealth after immigrating to America years before. She had rocketed up the corporate hierarchy, leveraging her facility with maths and biological systems to help orchestrate the trillions of interlocking networks that constituted the feed.

"It seems so." Sofia shrugged. "Sometimes I think they take it too far. But maybe that's why I'm an engineer and not an attorney."

"Better to build things than to sit around arguing about them."

Sofia laughed her distinctive laugh. "It's amazing how many words they use to say so few things."

Diana let the conversation hang for a beat. A hawk screamed far above their heads. Their shoes squeaked on the rocky path. The creek burbled down into the unseen valley below them. It smelled of sweat and forest.

"Friends can share things others can't," said Diana. "We can tell each other anything, when we know it'll be kept between us, right?"

Sofia didn't respond, just stared ahead as her legs churned beneath her. Diana admired her runner's physique, hidden by nothing more than shorts and a sports bra, sculpted by countless miles. Sofia had clawed her way over countless obstacles, never content to let herself be labeled a victim.

"Sofia," said Diana. "I'm asking you for a favor."

And there it was.

The request that could not be denied.

The world had turned its back on the hordes of refugees fleeing war-torn Europe. Fearing they would be overrun by traumatized outsiders, other countries had buttoned down their immigration policies and militarized their borders. Europe's own troubled history with immigration helped commentators rationalize the callous reactionary measures.

Led by her indomitable grandmother and after a series of trials and tribulations Diana could only half remember, her family had made it to the United States from Bulgaria many years before the crackdown. By the time Sofia's family tried to find their own way to friendlier shores, they had found themselves banished by bureaucratic indifference to die in war zones or survive refugee camps. But that was when Diana had been fresh out of Langley, dispatched with Helen's blessing and whatever favors she could requisition from Uncle Sam to continue to whisper secrets in his ear.

Unlike so many of those born into the privilege, Diana and Sofia knew that the American dream was real. For them, it wasn't some abstract idea of freedom, a marketing gimmick, or a sacrosanct Constitution. No. It was a ticket out of hell and a shred of hope for the hopeless. American authority had waned since its heyday as the world's only superpower, but the United States was still the only place where starting a new life from scratch wasn't just possible but normal to the point of being boring. Even though Congress was a deadlocked mess and rhetoric was viciously divisive, against all logic, America still believed it could make the world a better place. Americans still maintained faith in their ability to forge their own destiny, realize their wild and often misguided dreams. That faith, that belief, was the only active ingredient that real change required. That's why her grandmother had sacrificed so much to get Diana's family into the country.

And that's why Diana, with a blank check from a black budget, used her position as a case officer to offer asylum to people like Sofia. Diana was Moses, parting red tape as easily as the Red Sea. To a family fleeing the devastation of a town like Alba, there was no greater gift you could give. As the world became more callous to the barbarity that filled the feed during those long years, the value of Diana's intercession swelled. She was the guardian angel of their personal American dream.

And when the debt came due, Sofia would pay.

"What do you want to know?" asked Sofia.

The resignation in her voice was a hollow victory.

Even as Diana asked her questions, she had to hold back tears.

CHAPTER 5

Diana strolled along the crown of the levee that protected West Potomac Park from the rising waters of its namesake. As sea levels inched ever higher, people either abandoned low-lying cities after suffering storm surge after storm surge or went to extraordinary lengths and ever more expense to engineer safety measures. Washington, DC, would be a literal swamp without expensive Dutch hydrology firms, whose stock prices soared in concert with sea levels.

She had spent a few years stationed in Amsterdam, the Netherlands being one of the few nations to have survived the dissolution of the EU intact. The weird little country had always found a way to thrive on the edges of things, never big or powerful enough to have much gravity of its own. So the Dutch had cultivated an internationalist agenda that paired nicely with their age-old status as a world financial hub. Because their tiny nation was so exposed to the risks of climate change, they had become far and away the experts in finding ways to adapt. Ever pragmatic, they lost no time marketing that expertise to the world after securing their own home.

Amsterdam had been exciting. Diana would sip cappuccinos and nibble on fresh apple cake while probing members of the diplomatic corps for clues as to what their bosses might do next. She would sneak out for occasional excursions into the wasteland of what used to be

Germany, nominally in search of intel but really just seeking a thrill. Remembering her time in the Netherlands, so often the little things stuck with her even when the details of grand operations faded. The buttery taste of raw herring fresh from a street vendor. The colorful narrow buildings crowding the banks of the canals. The angled bike-lane wastebaskets designed so that cyclists needn't slow down to toss their trash. Holland delighted in its idiosyncrasies.

Diana knelt, scooping up a handful of the gravel that lined the path running along the crown of the levee. The hard little rocks bit into her palms, calling her back to the present.

Cars sped along Independence Avenue, weaving around each other on routes choreographed via feed, whisking staffers and lobbyists among the political dens of the capital. The White House was only a few blocks away. When she had first been summoned to the Oval Office as a budding spook, the rooms and hallways of the legendary building had seemed so much smaller than the feed dramas depicted. She could picture Lopez debating with his cabinet or maybe enjoying a rare moment of quiet between meetings. Then the hair rose on the back of her neck. If Lopez was in the Oval, Helen wouldn't be far away. Diana needed to keep a low profile while she was here. Far be it from her to disturb the hornets' nest.

Turning, she tossed the handful of gravel out into the sleepy waters of the Potomac. The pieces spread out as they arced through the air, creating a long ellipse of small splashes when they hit the surface. She had built a life here. She had been in the center of things. But when everything began to splinter apart, sometimes the center didn't hold. Diana's dangerous combination of curiosity and principles had thrown her out of orbit. By rights she ought to be rotting in a shallow grave by now. Maybe she should have picked up more of that Dutch pragmatism. On the other hand, was a pragmatism that had once rationalized financing the transatlantic slave trade worth cultivating?

Her feed alerted her that Kendrick was approaching.

Diana composed herself, pushing away the dull ache of resentment. There was work to do.

She called up the updated profile she'd assembled on Kendrick. He'd been busy since they last saw each other. Rising through the ranks at the SEC, he had recently transitioned from regulating financial services to tech and was now tasked with overseeing the behavior of the world's largest conglomerate, Commonwealth.

Kendrick was a big man with a quiet demeanor. He was dressed in a DC-issue suit and approached her with his characteristic rolling gait, trying not to scuff his shoes on the gravel.

"Diana." He wrapped her in a bear hug. "It's been too long."

"Kendrick," she said, her voice muffled by his shoulder. "You're taller than I remember."

He laughed, releasing her and looking her up and down.

"Damn," he said. "Remember the dives we used to haunt around here? I'm telling you, they're all gone, every last one. Freaky Pete's, Saddleback, Neumonon. All just poof." He mimed an explosion. "Now there are just fancy cocktail bars and dumpling joints."

"I could never figure out how Pete stayed in business with beer that cheap."

Kendrick shrugged. "Well, I guess he didn't. Or maybe he got tired of listening to everyone gripe as he polished the glasses. Oh man, that rag of his was foul."

"I swear he used it to wipe a bedpan."

Kendrick made a face. "Eck. Yeah."

"But I'm guessing you probably don't pull too many all-nighters anymore, with the little one."

Kendrick puffed out his chest. "Oh, I'm a model of paternal responsibility."

"I can only imagine."

He smiled with obvious affection. "Dena's a handful, for sure. But at least Rob and I have each other to lean on. Here, see for yourself."

He opened a shared feed and populated it with images and video clips. A toddler struggling up a set of carpeted stairs. The two proud fathers singing her "Happy Birthday." A golden retriever smothering her with kisses.

"You have a *dog*?" asked Diana.

"I know, I know," said Kendrick. "You know me, I'm a cat person, just like anyone with an ounce of class. But Rob just adores the dumb beast. And if I'm perfectly honest, it's starting to rub off on me."

Diana shook her head in mock disbelief.

"Kendrick, I know we haven't caught up in a while. I mean, a husband, a kid, I get it. But a dog? This is a whole 'nother level."

"Weird, I know," he said wryly. "Sometimes life just throws you a curveball."

"Well, hopefully *some* things haven't changed." Diana reached inside her jacket and pulled out a pack of neatly wrapped joints. "I brought you some legit California kush. They're from one of the fancy-pants markets in San Francisco. The curator said this was the best single-origin organic harvest he's had in this year. Apparently the terroir is magnificent. His words."

"Wow," said Kendrick, carefully examining the packaging and shaking out a joint. "Fancy-pants indeed. Shall we?"

"We shall."

Kendrick lit the joint, and they walked side by side up the levee, smoke tracing rococo curls out over the swollen river. Kendrick's domestic bliss highlighted Diana's domestic friction. She was proud of Dag for building a new life as an artist. But the public profile such a career implied made Diana want to fade into the background, and she was careful to avoid meeting Dag's agent, friends, or colleagues to protect the privacy her own career required. And that was just one of many tremors set off by the fault line of her love. She could neither imagine life without Dag nor a future with him. She fled into her work, into her feed, into realms she could more easily control. Less fight-or-flight than fight-and-flight. Now that she was on the other side of the country, she missed the sound of Dag's voice, his scratchy beard, the mildly dazed look he had when emerging from the flow state of sketching. But proximity would inevitably slip an off-key note into her affection, until the dissonance overwhelmed the joy and she made her next escape. Love was beauty and pain and profound confusion.

As the warm cannabis buzz buoyed them, Kendrick shot her a knowing smile.

"So," he said, "I'm assuming this isn't a purely social call."

Diana reeled herself in. "Are you familiar with Leviathan Partners?"

He frowned. "The hedge fund?"

"The very same."

"Sure," he said. "They specialize in high-profile shorts. When they find a company with a dirty secret, they bet against the company's stock and drag the skeleton out of the closet." He snapped his fingers. "Remember DysoTech? They released blockbuster drug after blockbuster drug until Leviathan found an inside source who revealed the company had been doing unsanctioned testing on displaced communities in Bangladesh. When the stock tanked, Leviathan made a fortune."

Diana nodded. That fit.

The bigger picture was starting to come into focus. A memory swept through her. The smell of fresh tobacco and sizzling burgers as Helen rolled an impossibly slim cigarette in their booth at Mauricio's. Diana sitting there, fidgeting, desperate to find new opportunities to impress her. Helen's baby-blue eyes flicking up as her quick fingers sealed the slender cylinder. *Step one of any op,* the older woman had said, *is to figure out who the principals are and what they want.* Her voice was always so light, so sweet, the dulcet tones belying the heavy implications of her words. *Until you've sorted that out, nothing else matters.* Diana had failed to follow that advice only once, and it had cost her everything. She wouldn't make the same mistake again.

Haruki was obviously a cutout. His cover story of needing whatever intel she could dredge up for an industry white paper on Commonwealth didn't justify the size of his budget. He had been far too generous to be credible. Plus, Haruki was amateur enough to be disposable if things went south. She had found feed footage of him drinking coffee with a Leviathan partner shortly after she had met him at Analog. If they were shorting Commonwealth, having her poke around in the company's dirty laundry made sense. They must suspect there was something damning hidden inside the tech behemoth. If she could sniff it out, they'd make out like bandits.

"Gotcha," she said. She took a puff, allowing herself a moment of reflection.

Commonwealth was the most valuable company on earth. It ran the feed. And the feed ran . . . everything. It was easy to forget, but cars were just computers that drove you around. Houses were computers you lived in. Hospitals were computers that healed you. Factories were computers that made stuff. Farms were computers that grew food. Utilities were computers that delivered power and water. Everything and everyone was connected to the feed, which made everything and everyone dependent on it. If Commonwealth was hiding something, Diana wanted to know what it was. Nothing was more intoxicating than the scent of intrigue.

She passed Kendrick the joint.

"All right," she said. "Let's switch gears."

"More?" His tone was incredulous, but she could tell he liked the attention. "What am I, an all-you-can-eat buffet?"

She nodded. "I love you, man. But Lady Liberty needs protecting."

His expression shifted from nostalgic to melancholic.

She waited.

He took a long pull, blew smoke out through his nose.

"Do you still believe all that stuff?" he asked. "I mean, last time we saw each other, sure, but we were both young, you know? Bushy-tailed and all that. After a while, though, you just watch the system grind. I don't know what you've seen, but from what I've witnessed . . . I dunno, man. I just . . ."

He trailed off and gave her a look that was almost a plea.

"Did I ever tell you that I spent a few years in Amsterdam?" she asked.

Kendrick shook his head.

"The Dutch build parallel dikes for redundancy," she said. "There are three kinds: watcher, sleeper, and dreamer. The watcher dike is right up against the water. If it fails, the sleeper is ready. If the sleeper fails, the dreamer is the last defense against disaster."

The end of the joint glowed bright orange as she took a hit.

"You asked what I've seen," she said. "I'm a watcher. That's my job." She failed to mention that she was no longer a federal employee, not even a hidden line item on a classified spreadsheet. There were few currencies as valuable as lies of omission. "I face the truly nasty bits of reality so that everyone else can rest easy." *The shield that guards the innocent,* Helen's favorite line. "If I fail, then the Luddites at the Pentagon have to get involved. If they fail, it's every person for themselves."

She paused to let that sink in.

"Sometimes I wonder if we're really the good guys we think we are," said Kendrick darkly.

"The people who run this town are snakes," she said. "The system we've built is inefficient and corrupt, no doubt about it. But it's our system, our country, our problem." She thought of Sofia, of what America meant to her family. "And from the fucked-up shit I've seen, it's the best of a bunch of bad options."

He took the joint.

"See them?" Diana pointed.

Tourists milled about the FDR Memorial, recording feed streams. A group of college kids played Frisbee on the lawns. Two old men threw crumbs to a squawking flock of pigeons.

"That's who we're protecting. Real Americans. Not the bullshit artists in Congress whose only constituency is themselves. Fuck them. Fuck the desk jockeys. Fuck the freeloaders and the hate-mongers and the con artists. This country isn't perfect, but it stands for something real. Freedom, democracy, second chances. It's corny because it's true."

Kendrick grunted.

"That's why I visit here whenever I'm in DC," she said, kicking up some gravel. "*Here*, here. This levee is a watcher dike. It's right on the river. Sometimes I wish that the Potomac would pour over it and wipe this rotten city off the map. But whenever I'm actually standing on it, I remember how beautiful it is. This berm that everyone ignores keeps everyone safe. I remember that even though Washington is full of creeps and megalomaniacs, there are still innocent Americans who need our help."

Kendrick took one last pull off the joint and crushed it beneath his heel.

"Okay, Captain America," he growled. "What are you here to pump me for?"

Some people needed a reminder of debts owed, some needed a credible threat, others just needed a pep talk. Knowing the difference made you an intelligence officer.

"What's going on inside Commonwealth?" she asked. "What off-the-record rumors are you hearing? What insights don't make it into the official reports?"

The color drained from his face, and his eyelid twitched.

"Look," he said. "Everything has already been requisitioned. I'm not going to back-channel with every branch of the goddamn government."

She recognized the brittleness in his voice.

Fear.

Someone else had been asking the same questions.

"I know, I know," she said. The Diana he thought he knew would know, and there was nothing to be gained from breaking the illusion. "Don't get paranoid. That's the weed talking."

"It's not paranoia if it's true."

"And he's back," she said, clapping him on the shoulder. "Witty rejoinders and all."

The playfulness might have been forced, but at least he cracked a smile.

"Look," she said. "Humor me, okay? For old times' sake."

Old times. Diana needed to get her answers and get out before this city ate her alive.

CHAPTER 6

Diana bit the tip of her tongue as she inserted the pin-size recording device into the center of the sunflower. Sunflowers actually sported two types of flowers. The long yellow petals, or ray flowers, formed their distinctive halo around the darker orange circle that was made of hundreds of tiny disc flowers. She turned the blossom this way and that, trying to catch any hint of something unusual, but the recorder was indistinguishable from the disc flowers. No glints of reflected light from odd angles. Nothing indicated that everything within range would be captured and transmitted. Satisfied, she moved on to the next sunflower in the bouquet.

Finding out the time and location of the Commonwealth board meeting had been straightforward. Sofia had provided inside intel, including typical amenities provided at board meetings and what facility-services contractors were on call that day. From there, Diana had arranged for the florist's regular delivery guy to win a backstage pass to see his favorite band, something he was guaranteed to skip work to attend. Trish at the nursery had provided a warm introduction to the florist, who was relieved to have someone who could cover the shift on short notice. With that, Diana had her ticket into Commonwealth. Espionage was mostly logistics.

After straightening her uniform, Diana collected the bouquet and opened the back door of the delivery van. The forest of sleek skyscrapers that was Commonwealth headquarters soared above her. The tops of the towers were lost in a blanket of fog, silver pillars holding up a gray sky. The conglomerate had gobbled up block after block of downtown San Francisco, and its employees filled the streets, sipping on macchiatos, sketching algorithms in their feeds, or debating technical problems and internal politics.

Summoning her feed to overlay the most efficient route, Diana made her way toward the entrance to one of the towers.

Governments around the world had long ignored Commonwealth's growing influence. The company's policy of maintaining the feed as a neutral piece of global infrastructure helped sustain the illusion that politicians were still the ultimate power brokers. The feed was a tool. A useful one, to be sure. But the people who *used* tools were the ones in charge, not the people who made them. That's why, from Washington's perspective, Silicon Valley was the nation's inventor, not its ruler.

But all that had changed when Commonwealth included a mandatory carbon tax in its terms of service update three years ago. Outrage was rampant, but pundits relied on Commonwealth just as much as countries did. Opting out of the feed meant opting out of the global economy. No nation could afford a denial of service, so the carbon tax immediately became de facto international law.

A few short years later, the decision remained controversial, but nobody could deny that carbon emissions were down and fossil fuels had been effectively phased out of mainstream use. Environmentalists crowed as unemployed oil workers protested. But only a handful of people on earth knew what Diana had done. That Dag had forced Rachel Leibovitz, Commonwealth's legendary chairwoman, to implement the historic policy.

Diana's stomach twisted. She didn't want to see the unread messages from Dag in her feed, didn't want to feel the weight of obligation. She had been avoiding him since getting back from DC, getting home late, leaving early, and keeping conversation to a utilitarian minimum. More than anyone, he should understand that the mission required total focus and that he was a distraction. The fact that he did seem to understand, was happy to give her space even though she told him nothing about her work, was the most maddening thing of all. Guilt leaked around her blunt denial until she plugged it with the affirmation that spies couldn't afford real relationships. She couldn't help what she was.

Pushing away the unwanted thoughts like spiderwebs, Diana stepped through the entrance and into the skyscraper. Her breath caught in her throat. She was standing in an atrium that took up the entire ground floor of the building and rose hundreds of feet into the air. But the cathedral space itself wasn't as surprising as the dozens of fully grown redwoods that filled it. It was as if she had stepped off the downtown sidewalk and directly into the grove on Mount Tam. Artificial mist circulated through the trees' upper branches, and flagstone paths connected the doors and scattered seating areas to a central elevator bank.

Diana's feed automatically logged her presence and authorization, prompting a welcome message. She dismissed it and hugged the bouquet to her chest. Much easier to secure an official excuse for being here than to try to outwit the world's most sophisticated security apparatus.

Her ears popped as the elevator whisked her up into the building's highest reaches. Emerging into what appeared to be an art gallery, she maneuvered through various abstract installations interspersed with lounge areas where employees chatted or stared off into infinity, fingers twitching as they manipulated data in their feeds.

The door to the conference room slid open at her approach. The interior was spacious and airy. Twelve chairs surrounded an oval table cut from a single piece of glass balanced on a granite boulder striated with tan and green mineral deposits. The entire far wall was a curved window. They were well above the fog, and its surface ebbed and flowed, the spires of the other Commonwealth skyscrapers rising from it like islands in a ghostly sea.

Diana circled the table, appreciating the quality of the light, listening to the soft echoes of her footsteps, getting a feel for the space. She deposited the bouquet into the glass vase that had been set out for it and slid the arrangement into the center of the conference table. Because the vase and table were both entirely transparent, they created the illusion that the sunflowers were hovering a few inches above the apex of the boulder. The effect was beautiful and strange, dreamlike green stalks and vibrant petals invigorating the room with life and color.

Summoning her feed, Diana ran a test. Audiovisual streams bloomed, each surveying the room from the perspective of one of the sunflowers. Seen from without, her own smile was a feral thing. Cut flowers were tributes to impermanence. But even as Commonwealth's board members perceived the short-lived beauty of these sunflowers, they would themselves become objects of scrutiny.

CHAPTER 7

"We need to press the Prideful Seven harder," continued a red-faced board member. "They've held out long enough. It's time we extended the network into their territories. Mexico was supposed to be buttoned up years ago. What's the problem? These people need their feeds to be faster, more reliable, more secure. Monopolizing hard fiber is a moat that nobody will be able to compete with."

Diana live-annotated the recording, dialing up visual opacity so it felt like she was staring out from the sunflowers. In the physical world, Diana was sitting in one of the lounge areas next to an impressionist sculpture the size and approximate shape of a bear made entirely from thousands of antique pennies. Having shrugged a blazer over her uniform, anyone walking by would see just another Commonwealth employee immersed in her feed. A few hundred feet away and behind closed doors, the board was two hours into their meeting, and things were getting heated.

The Prideful Seven. Russia, Thailand, Iceland, Ethiopia, Mexico, China, and France all maintained their own domestic fiber-optic networks, with varying levels of performance. National leaders within the Prideful Seven considered their independence a point of pride, refusing Commonwealth's repeated offers to update and standardize their physical telecommunications infrastructures.

"A waste of time," said Eddie Hsu, expression carefully composed. "That strategy is a straw man. Who cares whether or not we control the hard fiber? Everyone in the Prideful Seven still uses the feed. They're just as dependent on us as anyone else. It's the software that matters. The hardware is a diversion to keep them focused on the inessential. Extending Commonwealth fiber to the Prideful Seven is a PR stunt. We don't need another moat against commercial competition. At this scale, political risks are the only real risks we face."

Age had etched wrinkles into Hsu's weathered face, and his short gray hair and ramrod-straight posture gave him the appearance of an elderly general. But despite the fact that he'd orchestrated Taiwan's political ascendancy over the preceding decades, he'd never held an official military or government position. Diana understood the value of pulling strings from behind the scenes, and Hsu was a master puppeteer. In fact, one of his only missteps had been to secure a major stake in Lowell Harding's oil-and-gas empire right before the carbon tax had undermined the entire enterprise. Ever the pragmatist, Hsu had reinvested in Commonwealth via Taiwan's sovereign wealth fund and now served as its representative on the board.

"Look," said Hsu, rubbing the pommel of his walking stick. "What we really need to do is organize back-channel conversations with governments and their UN representatives, assure them that the carbon tax was a . . . one-time thing. We're not a threat to their authority. We're not encroaching on their sovereignty. We're a partner. We're here to make it easier for them to run their own countries. This Lopez interview was a shot across the bow. If we don't convince world leaders that we're friendly and obedient, they're going to ram new regulations down our throats."

"That's the absolute last thing we should do." All eyes turned to Javier Flores. Clad entirely in black leather, with dark-brown eyes, skin, and hair, his appearance might have looked affected if he didn't inhabit it so comfortably. He was slim, and the slender fingers whose gestures illustrated his every word reminded Diana of a Javanese ballet dancer she'd slept with on a bender in Yogyakarta. "Open your eyes. Nation states are dying. The economy, the environment, the feed, everything is global now. Governments are so focused on ensuring their institutional survival that they're failing the people they claim to serve. Even if they tried, they don't have the tools to deal with global problems."

Javier was a Commonwealth alumnus, a star software architect who had dropped off the map after helping engineer the feed's famously resilient security protocols. Three years ago, he'd reemerged at the head of a new foundation with a generous endowment and a sweeping mission statement. Investing the entire endowment in Commonwealth had earned him a seat at this table, where he lobbied tirelessly for user rights.

But secrets defined people, and Diana knew some of Javier's. He had spent the mysterious intervening years leading a group of activists who had hijacked the feed to manipulate what they saw as a broken system. Under the tutelage of mastermind Emily Kim, Javier and his team of hacker psychologists had finely tuned the feeds of linchpin individuals to sway major national policy decisions. Results included tax reforms that were empowering the middle class, liberalization of the draconian immigration laws implemented during the fall of the EU, better anti–human trafficking controls, and increased funding to education and scientific research. Nearly every progressive victory of the past decade could be traced back to Emily and Javier.

It was the greatest heist in human history. They were stealing hearts and minds.

But their crowning achievement had been their downfall. Having spent years tweaking Dag's identity by carefully curating his feed, they hadn't anticipated that their newest agent would slip the leash. Shocked at discovering that he was at once their tool and their target, Dag had gone to Rachel at Commonwealth. Trading knowledge of the security loophole Javier and Emily's ploys depended on for implementation of the global carbon tax via Commonwealth terms of service, Dag had achieved their mission and disarmed them at the same time.

Dag. Pride, awe, and yearning echoed within her. At his most vulnerable, at the moment when everything had been taken from him, Dag had discovered the capacity to fight for something bigger than himself. Picking up the shattered remnants of his life, he'd orchestrated a bloodless coup.

Diana remembered her shock when Dag had offered his entire feed archive to her, desperate for an explanation of the dark forces manipulating him. A person's feed archive contained their entire digital life, every binary breadcrumb, every piece of detritus from the journey from cradle to grave. Granting someone else access to your entire archive was the digital equivalent of unlocking your soul. It was a vault protecting your personal data, your most intimate moments. Javier and Emily had cracked those vaults to pursue their own idealistic ends. But what Dag had given Diana was different. It was a VIP pass to his own head, extended voluntarily without reservation or constraint.

There were discrete classes of secrets. There were the personal kind, secrets that orbited an individual life like moons, their gravity shifting behavior as easily as tides. And then there were the heftier kind, secrets that were stitched into the very fabric of world affairs, that directed the course of nations. Dag's had been both at the same time, which made it such a precious gift. There was only one other secret in her collection that might rival it.

Maybe the legacy of that secret was what made her relationship with Dag unworkable. She had peeled away the layers and peered into the deepest corners of his life. But as transparent as he was to her, she was opaque to him. Her life was secrets. Her life was secret. And romance could not bridge such a divide.

"Let Lopez rant," said Javier, emotion building up in his voice. "Instituting the global carbon tax was the greatest political accomplishment of the century. Politicians sat around debating the merits of this or that approach to reducing carbon emissions for decades as we burned through fossil fuels like a junkie through hits. The fact that the tax was implemented in the Commonwealth terms of service and enforced by the threat of denial of service is the only thing that made real change possible. Our terms are policies, and those policies are a tool that actually works in the modern, interconnected world. So let's bring those tools to bear and make that world a better place. Adapting to climate change. Reducing inequality. Improving education. Managing public health. Pushing forward scientific progress. These are global problems, problems only we can tackle. I have a plan to—"

"Enough." Silence fell like a curtain across the conference room. She might be an octogenarian, but Rachel's voice still carried the undeniable clarity of command. Her hands were on the table, and her silver hair was tied back in a ponytail. A thick scar ran from cheekbone to forehead, the eye it bisected dull and gray. Her good eye, violet and imperious, fell on each board member in turn. "This is a board meeting, not a forum for stump speeches."

She stood.

"We are adjourned," she said.

And that was that.

As the board members collected their things, Diana deposited the latest tranche of annotated footage into Haruki's cache. She was surprised to find a message waiting for her there.

Focus on Rachel. We need a detailed file on her. Key relationships, daily routines, physical layouts of home and offices, etc. Full take.

CHAPTER 8

As the board members filed out of the conference room, Diana did some last-minute mental gymnastics. Finding another excuse to get back into Commonwealth would require extensive planning, but she could still take advantage of her day pass as a facilities contractor. She would need to have a conversation later with Haruki about when and how to communicate changes to the project scope, but right now she had a window of opportunity if she acted quickly.

Dismissing the surveillance streams from the sunflower recorders, she buttoned up her blazer and stood. She let her fingers brush the surface of the adjacent structure as she circled around it to intercept the group as they made their way to the elevators.

She had to focus to keep her gait nonchalant as adrenaline flooded her system. Her senses sharpened. The pennies were cool to her touch, their textured edges tickling her skin. Instead of the typical HVAC staleness, the filtered air tasted clean and fresh. Her clothing hung loosely on her small frame, offering freedom of movement but risking getting caught on something if it came to a physical chase.

Which it wouldn't. Actually shadowing people was a far rarer occurrence in intelligence work than the general public assumed. Hot pursuits complete with parkour and fancy sports cars were, unfortunately, rarer still.

"Do I know you?" Javier's eyes were larger than they had appeared on her surveillance cam. His smile was friendly and curious. Behind him, the other participants walked to the elevators in ones or twos. Rachel was hanging back in the conference room, taking a call via feed. "I swear I recognize you from somewhere."

"I get that a lot," said Diana, giving him a small smile. "I look like everybody's cousin."

When Diana was a teenager, she'd envied beautiful people like Nell and Dag, whose looks made them magnets for attention. Her own banal appearance had driven her into hormone-laden bouts of depression. Average height, average weight, average everything. But she'd soon found that competence and intelligence were far more rewarding qualities. It was only years later, after settling under Helen's wing, that she realized ugliness was not beauty's opposite. Both extremes caught the eye, drew people in. The opposite of being beautiful was being common, for it attracted nothing but indifference. And that indifference was invaluable armor to a spy. Of course, the flip side was that people mistook you for the archetypal "someone."

Javier ran a finger along his jaw. "No," he said, shaking his head. "Not any of my cousins. Are you sure we haven't met before?"

As his eyes continued to search her face, Diana's skin went cold. Shit. She should have been more careful. Javier *had* seen her before, just not in person. He and Emily had spent years perusing and rearranging Dag's feed to their hearts' content, years in which Diana had collaborated with Dag on numerous ops. Javier would know that Diana had been the one to help Dag track Emily back to their secret island refuge. She needed to end this conversation and redirect his curiosity before any inconvenient memories surfaced in his mind.

She squinted at him, running a surreptitious feed search. "Wait." She let excitement bleed into her tone. "Were you at the Victoria Summit in April? Yeah, I remember now, you gave that talk about using the feed to improve human rights. I volunteer there every year. It's so stimulating!"

"Ahh," he said, cocking his head to one side. "That must be it."

"Is that real leather?" She peered at his jacket.

"It is," he said, holding out his arm so she could touch his sleeve. "There's this ranch out in Montana that does all the leatherwork in-house. They're great."

Diana shied away from the proffered sleeve.

"I'm vegan," she said shortly.

"Oh," he said. There was a moment of awkward silence in which he looked painfully at a loss. "Well, I should catch that elevator."

"Yeah," she said and stepped past him, losing herself among the sculptures.

She was getting rusty. That had been too close for comfort.

It took half an hour for Rachel to finish her call. Diana could only hear Rachel's laconic side of the conversation, which Diana inferred was about a pending acquisition. Then the older woman walked out of the conference room with a steady, efficient gait. Diana circled around behind the elevator bank, timing it such that she and Rachel arrived at the same time. A few other employees milled about, and Diana followed Rachel and a portly man onto an elevator headed down.

Diana had expected Rachel to retreat to a lavish office, some miracle of engineering that used every architectural trick to create the perfect aerie for the world's most powerful executive. Instead, after picking up some passengers on the intervening floors, the elevator deposited them at ground level.

Rachel explored the lobby until she found an unoccupied bench in a corner of the redwood grove. Sitting, she withdrew into her feed.

Being in the lobby made Diana's job much easier. With so many people coming and going all the time, all she needed to do was wander around with just enough purpose in her stride to appear to be going somewhere.

Rachel stayed there for the rest of the afternoon. Occasionally other executives would swing by for brief, intense conversations. Otherwise she appeared content to do whatever was required of a magnate overseeing her dynasty from the safety of her feed. While Diana waited, she mapped out the space as Haruki had requested, noting doorways, pathways, trees, and countless other details that seemed hopelessly irrelevant.

Finally Rachel stood and stretched. She removed her hair tie and shook out her mane. Diana was surprised by how much this changed her appearance. Without her ponytail, Commonwealth's fearless leader was somehow less distinctive. The silvery halo called attention away from her scarred face.

Rachel walked toward an exit. As soon as the chairwoman stepped outside the skyscraper, her four-person security team appeared, following at a discreet distance. Diana tagged Rachel on a live, high-definition satellite stream and tracked her progress via feed, staying far enough behind to remain invisible. Rachel surprised Diana again, eschewing a car and making her way north on foot to a public indoor pool where she proceeded to swim laps for an hour. One of the bodyguards stood off to the side in a largely failed attempt at discretion while the others covered the street outside. Diana had ditched the blazer and donned glasses as an extra precaution, but it was hard to imagine being recognized among the troupes of begoggled, chlorine-infused San Franciscans in various states of undress.

After a quick rinse, Rachel was out on the streets again, heading toward what Diana could guess was her home on the slopes of Telegraph Hill. Diana kept an eye on Rachel and her bodyguards via satellite feed, noting the route, distance, and time stamps. Diana herself walked one block over, speeding up as they neared their destination so she could arrive first.

The sun was setting behind the Golden Gate, bathing the hill in amber light. Diana sought cover in one of the narrow bamboo-shaded stairways that led up to where Coit Tower stood on the summit.

Pretending to be on the lookout for one of the neighborhood's famous feral parrots, she found an angle that gave her a direct view down onto Rachel's home. While no houses in San Francisco were inexpensive, Rachel's was far from ostentatious. Nestled between a small apartment building and a pedestrian byway, the narrow two-story Edwardian looked out over the Bay Bridge and downtown skyscrapers.

Rachel climbed the stairs and went inside. Using her feed to zoom in, Diana could see through the bay windows and into the first floor. The kitchen, dining room, and living room were all connected in an open plan. Two men were chopping vegetables in the kitchen: Omar, her husband, and Leon, their lover. Rachel greeted them each with a kiss, grabbed a chef's knife, and began dicing tomatoes.

Outside, Diana suppressed a shiver. The temperature was dropping fast, and she now regretted abandoning her jacket. Sighing, she created an approximate blueprint of the house's internal layout based on what she could see and what she could deduce from the roofline, window placement, and internal stairwells.

What was she really doing here? Watching the trio cook, eat, gossip, laugh, drink a bottle of wine, and wander up to bed together, Diana felt like little more than a voyeur. If this had been the twentieth century with its puritanical gender and sexuality norms, maybe a sex tape of a senior-citizen threesome would be scandal-worthy. But in today's world, it wouldn't cause so much as a hiccup in the feed's media maelstrom. Rachel was openly polyamorous anyway. It wasn't even a revelation.

Adding a thermal filter to the satellite footage now that darkness had fallen, Diana prompted her feed to notify her if anyone entered or exited Rachel's house. Then she stood, stretched cramped muscles, and began climbing the steep stairway. Bamboo leaves whispered above her head, and she had to focus to keep her footing on the cracked concrete stairs. Her calves burned, and her breath formed little puffs of condensation.

When they find a company with a dirty secret, they bet against the company's stock and drag the skeleton out of the closet. It made sense that a hedge fund like Leviathan, and by proxy a cutout like Haruki, would covet covert recordings of a Commonwealth board meeting. Mapping out the alliances among major shareholders and seeing what strategies were being discussed would make it easier to predict key decisions before the rest of Wall Street knew what was happening. There was clearly tension between Hsu and Javier, and between both of them and Rachel. That was good intel. Even better was that the board viewed the company's push to bring the Prideful Seven under Commonwealth's wing as a straw man. Leaking that juicy tidbit could create havoc all by itself.

But a full take? Physical layouts of Rachel's environs? A schedule of her daily routine? Those quotidian details hardly seemed worth the effort or expense.

As she climbed, Diana summoned her feed and pulled up Leviathan's portfolio and trading history. Kendrick had mentioned the biotech firm DysoTech that Leviathan had bet against and then exposed for conducting illegal drug trials. But there were at least a dozen others. Scanning through the outraged news reports and lucrative financial windfalls each scandal had provoked, she saw that a number of them had focused on key executives. A banking CEO who had personally approved initiatives that violated international law. A CFO who had been making insider trades on his own account. A VP who had sexually harassed a dozen employees. It was plausible that they had her shadowing Rachel as a fishing expedition for some unknown personal wrongdoing.

But plausible didn't cut it, not when it came to espionage.

She reached the park at the top of the hill. Coit Tower thrust into the darkness above. It smelled of brine and honeysuckle. The fog had cleared, and stars glittered in the night sky like a reflection of the thousands of lights in the city below.

This hill had once housed a semaphore, which was why the neighborhood was called Telegraph Hill. When sailboats and steamships crossed from the ocean into the bay, a crew would adjust the mechanical arms of the semaphore into shapes that merchants down in the streets of San Francisco could interpret. Each shape referred to a particular kind of ship with a particular kind of cargo. Armed with foreknowledge of what the incoming vessel carried, shopkeepers could adjust their prices in advance to arbitrage the influx of new supplies about to hit the docks.

That's what Leviathan should want, a hot tip that they could arbitrage ahead of the market. They weren't going to find that by having Diana report back on Rachel's office furniture, how many laps she swam, or the ingredients of the salad she'd prepared for dinner.

A shiver ran down Diana's spine that had nothing to do with the cold.

If you suspected you were being played, the only move was to raise the stakes.

CHAPTER 9

"Cream, extra sugar for Gerald, and black for Sam." Diana handed a steaming cup to each muscled bouncer. "Let no one say I don't take care of my own."

Gerald inhaled the scent of his fresh coffee, and an ecstatic smile spread across his wide face.

"You're an angel, D," said Sam.

"You better believe it," said Diana as she pushed through the heavy oak doors. "Just wait till you see me spread my wings and bring justice to the unworthy with a big-ass flaming sword."

Nell looked up from the podium, radiant as ever.

"You again." A dimple ruined her deadpan expression.

"Hardly the way to greet an old friend," said Diana. "I am shocked and appalled by your impropriety. Call the guards."

Nell grunted. "Good to have you back," she said. "Your booth is empty at the moment."

"You're a dear," said Diana, stepping past her but stopping with her hand on the red satin curtains. "Oh, silly me, I almost forgot. I've got something for you. Actually, it's for Jorani."

Diana placed a brown paper bag on the podium, and Nell opened it curiously. She pulled out a collection of comic books sealed in thin layers of protective plastic.

"Original English-language *Akira* reprints from the early 1990s," said Diana. "It's a masterpiece. A sci-fi epic from the golden age of manga. Jorani will love it."

Nell bit the tip of her tongue as she flipped through the collection. "This is too much, Diana," she said. "These are collector's items."

"Don't worry about it," said Diana. "*Akira* was foundational for me when I was Jorani's age. It's about this kid growing up in Tokyo after World War III destroys the city. He discovers this secret that everyone's trying to cover up. There's action, violence, supernatural powers, weird philosophy, and bad influences galore for a growing girl." She nudged Nell. "Seriously though, it would mean a lot to me to give them to someone who'll appreciate it."

Nell hesitated, and Diana put a reassuring hand on hers. "Take them. Just promise me that you won't lecture her on how she needs to keep them pristine. They're comic books. They're meant to be read and loved. I'll be disappointed if they don't end up a tattered mess."

Nell shook her head. "Okay, then," she said. "Well, thank you." She met Diana's eyes. "Thank you."

"My pleasure," said Diana with a devilish grin. "Now you're never going to be able to pull her away from manga."

Nell gave an exasperated sigh. "Oh, I know," she said. "I keep offering to take her up and give her some flight training, but she'll have none of it. Parents always wish their children shared their hobbies." She shrugged. "All right, off with you." Shooing Diana inside, she said, "Get out of my sight before you cause more trouble."

After slipping through the satin folds, Diana gave herself the requisite moment to adjust. The ambient-beats playlist she'd had running on low volume was gone, as were the bulleted notes she'd taken on Leviathan's trading history. The collated report on the mission's progress that she'd submitted to the cache this morning vanished from her peripheral vision.

No notifications.

No connections.

No feed.

Rubbing her eyes with her knuckles, Diana wove through the crowded tables to the back corner of the club. Virginia waved at her from behind the bar and got to work preparing a Caesar. An oil lamp guttered. A young woman in an outfit of finely patterned white lace played wild folk tunes on an accordion.

Analog was in fine form.

"How are you three holding up?" As always, Diana knelt beside the vizslas curled up in front of the enormous fire and slipped each dog a piece of jerky. They thanked her with rough licks, and she scratched them each under the chin before retreating to her nearby booth.

A brooding darkness welled up inside her as she waited. The silence left in the wake of her absent feed forced uncomfortable reflection. Without the information mainline, nothing stood between her and the disturbing truth that there was more going on here than she understood.

Haruki appeared shortly after Diana's Caesar. She had to suppress a smirk when he ordered a gin and tonic instead of a martini. Baby steps.

She briefed him on her findings. Sofia had helped Diana map out the political hierarchy within Commonwealth and given her details on specific internal priorities and operations. Kendrick had shared what his auditors and analysts had found as well as insights that they suspected but could not prove. The board meeting footage had illuminated leadership's key strategies, lines in the sand between high-level factions, and the pressure Rachel faced from her directors.

The overall picture was consistent with what Diana had expected. Commonwealth was a large organization that was as powerful and as conflicted as other major institutions. They weren't, and couldn't be, squeaky clean, but neither were they sitting on a ticking time bomb. Diana's snooping on Rachel's personal life added color to the narrative, but little else. There was enough material for a hedge fund like Leviathan to make a bet, but nothing that would yield a slam dunk.

Emily and Javier's hack was just the kind of explosive secret they were after, but one that Diana would never reveal.

"This is fantastic," said Haruki. "Great work."

"You bet your ass it is," said Diana. "Great is the only work worth doing."

Haruki grinned and leaned in across the table conspiratorially. Diana lifted an eyebrow, and he sat back up, chastened, before speaking in a hushed voice.

"Your file on Rachel's relationships and routines was particularly useful," he said. "We want to really differentiate this white paper from other market intelligence reports. Our clients are looking for insights that they can't get anywhere else. This is unique intel, and we want more. Expand Rachel's personal file, and open files on the other top executives and key personnel. That's what we'd like you to focus on during the next phase of the project."

White paper. What a crock of shit. She wanted to reach across the table and slap Haruki across the face. Or yank him close by his fancy tie and whisper the truth in his ear, *You're only here because you're expendable.* Did he really think that someone who could deliver this kind of material couldn't see through his paper-thin facade? Was she falling for a long con? Could he be such a savvy operator that he could pull off playing a baby spy and beat her at her own game?

She threw a sidewise glance at the dogs. They napped peacefully in front of the fire, pink tongues lolling. She tried to douse her growing anxiety with some of their tranquility. Haruki was no mastermind in disguise. Paranoia was a spy's best friend. You kept it close, confided in it, watched it grow and mature with a certain measure of pride. But like a best friend, you couldn't let paranoia get the better of you.

Haruki was a rookie. He was so mesmerized by the thrill of his first cloak-and-dagger assignment that he thought cover stories should be relished. Diana could identify with that. She had been a rookie once.

That's why he drove her crazy. She could see herself in him. She could see that thrill holding him in its thrall. How it bled all other experiences of their vitality. Intrigue was an addiction, and Haruki was riding his first high.

She considered smashing her cup on the edge of the table, holding a shard to his neck, and demanding answers. She could call for Gerald and Sam, claim Haruki had groped her, and oversee them beating him in the back alley. She could even kick off a shoe, run her foot up the inside of his thigh, and turn his libido against him. Perhaps the most elegant play would be to deploy her knowledge of what he thought was hidden, destroy his eager confidence blow-by-blow until he stood naked before her, the ashes of his ego scattered to the wind and his mind opened up to her like a steamed oyster.

But she would do none of those things. Not because it wouldn't be fun but because there was no pearl inside this particular oyster. Cutouts didn't know the real reasons for anything. That's what made them good cutouts. If her hypothesis was wrong and Leviathan wasn't hoping to short Commonwealth after all, then Haruki couldn't help her.

The accordion held an oscillating high note before plunging into consonant resolution.

That wasn't entirely true. Haruki could help her, even if he didn't realize it. Cutouts shuttled information back and forth. He was her messenger as much as his boss's. And as long as she played nice, Haruki would deliver her A++ report to his betters. That report would eventually reach a principal, one way or another.

Diana sipped her Caesar, imagining barbarians massing at the gates of ancient Rome.

What Haruki didn't know, what he didn't have the experience or imagination to suspect, was that she'd spiked the report with a tracker.

CHAPTER 10

Diana arranged everything. She sought out Dag's favorite art-supply shop in Berkeley, a strange hole-in-the-wall with matryoshka dolls in the window and an ancient feedless proprietor. After sharing a shot of his eye-watering homemade gin, he had offered to sell her something special, a set of premium drawing charcoal that he swore was peerless. From there, she'd greased the palm of one of the young waiters smoking a cigarette in the alley behind Dag's favorite restaurant. Finally, she'd secured tickets to a hush-hush soft opening of a new gallery show that was hosting a painter whose work Dag adored.

Throughout it all, she followed the digital trail of the report she'd submitted to Haruki. She could see where it was sent, how it was opened, and a slew of other metadata. Making a move on her own initiative was rejuvenating.

She opened the cottage door, and Dag looked up from where he stood working on a sketch. He smiled and swept her up in an embrace.

"Look who decided to take a break from life in the shadows," he said.

"The shadows are all well and good," she said. "But I get frustrated without my boy toy." She pinched his ass. "And you know what I'm like when I get frustrated."

"The world trembles, the dead rise again, and far-off galaxies go supernova."

"Exactly," she said matter-of-factly. "And who wants that?"

"Very public-spirited of you to return."

"I'm nothing if not beneficent. When you're as supremely intelligent, inspiring, and humble as I am, there's really no other option."

"The rest of us live in awe of you, my love. You are a god among men. Or a goddess among women, or a deity among people. Whatever."

"If only the other lowly humans did not deny the reality of my holiness, we could dance naked through the streets, open the gates to heaven, and enjoy peace on earth."

She kissed him on the mouth.

"Hey," he said, his expression softening. "I've missed you."

"You too, babe," she said, surprised to realize it was true. Over his shoulder, her eyes found the sketch mounted on the drafting table. "Wow, that's incredible."

Color touched his cheeks. "Oh, come on," he said. "It's nothing special. I'm just getting started."

But it was special. La Jolla Cove spread out before her in all its apocalyptic glory. Warped steel beams and crumbling concrete reached up like bleached bones from where the town used to be. Asphalt appeared to froth and flow where it had solidified after the extreme heat had turned the streets into slow-motion rivers of hydrocarbon. Ash fell from the sky thick as snow, obscuring the horizon. These were the only remains left behind by the infamous fire that had consumed all of Southern California, the single most destructive natural disaster in American history. Thousands had died and millions had fled, flooding neighboring states and filling the vast new housing projects that Dag had once helped oil magnate Lowell Harding build as a part of the billionaire's multipronged scheme to profit from the privations of climate change. As she moved closer to inspect it, she noticed a fantastical element that gave the piece the surreal aspect of magical realism. While the land held nothing but debris, fish leapt from the waves that lapped against the beach, and sea lions soaked up sun on the rocks.

Diana glanced sidelong at Dag, saw him regarding her, watching her reaction. She wasn't the only one driven by guilt, haunted by misdeeds she'd rather forget. This was a man who had given up everything for a chance at redemption. That made him at once fascinating and somehow inaccessible to her, a combination that either drove her mad with lust or just plain mad. She reached out and touched the paper, feeling the grain. Even incomplete, the sketch had a raw power to it, an authenticity that their conversations often lacked.

"I brought you something," she said.

Dag smiled in a way that said, *Of course you did*. He opened the box and inspected the charcoal. Holding up a single piece, he sniffed it, touched it to his tongue, and etched a sharp line across the ridge of Mount Soledad where it rose behind La Jolla.

Diana gasped. The movement had been quick and violent, the gash of darkness stark amid the slim and graceful pencil lines.

"It's magnificent," he said. "Thank you. I think I might be able to guess where you found it."

"Can you guess where I'm taking you to dinner?"

They took a car into Oakland, and Diana led the way down the short flight of stairs. When she opened the unmarked wooden door, the smells of pork, garlic, and onion enveloped them. The beaded curtain chittered as they passed into the low-ceilinged ramen bar filled with noise, steam, and smoke. The walls were covered in detailed murals of ancient mythical beasts invading modern cityscapes. It was hot and crowded, but Diana's waiter waved them over to a table tucked into a nook, winking at her as they sat. He returned a few minutes later with huge steaming bowls of *tonkotsu* ramen and pints of cold beer.

They slurped the thick broth, relishing the handmade noodles and slow-cooked pork. It reminded Diana of operations in Tokyo, slumming with yakuza informants and liaising with Naichō, the Japanese intelligence agency. That made her think of *Akira*, which made her think of Nell, which made her think of Haruki, and then, even as they finished their bowls and ordered another round of beers, Diana put the conversation on autopilot and summoned her feed.

The report had been sent through San Francisco to Singapore and then Washington, DC, ping-ponging up the hierarchy of Hoffman and Associates, Haruki's employer. She flagged the accounts of each individual the report passed through, pulling up their profiles and cross-referencing against Hoffman's track record of private investigations. A few opened the file and perused it at length. Others simply forwarded it along.

Diana's tracker was a tiny sliver in the vast and overwhelming Commonwealth security apparatus that protected the feed, only possible through a combination of favors from a brilliant Austrian coder who owed her his freedom and Cynthia over at NSA, who had conveniently "forgotten" to wipe Diana's official log-in credentials.

Whatever small ways Diana managed to subvert the feed paled in comparison to Emily and Javier's unprecedented hack. Diana remembered her abject shock as she had plumbed the depths of Dag's feed archive to discover that someone had root access to Commonwealth's systems. It was the exploit to end all exploits. It cracked the entire feed open like a ripe fruit, laying bare every log, every connected system, every life on earth. It was an exceptional, terrifying masterpiece, an extravagance of riches for any secret-hoarder.

Was it possible that was the dirt Haruki's masters were after? Had they smelled something rotten? No. There were too few people who knew that anything had occurred, let alone what had really happened. And every single one of those people had every incentive to keep their mouths shut, including Diana and Dag.

More impressive than Javier's exploit was how Emily had used it. With her team of hacker psychologists, she had burrowed into the feeds of key decision makers and manipulated every detail of their lives for years until they saw the world the way she wanted them to. She had done that to Dag. Had even implanted within him a fascination with her own visage, slowly turning herself into an object of sexual obsession long before he'd even known she existed.

Something quickened inside Diana. Emily was a genius and a snake. Diana had tracked her down based on little more than Dag's lovingly rendered sketches of Emily's remembered face. How eager he'd been, how full of burgeoning desire. And yet Emily had inspired him to trade cynicism for hope, to do what he thought was right even as she carefully curated the substrate that fueled his motivations. Could Diana honestly say that she was bringing out the best in Dag, or he in her? Instead of encouraging each other's best qualities, was their relationship eroding the very things that made them special? Or maybe her own delusions were reflecting back on each other. Diana was living her love life in deep cover, refusing to extend trust even as she relished receiving it. But despite herself, details shone through the fissures of daily life, details she never planned to disclose, details that kindled the thrill of shared intimacy even as they tarnished the sacred rules of tradecraft. The whole thing made Diana sick to her stomach. It made her despise Dag for being a puppet and pity him for being taken advantage of. She wanted to sever Emily's reins and take him all for herself. But at the same time, she wanted to rid herself of the shameful desire to possess him, to excise the shadows from her heart.

"Forget the gallery," she said with sudden intensity. The meal was over, but a different kind of hunger rose within her. "Let's go home. My frustration's getting out of hand."

Even though it took what felt like an eternity to get back to their bedroom, they started slow. She slipped out of her dress, letting it fall around her ankles as she unbuttoned his shirt and stripped him naked before pushing him down onto the bed. His skin was hot under hers, his barely restrained desire enflaming her own. They kept their touch light, all lips and fingertips and feathery sensation. Then his hand was between her legs, and a small whimper escaped her. She found him, relished his hardness, but even as they played with each other, whispering nonsense, the anticipation became too great to bear.

Swinging her leg up and over, she mounted him. They found a deliberate, unhurried cadence, stepping to the edge of ecstasy before reeling themselves back in. Their breaths, their hearts, matched the tempo measure for measure, until everything was a single interlocking pattern. Every inch of Diana's skin was electric, and a light kindled deep inside her. With each salvo, the light pulsed bigger and brighter. Their hold on self-control began to loosen, and time lost its constancy. The smell of sex and sweat, the desperate panting, the pyrotechnics of a million nerve endings, the guilt and lust and raw compassion, all bled into each other until they were everything and nothing. And then the light spread and swelled and burst within her, pouring from her eyes, her mouth, her heart, her mind, transforming her into a Valkyrie of pure energy that illuminated the entire universe and was illuminated by every star, every galaxy, and she was in a house of a thousand mirrors where every reflection amplified the power of the light, and she was riding the crest of a wave a hundred miles high, and she was shining, shining, shining until she wasn't and it was fading and it was done.

Diana collapsed onto the bed. As the echoes of infinity receded, she coasted back from oblivion into self-awareness, self-possession. Dag's breath was ragged beside her, his body slick with sweat, the bed soaked. The air was close and humid, goose bumps rising on her naked skin as the heat of their union dissipated.

Buoyed by trailing jolts of pleasure, Diana summoned her feed from the periphery. Orgasm had wiped her mind clean, laying bare a simmering anxiety. Why had she been tasked with collecting a full take on Rachel? Who stood to benefit from that information? What could they possibly want to use it for? Diana had built many such profiles in the past, but only in advance of a specops mission. Assassination, kidnapping, countersurveillance, all of them required rigorous physical surveillance. But an industry "white paper" or betting against a stock? Hardly.

The report had finally left Hoffman's orbit, pinging through a few different servers before arriving in Manhattan. She cross-referenced the recipient. A managing director at Leviathan. Bingo.

That confirmed her initial hypothesis. Haruki was a Leviathan cut-out. But it didn't clarify the issue at hand. Was she overthinking this? Could this simply be amateurs asking the wrong questions, Haruki letting his spy-envy get the better of him? Or was Leviathan working some other angle, looking to find an excuse to oust Rachel rather than short the stock? Maybe Diana was just a washed-up ex-agent so desperate for a taste of the old game that she'd chase her own tail into psychosis, let her life crumble around her as she tilted at windmills.

And then the managing director sent on the report, and Diana's breath caught in her throat. He used a secure connection, routing it through Kathmandu, Seoul, La Paz, Calgary, Amsterdam, and a hundred other locations. The encryption did a decent job of protecting the transmission from prying eyes but did nothing to her tracker hiding safely inside the Trojan horse that was the report itself. And then it arrived at its destination.

Washington, DC, area. More specifically, McLean, Fairfax County, Virginia. McLean was an exclusive Beltway suburb populated by the capital's political elite. Shuffling data in her feed, she zeroed in on the identity of the recipient.

Sean Bancroft.

A ripple of disorientation swept through her. Sean was Dag's mentor. Just as Helen had trained Diana to be a top intelligence operative, Sean had helped Dag become a rising star at Apex, the preeminent political lobbying firm. Even after Dag had left the firm three years ago, Diana knew he had stayed in touch with Sean. Sean and Diana knew each other, or at least knew *of* each other, because of the freelance missions she'd run for Dag when he was still at Apex. If Sean was commissioning this project, why had he used cutouts instead of reaching out to her directly? What was he hiding? Or, more likely, *whom* was he hiding?

Dag knew Sean better than anyone. Should she ask Dag what his old boss might be planning? Perhaps he could provide some much-needed insight. But that would require her to brief him on the situation, and that was a bridge too far. Dag was already here, in her home, in her bedroom, in her heart. He had already slipped through too many layers of the armor with which she protected herself. Already a liability, the risk of further contamination was too great.

Uncertainty compounded into nausea. Could Dag know about this? Was he the reason Sean was taking so many precautions? Was her and Dag's relationship nothing more than a stratagem in some larger game? Were the secrets they sought not Rachel's but her own? Unlike Haruki, a childhood spent shuffling between foster homes, years of high-level lobbying, and his specops course in Namibia had made Dag an expert social hacker. He could lie as well as anyone and was as much of a survivor as Sofia or Diana.

Dispelling her feed, she appraised the man beside her.

Dag was propped up on an elbow, staring at her.

"Where are you?" he asked.

"I'm right here," she said, hating the defensiveness that infected her words.

He paused, tried again.

"I know your body's here," he said. "But *you* are somewhere else. In your feed, in your thoughts, in the clouds, somewhere else. Take me there."

"It's nothing," said Diana. The last thing she wanted was to invite him into her head. "I was just daydreaming."

"Daydreaming's not nothing," he said. "Daydreaming is the bulk of the work of any artist. What were you daydreaming about?"

That just like Haruki, I'm the pawn in someone else's game. That I can't escape my past. That you're not really my boyfriend. Suddenly she just wanted to get out. The fresh-baked-bread scent of cum, the sticky sheets, his demanding gaze, her tainted home, her broken self, everything disgusted her.

She sat up.

"What was I daydreaming about? I was daydreaming about having the freedom to do whatever I want, of being able to come home and just relax and have time alone, of you not besieging every aspect of my goddamn life like it's one of the fucking medieval castles you love reading about so much. Can't I even have my own thoughts? Jesus."

There were moments when you regretted words even as you said them but couldn't swallow them any more than you could turn back time.

He lay there, looking stunned.

"I'm sorry," she said. "That came out all wrong."

He shook his head.

"You're not sorry," he said. "You're being honest. You think I'm some kind of leech. Well, how do you think I feel? Sitting around here waiting for you to come home. You never tell me where you're going, what you're doing, when you're going to be back. We've been living together for three years, and I've never met a single one of your friends, never heard a single thing about your family. I get it, your work is important to you. Your privacy is important to you. But come on. You have more borders and treaties and NDAs in your head than the fucking United Nations. It's like you're a shadow of a person. You know what I think about when I'm working on a piece? I think about all the ways you might die out there, all the horrible things that could be happening to you, what I would do if you just never came home. It's like some sick fascination. I can't get it out of my head. It drives me nuts. And then you just appear out of nowhere and try to win me over with gifts, favors, and a good fuck. So if I'm a leech, you're a . . . a . . . a ghost."

Diana saw her regret mirrored in his eyes and needed to escape it. "I've gotta go," she said, pulling on jeans and a T-shirt.

"Of course you do," he said. But his voice was more sad than venomous. "Whenever there's a chance to get real, you run for your life. I guess it must be easier to cling to God and country or whatever it is that makes spies tick."

"Why don't you go draw a picture or something?" she said, grabbing her go-bag from under the bed. "I've got actual work to do."

CHAPTER 11

The problem with hiding in a pantry was that there was nothing to distract Diana from hating herself, except the feed. So she binged, drowning heartache in a tidal wave of information. She responded to every outstanding message. She followed up with contacts she hadn't touched base with for a while. She watched slow-motion highlight reels of the World Cup qualifiers, the latest critically acclaimed immersive short from Sundance, and a video of a goat skydiving. She devoured news like a famine survivor at an all-you-can-eat buffet. Commonwealth had announced yet another acquisition. The next day, Javier had penned an op-ed outlining a radical plan to make the tech giant more accountable to its users, and pundits were at each other's throats. An international scientific commission was reporting that although carbon emissions were down, the impacts of climate change would continue to shape the world for centuries. The superstorm bearing down on Europe underscored their projections. Rumors circulated about why Alexis Hamid was dropping out of the world BASE jumping championships. The *New York Times* had profiled President Lopez, recalling how he'd taken the reins after President Freeman's tragic heart attack and then returned years later to win a nonconsecutive second term. Diana thought it was a good story, even though it missed the only truly crucial detail. Through it all, her feed played *Izlel je Delyo Hagdutin* and other Bulgarian folk classics in the background, and Diana dreamed of the empty space between the stars.

And then Sean came home, interrupting her orchestra of diversion. She killed her feed, focused on her senses. Not wanting to risk a light, she had been waiting in utter darkness. The air in the pantry was thick with cumin and allspice. She heard the front door open and close and tried to match the muffled footsteps to her mental map of the house.

Sean was talking to someone about a congressional bill that would be killed in committee. Did he have a guest? That might pose a problem for Diana. No. Only one set of footsteps. He must be talking to someone via feed.

The light in the kitchen came on, the glow coming under the pantry door the only illumination in the cramped space. The clickity-clack padding of a dog's paws on tile signaled the halting arrival of Mr. Snufflebunch, Sean's doddering old Irish wolfhound, whom Diana had won over with treats and affection during her clandestine entry earlier that evening. Sean ended his call.

"Ooo, who's a good boy?" he cooed to the dog. "Yeah, you are, you big old beast. Want a piece of cheese? Only if you've been good. Oh yeah? Want it? Okay, okay. Let me put down these groceries, and I'll hook you up with some top-shelf gruyère."

She heard the fridge door open and close, followed by some banging around in the kitchen.

"Here you go, buddy," said Sean through a mouthful of his own. "That's it. Yummy, right? Your favorite. I wish my dinner could be as delicious as yours. But Doc's orders say nothing but smoothies. You'd hate 'em, believe me."

Mr. Snufflebunch panted happily. Sean busied himself preparing dinner, or that's what Diana guessed from the alternating sounds of the sink and a knife thwacking into a cutting board.

Diana had once taken a surfing lesson during R&R after an op in Jakarta. She remembered how it had felt to get tossed around underwater, raked across reefs, and generally beaten senseless by the ocean. At least that was offset by the heady rush of actually riding a wave, flying along the turquoise face in perfect symmetry with nature. But the most memorable part of the experience was how it felt right before you dropped into a wave. Paddling as fast as you could to match its speed, feeling it rise beneath you from behind, the visceral flash of your insignificance in the face of the ocean's strength, the moment when you had no choice but to commit.

There was a moment like that in every operation, when you could feel the momentum building and second thoughts urged hesitation, but you had to push through, drop in, and catch the wave.

She opened the pantry door and stepped out into the kitchen.

"What's up, Sean?" she said. "Fancy seeing you here."

Sean jerked around. He had been facing the far counter under the windows that looked out onto the backyard of his McLean estate. A kitchen island separated them, and the room was appointed with pristine stainless-steel appliances that appeared to get little actual use. A large blender sat next to the cutting board, two-thirds full of spinach and fruit.

Sean's bright-green eyes blinked rapidly. With his bulky build, thick red beard, and shocked expression, he looked like a hoodwinked giant. His tie hung loose, and the top few buttons of his fruit juice–splattered shirt were open. A large chef's knife hung limply from his right hand, and Diana saw that he had been hacking the husk off a coconut, which had rolled over on its side on the cutting board.

While his master tried to get his bearings, Mr. Snufflebunch tottered over to Diana, tail wagging, tongue lolling, nose twitching in the hope of another offering. Diana crouched and ruffled his ears.

"Hey there, handsome," she said. "Such a good doggie."

Mr. Snufflebunch nuzzled her face, and she got a whiff of gruyère.

Her comfortable familiarity with his dog seemed to throw Sean even more off balance.

"Who—"

"If I wanted to kill you, you'd be dead already," she said with a casual matter-of-factness that belied her pounding heart. "So don't do anything silly like calling the police."

Sean looked taken aback. She could see the gears turning in his head, the realization dawn that she very well might be there to kill him and that he should have been doing something, anything, like using his feed to call the police. Working with civilians always reminded her of what it took to be a professional. Good training made everyone else's reactions in crisis situations look like slow motion. Sean had been smart to send Dag to commando camp in Namibia all those years ago. In the messy world of geopolitical lobbying, you needed somebody who could handle the dirty work.

"What—"

"Hi," she said, smiling brightly. "I'm Diana. We've never met in person before, but you know who I am. I've helped out Apex over the years, and you were generous enough to commission me on this new project. Always good to put a face to a name, right?"

"Look, Diana—"

"Now don't get me wrong," she said. "I really appreciate you thinking of me. Everyone loves a loyal customer. I'm honored. Humbled, even."

This time he just swallowed.

"I just have a few questions. Barely questions at all really, *clarifications.*"

She shrugged.

"Like, for example, why are you using Leviathan Partners *and* Hoffman and Associates to pretend that you're not the one hiring me? And for that matter, what is the point of having me shadow Commonwealth execs?"

"I—"

"And don't feed me some bullshit about how Apex is looking for 'differentiated market intelligence.' We're past the buzzword cover-story phase. It's time to get real. You're a lobbyist. That means you represent your clients' interests. I don't believe for a second that you're commissioning this operation on your own account. So who's the client?"

"You're angry," said Sean. "I get it. I didn't want to do it this way either."

"I get it too," she said. "You need to put up a good fight for client privilege. You don't want to throw them under the bus. Very commendable." She gave him a double thumbs-up. "Now this may seem like a bit of a tangent, but I was very sorry to see the evidence of recurrence in your latest oncology report. Nasty thing, cancer. Especially when it comes back to haunt you after remission. I'm with you on the diet regimen. Once the docs have thrown everything they've got at it, sometimes you just need to ride the damn thing out. Better to enjoy whatever time you've got left than turn yourself into a medical experiment." She pointed at him and then at her own chest. "You and me? We're kindred spirits. I have an intuition for these things. We play the greatest game there is." She gestured to take in all of DC. "Once you get a taste, there's nothing else like it. So I'm guessing you would really prefer that your partners at Apex and the clients you so loyally serve don't find out that you're terminal. Cuz, let's be honest, nobody wants a dead man representing them."

All the color drained from Sean's face, and he seemed to shrink into himself.

"I don't know what they want," he said quietly. "They just had me hire you anonymously and feed you their instructions."

"Who, exactly?" Her tone was sickly sweet.

He shook his head.

Diana vaulted her hips up onto the kitchen island, slid across the smooth surface, and landed immediately in front of Sean. He flinched, bringing up the chef's knife instinctually. Anticipating the move, she brought her right hand up from below to deflect the point, grabbed his wrist with her left hand, sidestepped past his elbow, twisted his wrist with her until the knife popped out of his grip, and caught the handle as it fell. Then she shoved him back against the counter, spun, and put all her weight and strength behind an overhand chop.

The coconut split in half with a sharp crack. Juice poured off the counter onto the tile floor, and bits of husk and thick white meat flew everywhere. She left the knife quivering in the wooden cutting board.

Standing on her tiptoes, Diana whispered into Sean's ear, "I said I didn't want to kill you. A girl like me deserves to get what she wants, wouldn't you agree?"

She smelled the sharp tang of urine.

"Lowell Harding." Sean's voice shook. "The oil baron. Or ex–oil baron anyway."

"No need to be coy," said Diana. "Give me details."

"I don't know what he's up to," said Sean, his tone begging her to believe him. "After the carbon tax ruined his oil cartel, he sold off most of the assets and had me set up meetings for him with government officials all over the place. I'm sure Dag had you work on some of his projects over the years. He said he needed you for something but that it was sensitive and needed to be safely insulated. I set up a couple of cutouts and have just been passing things through."

"He asked for me, personally?"

Sean nodded. "He threatened consequences if the operation wasn't kept compartmentalized and strictly need-to-know. Lowell's an . . . asshole. Sees himself as a player, a real tough guy. No qualms about doing whatever he thinks needs to be done. Rules don't apply when he decides to squash his competition or open up new markets. Let's just say that he's not a client I'm proud to serve."

"Which is why you took his orders and his threat seriously."

"It's my job."

"So said the Nazi in charge of the gas chamber."

Sean shrugged. "And you haven't done things you regret?"

"I do what I do for my country."

"Seems to me the Nazi could have claimed the same. And if you're such a patriot, why are you working for hire?"

He was regaining some nerve. Diana had to make the call. Should she press Sean for more, try to squeeze him to the last drop? She thought back to Dag's descriptions of him, the impression of Sean she'd gleaned from Dag's feed archive.

"All right, all right," she said, patting Sean on the back and retreating a step. He was a good man, and she couldn't blame him for trying to be loyal to his client. More to the point, this particular well of information had run dry. "That wasn't so hard now, was it?"

Sean looked down at his damp slacks. "I'll take the dry cleaning bill off your fee."

"And I'll pad my invoice with expenses incurred figuring out who the hell was behind this."

Diana gave Mr. Snufflebunch a final belly rub.

Then she waved to Sean and headed for the exit.

"Pleasure working with you, old boy," she said. "Oh, and here's a hot tip. You'll ruin the blade of your chef's knife prying open coconuts like that. Buy yourself a machete. While you're at it, clean out your pantry. You have some pickles in there that expired before I was born. Sometimes it's the things we forget that refuse to stay hidden."

CHAPTER 12

Diana double-checked her harness, let out a slow breath, and stepped off the roof of the Hay-Adams Hotel. She rappelled down the side of the building, keeping her footing sure but soft on the stone siding as the line whined through her gloved hands. The stars formed a dome above the capital, their dim light and the dispersed city glow bending around the specialized material of the stealth jumpsuit that covered every inch of her body.

In her feed, she overlaid a digital blueprint of the hotel and checked her position. Perfect. Locking the belay device, she stopped her descent, the harness digging into her thighs. Her feet were braced on a stone pillar, and she sidestepped to the right into the yawning mouth of the adjacent archway. Using her body weight to swing beneath the arch, she hooked a heel over the iron railing, slowly let out slack, and pulled herself onto the balcony within. Standing on the balcony, she recalled her grapple via feed, and the spidery device skittered down after her, attaching itself to a loop on her harness as she collected and secured the line.

Just as a seasoned public speaker knew the power of a pregnant pause, Diana respected the prime importance of brief moments of respite in the middle of an op. She did an inventory. No sign that anything out of the ordinary had been noticed by the various algorithms she had deployed to scrape the feed. No shouts, sirens, scuffles, or alarms going off. She hadn't tweaked an ankle rappelling, her gear was all where it should be, and her heart rate was returning to baseline.

Across the forested grounds opposite the Hay-Adams, the White House glowed. The stately Ionic columns supporting the portico were silent sentinels, and from this angle, the distant, glowing spire of the Washington Monument appeared to rise from the roof as if the executive residence had been impaled by some godlike spear.

If you're such a patriot, why are you working for hire? Diana remembered the last time she had walked those halls. Then—Vice President Lopez had nodded to her as she passed, his soul as yet unburdened by crisis and hair still unsullied by gray. She savored the tangible history of those narrow passages, the satisfaction of a mission on the verge of completion, the sense of quiet pride she'd felt knowing that she was there for a reason, that her adoptive country needed her just as she needed it.

That particular journey had started on the wide avenues of Buenos Aires. The city's famous jacaranda trees were dropping their delicate blossoms, carpeting the streets in lilac. The black market biochemist was professional and discreet. Diana smuggled the synthetic compound through customs in a diplomatic pouch and ferried it all the way back to Washington under strict orders from Helen that nobody, not even the director, could know about this particular operation. The directive came straight from the Oval Office, and it was there that Diana was to deliver the package to Helen in person. That she had accomplished, President Freeman having been called away to a meeting with the Joint Chiefs. In an unusual display of pride, Helen had squeezed Diana's shoulder, congratulating her on a job well done. Enjoying the warm afterglow of rare praise, Diana had set off with a bounce in her step, unaware that her life was about to change forever.

A faint whiff of ash interrupted her reverie. Two half-smoked cigars rested on the arm of one of the balcony chairs, a slim cigarette stubbed out beside them. Time to get this show on the road.

Turning away from the view, Diana saw that the glass-paneled door had been left ajar. She wouldn't even need to use the laser cutter. Instead she snatched a miniature canister from her belt and applied WD-40 to the top and bottom hinges. Satisfied, she drew her silenced sidearm. *Never hesitate. He who hesitates, dies.* Those words of wisdom from her old shooting instructor had saved her life more times than Diana would like to admit. Cracking open the door a few more inches, she slipped inside.

There was enough ambient light filtering in through the windows that she dismissed her feed night vision. The Federal Suite was a favorite for incoming presidents on the eve of inauguration, and the rooms were enormous and opulently appointed. Golden chandeliers hung above dark wooden tables sporting vases of white roses. Tasteful photography hung on the cream-colored walls. Sofas and chairs were arranged into a variety of seating areas and conversation nooks.

She moved from room to room with the silent gait of a nocturnal predator, clearing the full kitchen, wood-paneled office, conference room, and entrance hall. Good. No internal security personnel. She removed the *shemaugh* of stealth textile wrapped around her head. Returned to the main entertaining area for a more thorough inspection.

While much of the space was pristine, the large circular table in the corner was covered in half-empty bottles of Scotch, tumblers, and scattered playing cards. One of the chairs had been knocked over. Poker chips were stacked haphazardly, and a few stray salted nuts were strewn around the crystal bowl. There was a hunting knife standing vertically, its tip embedded in the lacquered wood. When Diana leaned close, she identified the distinctively spaced notches of a game of five finger fillet. The heady smell of sweat and liquor underscored that this must have been one hell of a poker night.

Looking around, she spotted the humidor on a side table. Opening the lid, she removed a fat cigar, using the adjacent guillotine to snip the end above the seam. She raised it unlit to her lips. A nice smooth pull.

Excellent.

Holstering her weapon, she palmed a wooden match and made her way to the bedroom. The door had been left open, so she leaned against the frame, struck the match on her harness, held the cigar at a forty-five-degree angle, and slowly rotated it above the tip of the flame until the entire circumference smoldered. Then she puffed on it gently, continuing to rotate it over the match until the flame flashed up and ignited the tobacco.

The brief flare filled the bedroom with a burst of blood-orange illumination. The light caressed three naked bodies stretched out on the king bed. A short-haired young woman with umber skin rested on her stomach, the geography of her body a fantasia of nubile curves. Another woman slept curled up on her side, her hair long and black, her skin as fair as the other's was dark.

Between them lay Lowell Harding.

CHAPTER 13

Lowell had the physique of an athlete gone to seed. He lay on his back, flaccid penis between splayed legs, paunch rising and falling in time with his irregular snoring. He had a baby face and a mussed-up mop of light-brown hair with rakish gray streaks along his temples. His right hand cupped the ass of the woman beside him. Thick curls matted his chest, and his foot twitched in reaction to whatever sordid dream his unconscious was staging.

Diana sipped her cigar, the glowing tip throwing another splash of light across the scene. She held the smoke in her mouth, and notes of cedar, moss, and pepper danced on her palate. Letting the smoke out through her nose, she tasted licorice in the finish.

Growing up in a Texas ghost town, this man had built a commercial juggernaut from scratch. Following the wildcatter tradition of his home state, he had struck oil on a few wells drilled into mature reservoirs everyone else thought had run dry. He parlayed that early success into an incredible run of highly leveraged growth, taking on as much debt as he could get his hands on to scoop up leases for reservoirs deemed too difficult to produce. Then he'd brought on petroleum engineers who went to extreme lengths to milk fossil fuels from Mother Earth. This strategy had found its ultimate expression when Dag had helped him secure rights to drill the Lomonosov Ridge, the underwater mountains below the Arctic Ocean that held the largest reserves of oil left on the planet. Climate change had thawed the Arctic, which made accessing the oil easier, the use of which further accelerated climate change, which increased the value of Lowell's large real estate holdings, which he carefully invested in based on their relative resilience, making him a billionaire many times over.

You didn't pull off a scheme like that without a lot of subterfuge. Lowell played well and played dirty. In his bid for global natural-resource domination, he had left a trail of political corruption, corporate espionage, financial shenanigans, blackmail, human-rights abuses, and even targeted assassination. That didn't even take into account the destructive cynicism of the overall business plan.

Even while she was an official spook, Diana had run some operations that supported or protected Lowell's various gambits. After her exile, she had continued to aid in his efforts whenever Dag came to her for help with things he couldn't handle. Lowell might be an asshole. But Uncle Sam wanted *our* asshole to win. God forbid the Taiwanese, the Russians, the Indonesians, or the Saudi royal family lock up the last of the world's oil. So the US government turned a blind eye or even lent a hand, often in the form of Diana. It was shady. But life was shady. And it was her job to sweep up the mess so that American civilians could live in self-satisfied peace.

Of course, the global carbon tax had dashed aside Lowell's house of cards in one fell swoop. But he wasn't the type of person to waste away the rest of his days in luxurious retirement. He was up to something. She was here to find out what.

The pale woman murmured something to herself. Then she stretched, arching her back like a cat. Rolling over, she tried to get comfortable again. A frown creased her elegant forehead. She sniffed. Sniffed again. Yawning, she rubbed her eyes. Sniffed a third time.

"Do you smell smoke?" she muttered, the words muddled by sleep. "I smell smoke."

Blinking slowly, she turned her head from side to side, looking around the room.

Diana sucked on her cigar, the ember setting her face aglow.

"Jesus fucking Christ." The woman jerked up to a sitting position and shimmied back against the headboard, pulling up a corner of the sheet to cover her naked breasts. Her exclamation was pitched high with terror and panic. "Noel! Wake up!"

Her companion stirred. "What the fuck, Sandra? It's the middle of the night."

Sandra just pointed a shaking finger at Diana.

Diana imagined what they must see. A disembodied head smoking a cigar in the doorway, her stealth jumpsuit turning the rest of her body into a shimmering pool of shadow.

Noel hit the light, and the bedroom was flooded with harsh illumination.

Lowell snorted, and Sandra slapped him. "Wake up, asshole," she said.

"Who the fuck are you?" Noel addressed Diana.

Diana was struck by the fire in the woman's eyes, her blunt refusal to be intimidated. These women were top-tier courtesans, a profession once reviled, now held in high esteem.

"I'm here for him," said Diana, flicking ash in Lowell's direction. "You two can feel free to go and to charge him double for the trouble."

Noel and Sandra traded glances over Lowell, who was shaking his head blearily. Without another word, they stood and dressed in quick, efficient movements.

"Mmmphgg, where are you going?" Lowell was shaking his head. He looked hungover.

"You've got a visitor," said Noel, and followed Sandra past Diana and out of the suite. Even their exit was imbued with an apparently effortless grace that Diana knew must be the result of years of training.

"A visitor?" Lowell grunted and pushed himself up to a sitting position, finally looking up at Diana. She would appear even stranger when lit, her body a glistening liquid absence, her head and cigar the only things his eyes could latch on to. She blew a smoke ring, watched it tremble and dissolve as he got his bearings.

A predatory grin spread across his face.

"My, my, my," he said. "Look who we have here. Welcome to my humble abode, Diana. You missed the party. But I'm sure I can find some way to entertain and delight you." He patted the bed beside him. "I'm nothing if not a generous lover."

She waited him out.

He shook his head in mock disappointment. "Ah well, playing hard to get, are we? Well, at least be a doll and ring room service to bring up some coffee. This hangover is a motherfucker."

Diana wasn't above using other people's sexism against them. It was as useful a tool as any other. But she certainly wasn't going to play along with his blatant attempt to signal social dominance.

She took another pull on the cigar.

"I've always found vanity to be the most unfortunate aspect of megalomaniacs," she said. "They say it's about the world, but it's actually just about them. All those grand dreams are rooted in nothing more than personal insecurity. Puffing out the chest, raining terror upon enemies, declaring strong opinions in loud voices. You're so obsessed with yourself that you think I must be too. I think it's rather pathetic. What really surprises me about this situation is that you appear to be equally obsessed with me." She paused for a beat. "Why?"

Lowell threw up his hands. "Really? This is the conversation you woke me up at four in the goddamn morning for? For heaven's sake, Diana, life deserves flair. Add some pizzazz. Stick a finger up his butt. Something, *anything*." He sighed. "Why you? That's a ridiculous question. Because you're the best. And this is important. You think I'm going to hire some fucktard like Haruki when it's for real?"

"Ahh, flattery. What a devious little man you are. Just praise my virtues and win me over, right? Well, if I'm just the star student you've been looking for, then why use so many cutouts?"

"Would you have taken it seriously if I didn't? Compartmentalize information, each cog knows only its own task, etcetera, etcetera. Isn't this right out of your playbook? You secret agents just *love* to lecture me on operational security. Now you're criticizing me for being careful? I just can't win, can I?"

"Interesting that you would choose this particular moment to brag about being so very careful." She took a puff. "If you anticipated I'd slice through the cutouts, then forcing me to do so risks blowing the op."

"Look," he said. "Honestly? I'm happy you're here. We can cut the bullshit and do this like good, honest spooks. Plus, even if your questions are lackluster, I can't fault your entrance." He looked her up and down. "My security detail didn't peep, and whatever that is you're wearing is slick as a wet pussy. You'd be amazed at the utter *dullness* of some of the people in this town. Their cheap suits, their endless acronyms, their zero-sum-game thinking, their patent inability to dream big. They have no sense of adventure, no joie de vivre. It's stage-four boring. Sometimes I worry it might be catching. So even though you chased away my lovelies, I must admit, you're a blessing in admittedly heavy disguise."

Dag had always said that the one thing Lowell hated above all else was boredom. In fact, the primary factor that had kept Dag in Lowell's employ even as other colleagues dropped like flies was that

Dag challenged Lowell and could keep up with his antics. But as Dag became less and less comfortable furthering his client's schemes, he'd come to regret his status as a favorite lieutenant.

I'm sorry. That came out all wrong. All the emotions that Diana had been smothering with continuous action threatened to boil up and overwhelm her. Nothing Sean or Lowell had said so far implicated Dag in their plot, but did that mean he was innocent? Was it coincidence that Dag's mentor and his former client were both so intent on engaging her? Helen had taught her never to believe in coincidences, and this one was too big to swallow. Even so, Diana had lashed out at Dag without evidence of wrongdoing. She very well might have fatally wounded their relationship. A relationship that, for all its many faults, was also the one constant in her changeable life. Sometimes it felt like Dag was smothering her, but there was no one else looking out for her, no one else offering her small kindnesses with no expectation of reciprocation. It was the very lack of a quid pro quo that made her feel so uncomfortable, so out of her depth. Sparring with Lowell was so much easier, familiar in its stark self-interest.

"Seems like the guy who claims to want to cut the bullshit is the one spewing it," she said. "For all the words you've said, there's surprisingly little actual information. And if that's not a red flag, I don't know what is."

The color drained from Lowell's face, and his eyes widened. Diana's hand went to her holster, and she twitched her head to the side to check the room behind her. But there were no henchmen sneaking up behind her, and her feed scans were still coming up clean.

Then Lowell leaned over and projectile vomited onto the carpet. It was a slimy yellow sludge, mostly liquid. He wiped his mouth with the corner of the sheet.

"Whoo," he said, as the acrid smell reached Diana's nostrils. "I feel *so* much better. I'm telling you, DC people are so inane that I have to drown my frustrations in liquor. Their tediousness is hell on my liver. Next time drop in a few hours earlier, and I'll find a boy, girl, or whatever you're into who can loosen you up a bit, if you know what I mean."

"Despite appearances, I have better things to do than listen to a crackpot and not-so-well-endowed old man. If you don't get to the fucking point, I'm either going to torture you or leave."

"*Zing,*" said Lowell delightedly. "Yes! For the love of all things fuckable, I'm glad you're here. Okay, you wanna know why I have you looking up Rachel's skirt?"

He bounded off the side of the bed, strode to the window, and pulled back the curtains. The lights of Washington twinkled in the darkness beyond. Lowell pressed his palms against the glass.

"Everyone worries about the future." His voice lost its affected madness. He was quiet now, incisive. "They freak out about technology. They obsess over how tomorrow might be different. But it's the things that do *not* change that we should pay attention to. If you want to make sense of the world, focus on finding the constants. They're the rare truths that everyone's too busy to bother with. This town"—he tapped a finger on the glass—"has forgotten its most basic truth. These politicians and bureaucrats are so consumed with their petty institutions that they don't even realize they're ceding the only thing that matters. Power. During the Revolutionary War, Americans beat the British because they didn't engage in open battle, sapping their enemy's strength with a thousand guerrilla raids instead. Today Commonwealth has infiltrated every corner of our lives. Our houses, our cars, our planes, our jobs, our cities, our armies, our communications, our money, everything runs on their software. We invited them in, handed ourselves over willingly. We're all so dependent on the feed that we can't do anything without it. It's death by a thousand small conveniences. When Rachel announced her cute little carbon tax a few years ago, it didn't just blow up my business, it sounded the death knell of the nation state. Countries can't even make their own damn decisions anymore, not without Rachel's permission anyway. And this is just the beginning. The balance of power has shifted. And this town"—he tapped the window again—"is on the losing side."

Diana puffed on her cigar.

Fifteen years ago she had lost her first agent. As a case officer, her primary job was recruiting, managing, and protecting a network of agents who could feed her secrets. Sometimes they shared intel under duress. She might blackmail an official if she could find suitable documentation of scandal. More often they did it for greed, revenge, or a ticket out.

Hamza had been none of these. He was a principled spy, so fed up with the endless corruption over water rights in drought-ravaged Morocco that he had walked straight into the American embassy and demanded to speak to an intelligence officer. From that day on, Hamza had been a font of useful intel, passing along classified documents, secret blacklists, and details of clandestine payouts in the hope that the Americans would force out the worst offenders.

Hamza's information was pristine, but Diana started to worry that the bosses he was reporting on might get wise to his efforts. She petitioned for help, but Helen refused on the basis that agency algorithms were turning up no such evidence of conspiracy in the feeds of the targets. Resources were needed for more pressing problems. Diana then urged Hamza to take a break, or at least slow down. But in his zeal to empower his supposed benefactors, he wouldn't think of it.

One dusty afternoon he missed a meeting. Diana had sat there sipping on too-sweet mint tea and wondering where she'd find his body. After he didn't show up at the backup location, she began searching his haunts. He was in his bathtub, hair still sticky with shampoo, throat cut, resting in scarlet water thick with soap bubbles.

Diana had lost it when she got back to Washington, shouting down Helen right there in the middle of Mauricio's. The agency had become so reliant on the feed for intelligence gathering that it had divested its expensive and risky human networks. Why bother running agents when you could scrape a trillion data points and filter them for statistically significant intel? The problem was that data told you what people did and how they did it. But it revealed little as to why they did what they did. In the special kind of blindness brought on by apparent omniscience, they were hemorrhaging their best people.

Lowell was an asshole, but he was also right. When everything from the grappling hook at her side to the national power grid depended on the feed, the world had slowly but surely divorced power from official politics, people not even cognizant of what their reliance on Commonwealth might foretell.

"Sounds like you're working on a campaign speech," she said.

Lowell's head snapped around to pin Diana with a stare.

"It doesn't have to be this way," he said. "We don't have to scratch our balls and watch our country wither and die. If I learned anything as a businessman, it's that opportunity hides in every disaster. Commonwealth is a threat to every government on earth because every government on earth depends on Commonwealth. But it's headquartered here on American soil. It's a prize waiting to be seized."

Dominos fell in Diana's head. Collecting dirt on Commonwealth and progressively more personal intel on Rachel. Surveilling her daily routines. Mapping key physical locations. It wasn't about shorting their stock. It wasn't even about ousting her as CEO.

"You want to *nationalize* Commonwealth?" Diana couldn't contain her shock.

Lowell beamed. "All we need to do is work up a good excuse and send in the FBI. Countries nationalize big companies all the time. Hell, we saw too much of it in the oil industry. Rachel can do what we tell her or go to prison while we install a more reasonable leader. Shareholders will throw a hissy fit, but we'll promise to remunerate them at some point, and they won't be able to do shit about it. It's our public duty, for heaven's sake. We can't just abdicate the sacred mantle of American sovereignty to Silicon Valley, can we? Endangers the Constitution and baseball and apple pie and all our other brilliant traditions and blah, blah, blah."

It was totally insane. But it would finally provide the oversight that techno capitalists like Rachel had evaded for so long. It would put voters back in charge of critical infrastructure. It would clarify what had long since been obvious: the digital world was just as important as the physical one and ought to be a public jurisdiction, not a walled garden.

Lowell dropped Diana's report into a shared feed. Images unfurled. Board members arguing, Sofia's map of the corporate hierarchy, Kendrick's financial highlights, Rachel working in her corner of the lobby, Diana's rough outline of the house on Telegraph Hill.

"As your report illustrates, Rachel is not even close to being prepared for such an eventuality. If we strike hard and fast, she won't even know what hit her. These tech gurus still live in a fantasy universe where they're the peaceful purveyors of a benevolent future. That's the problem of living in a bubble. Can you imagine trying to develop an oil field in Nigeria with an attitude like that?" He roared with laughter. "You'd be eaten alive. Welcome to the real world. I mean, shit, Rachel swims laps at a public pool. Minimal security detail. Pfft. With a few guns and a lot of lawyers, Commonwealth will be the rightful property of the United States government. God bless America. Problem solved."

Lowell gave himself a round of applause and dismissed the shared feed. He bit his lower lip and raised his eyebrows, leaning in toward Diana with feverish intensity.

"The thing is," he stage-whispered, "we can't do it without your help."

Diana looked beyond Lowell, through the haze of cigar smoke, and out the hotel window. She found the apex of the Washington Monument, followed the shining obelisk down to where it appeared to emerge from the roof of the White House. It was to this beacon that her family had fled the destruction of Bulgaria. It was here that they had finally discovered what it felt like to live free of constant fear. Diana had dedicated her life to protecting that feeling, to serving this symbol and the people who believed in it. Was this lunatic plan its unlikely salvation from the descent into irrelevance or the harbinger of its self-destruction?

CHAPTER 14

Diana dangled her legs off the edge of Indian Rock and gazed out over the Bay Area. From this vantage high in the Berkeley Hills, she could see everything from the angled slopes of Mount Tam to the iconic cranes at the Port of Oakland. She smelled a faint hint of ash on the wind, doubtless carried up from the blackened remains of Southern California. The rock was warm underneath her, having soaked up the afternoon heat.

Now that the baseline adrenaline of her trip to Washington was receding, she couldn't escape the mess that she'd made of her personal life. Indian Rock was where she and Dag had shared their first kiss. She remembered her surprise when he'd offered her a gift, how she'd almost refused to believe that the lovingly rendered portrait of herself was real. *I can make pancakes.* She smiled. Usually so suave and confident, he'd fumbled for words even as she'd struggled to come to terms with her own budding affection. His vulnerability and awkwardness had drawn her to him, sparked something inside her, inspired her to take the unprecedented step of bringing him home with her.

It was unprecedented for a reason. Taking Dag home had been a breach of protocol. *You have more borders and treaties and NDAs in your head than the fucking United Nations.* Diana didn't live one life. She lived dozens of lives, each carefully calibrated for the people from whom she needed something and who needed something in return. Letting a client become a lover, inviting him to move into the cottage with her, these were painfully obvious missteps. Helen would have unleashed hellfire on any subordinate stupid enough to blur such important boundaries.

Diana wasn't stupid. But in Dag she'd found something that made all her rules fade into the background. It was harder to feel that her strictures should always take precedence, easier to let things slide.

Sloppiness invited chaos. But maybe chaos was exactly what she needed.

A container ship crossed beneath the Golden Gate, dwarfing the sailboats tacking in and out of Sausalito. Diana imagined matte-black helicopters skimming over the open water, their rotors kicking up spray, ascending at the last possible moment to swoop into downtown San Francisco, hundreds of small drones flying cover, weaving through the vertiginous skyscrapers. The FBI team would leap out in formation before the chopper touched down, pedestrians fleeing or watching in slack-jawed amazement as black SUVs poured in from all sides and the heavily armed squad charged through the doors of Commonwealth headquarters, spreading out to cover the redwood grove within, hijacking elevators and pounding up emergency stairwells to detain the entire executive team, bursting in to ambush Rachel, the aging mogul looking up with undaunted poise, her purple eye assessing the hardened veterans not with surprise but resolve. Ranks upon ranks of attorneys would invade in the wake of the tactical strike, drowning dissent in dense legalese, self-referential rationalization, and bland nonanswers at endless press conferences. Diana smiled to herself. Surely nothing so cinematic would come to pass. Complex legislation and detailed regulations would precede indictments, no less effective for their lack of melodrama.

Lowell must indulge himself in similar daydreams. Commonwealth's global carbon tax had undermined his oil empire, and nationalizing the tech conglomerate would be vengeance incarnate. They would need some kind of pithy justification for the public. It might even call for a false-flag operation, orchestrating some disaster for which Commonwealth was clearly at fault so that the takeover would appear legitimate.

Seizing the paragon of American technological innovation was absurd, an affront to the economic freedom the country had been founded to uphold. But the feed rendered so many of the founding principles obsolete, operating at such vast scale and individual intimacy that it defied any traditional definition of a private firm. Was the ubiquitous flow of data any less a natural resource than the Rockies or the Mississippi? Shouldn't the digital world be subject to the same checks and balances as the physical one? What right did Commonwealth have to authoritarian rule over the feed, even if it was their creation?

Lowell was an opportunist, not a patriot, and his professions of public-mindedness were an odious mix of selfish grandstanding and ironic condescension. He was looking for revenge and the thrill of a dangerous bet that could win him more power than his climate-change flywheel ever had. He might be angling to take Rachel's place at the helm of Commonwealth, salt in the wound of her fall from grace. Or maybe he would be content to pull strings from behind the scenes, play people against each other until everyone owed him their standing.

But his lack of ethics didn't mean his argument was unfounded. Just as his fossil-fuel play had required insight as well as deviousness, nationalizing Commonwealth had a certain ruthless logic to it. The private health insurance industry had fought tooth and nail against government encroachment, but the ultimate reform to a single-payer system had improved quality of care, reduced costs, and benefited millions of Americans. Perhaps a parallel effort to reform governance of the feed would yield similar public dividends. Positive outcomes could outshine malign origins.

I guess it must be easier to cling to God and country or whatever it is that makes spies tick. Dag was more right than he knew. Diana had done unspeakable things in the name of patriotism. America was a force for good, a respite for the desperate, a land where even if you didn't achieve your lofty goals, you might still dream. So despite the fact that Helen had dismissed her from federal service, Diana still served in the best way she knew how.

But what was the right course to chart now? Should she forge ahead or blow the whistle? What happened when you pitted America's top entrepreneurs and innovators against America's preeminent politicians and policy makers? She needed someone with more information, someone with deeper insight into Lowell's thinking, someone with whom to brainstorm scenarios and contingencies, someone she could trust.

Fuck who you like as long as it doesn't endanger the mission. Love if you can't help it. But trust? Never. Diana would never forget Helen's honeyed words or the steel behind her baby-blue eyes. Falling in love with Dag had illustrated the self-denial such a maxim required with brutal clarity. Diana's stomach clenched. Despite her finely wrought facade, Dag saw right through her. She was a ghost, a shadow of a person, unworthy of the tenderness he showed her. Her entire life had been spent weaving a web of lies around a horde of secrets.

There was a green acorn lodged in a crack beside her. She plucked it out, rolled it around with her fingers. It was small and smooth and hard. The Ohlone Indians had called these hills home before Spanish conquistadors colonized the region. At that time, acorns were a staple food. They shook the oak trees, collected the acorns, and ground them into a fine flour with stone mortars and pestles. But acorns contain tannic acid, making them both bitter and poisonous. So the Ohlones rinsed the flour over and over and over again until they leached out the acid and were finally able to prepare the porridge that sustained them for generation after generation.

She dropped the acorn between her legs, watched it roll in little zigzags toward the edge, gaining momentum until it tumbled down the face of Indian Rock and out of view. *Whenever there's a chance to get real, you run for your life.* Difficult truths were as bitter and poisonous as acorns, but maybe they were just as critical to survival.

The cottage was only a few blocks away.

Diana pushed herself up and walked home.

She wanted Dag. She needed Dag. She loved Dag.

No matter what, she didn't want it to end this way.

It was time to face the fact that she hid things out of fear as often as professional discretion. The only way to win him back, to earn his trust, was for her to open up, to start sharing more with him. It would be a major risk, but so was inaction.

Few people knew Lowell better than Dag. If she was able to salvage things and tell him what was really going on, he might provide invaluable counsel. Maybe the solution to this whole mess was just around the corner.

As she walked up the path to the cottage, something caught her attention.

The front door was ajar.

CHAPTER 15

"Dag?"

Diana tamped down panic as she stepped through the front door. She had to remember that just because she rappelled into hotel rooms and had seventeen confirmed kills didn't mean that the rest of life was spy versus spy. Most people worried about their mortgages, jockeyed for promotions, and tried not to fuck up their kids too much. Since leaving Apex, illustration, not intrigue, had filled Dag's days. She would never leave the front door open, but he probably just wanted fresh air circulating through the house because it was a warm afternoon and they didn't have air-conditioning.

The drafting table in the living-room-turned-art-studio was empty, but the charcoal set she had given him rested beside his extensive collection of pens, pencils, and other implements. When she had stormed out after brunch a few weeks ago, such evidence of Dag's presence in her cottage had felt like symptoms of an infection. Now they inspired regret at how easily she had taken him for granted and a selfish hope that she might be able to glue the pieces back together.

"Dag?"

She still had no idea where she should start. She could explain how her grandmother had never spoken of what she'd had to do, what she'd had to endure, to get their family out of a war zone. She could remind

Dag of what she'd taught him and his cohort in Namibia about the critical importance of infosec and the hard-earned habits that Helen had drilled into her with brutal efficiency. She could describe how Haruki had hired her and how Sean and Lowell had been behind it. She could start with the big picture and map out Lowell's scheme. She could make a joke and try to defuse things with humor. She could pull him into bed and try to defuse things with sex. She could simply apologize and beg forgiveness. Every imagined monologue ran in parallel, filling her mind with a symphony of remorse.

Upstairs the bedroom was empty. It was hot and stuffy, the primroses in the small vase on the dresser slightly wilted next to that first portrait Dag had drawn of her. The glow-in-the-dark stars she had pasted all over the bedroom walls and ceiling looked a little sad in the bright afternoon light. At night they imbued the room with magic. By day they were just dull stickers.

Was it possible that Dag wasn't actually here? She touched the comforter. Maybe after their fight a few days ago, lying naked on this very bed, he had decided enough was enough, taken a page from her book, and simply left. Maybe he was fucking a star courtesan right now or running off in search of his programmed obsession, Emily. But he wouldn't have left the door open if he'd moved out, would he? Could it be a spiteful send-off, a small act of bitter vengeance demonstrating the persistence of her absence? Or perhaps he'd left and locked the door, but an opportunistic burglar had guessed the house was empty and made a move.

Diana tried to calm her racing heart. More likely he'd run out for a macchiato and was so caught up in imagining a new drawing that he'd neglected to double-check that the door closed behind him. Dag got lost in his own head all the time.

She descended, faster now, the balls of her feet skipping off each step. One, two, three knocks on the bathroom door. You never thought

you'd arrive home while your lover was pooping, but sometimes life threw curveballs.

"Dag?"

No answer.

She opened the door. The sprig of lavender hung from its string by the small window. Her family of rubber duckies was arranged in ascending order on the edge of the bathtub, and a complete collection of Borges's short stories rested atop the toilet tank.

Diana placed the book next to the sink, removed the top of the toilet tank, and pulled out one of her backup handguns from its waterproof case within. You kept paranoia on a tight leash, but once it started barking loud enough, you loosened your grip because it might be onto something. Even the reassuring weight of the pistol didn't prevent hairs rising on the back of her neck.

Anger flared. This was why she was so careful. So stupid shit like this didn't happen. Let down your guard for even a moment, and you're prey. As quickly as it had come, the feeling passed. She didn't know what was going on here. What she needed right now was to collect more data, not pass judgment. She had to keep her mind open, her senses alert.

Diana stepped out of the bathroom and into the kitchen, this time cognizant of maintaining her line of fire, keeping her center of gravity low, and letting her eyes flick around the room in practiced patterns. Faint aromas of cilantro and ancho chili greeted her. Pomegranates were piled in a basket on the counter. An empty coffee cup sat next to the sink. A single drop of water elongated and fell from the faucet. Cast-iron pans hung from hooks on the wall opposite a fading photograph of a coastal Greek village, one of the only remnants from Diana's childhood, a gift from a fellow refugee, bestowed in the crowded darkness of a smuggler's hold along with halting stories of Aegean life.

No Dag.

With predatory grace, she moved across the tile floor. There was one last place where Dag might be, must be. He probably hadn't been able to hear her from back here, didn't even realize she was home. Leading with the gun, she opened the back door to the attached greenhouse.

And froze.

No. It made no sense. Her heart thudded against her rib cage as if trying to escape. This was some sort of strange dream, the kind that left an uncanny emotional hangover that lasted for days.

The greenhouse was empty. Not just empty of Dag. Empty.

The dewy ferns, hanging vines, thrusting roots, rough bark, thick stems, veined leaves, sinewy stalks, vivid flowers, whispering fronds, the vibrant, encroaching, irrefutable life, even the silky lace of spiderwebs, all of it was gone.

She grasped the doorframe for support.

The botanical wonderland wasn't destroyed. It hadn't been savaged by pests or eaten by flame. Her plants were simply absent. The muted light falling through the greenhouse panels illuminated flat, even dirt. Nothing more.

Diana stumbled down the steps and knelt. She rested the gun beside her knee, dug her fingers into the earth, and raised a double handful of cool, moist soil that she let trickle through her fingers. Raw disbelief hit her like a double shot of grain alcohol. It was as if all her plants, the horticultural cornucopia that had been her respite, her labor, her shrine, had been nothing more than a figment of the imagination, a spectral hallucination instead of a sanctuary.

Looking down at her muddied hands, she saw dirt under her nails and raised a finger to touch the tip of her tongue. She tasted minerals and clay, had a momentary vision of a mole burrowing deep within the earth. She pressed her eyes shut. Opened them again.

This wasn't a hallucination. This was real.

Retrieving her gun, she pushed herself to her feet and tried to think.

The greenhouse wasn't entirely empty.

The mosaic path was still there. The bright tiles wound across the expanse of bare dirt to the small patio table at which she and Dag had eaten brunch. Without the attendant greenery, the arrangement was simultaneously forlorn and threatening.

Driven by a compulsion beyond her control, Diana walked up the path, stepping from tile to colorful tile, following every twist and turn until she reached the center of the barren greenhouse. She had come to seek forgiveness, to make amends, to turn a new page. She had dared to hope for counsel, companionship, someone she could rely on in a time of need. She had forgotten the inescapable core tenet of espionage.

All trust ended in betrayal.

A small envelope lay on the table, her name scrawled across it in ornate script. The world spun lazily in her periphery as she lifted the envelope, tore it open, and plucked out the card. The paper was thick, and the stylized head of a longhorn steer had been pressed into it.

She turned the card over in her hands.

Dearest Diana, it read. *If you would care to join us for dinner at the Ranch, details below, at 7 p.m. on Friday evening, we would be ever so much obliged. No plus-ones, I'm afraid. I dare say that the chef is quite good and that we should be able to clear up a few niggling questions for you. Sincerely, Surely-you've-guessed-by-now*

Diana swayed on her feet as the translucent walls closed in around her, darkly indistinct memories swimming behind them like denizens of an inimical aquarium. She recognized the handwriting.

Helen.

CHAPTER 16

The deck thrummed beneath Diana as the boat piloted itself away from the dock. Wavelets slapped against the hull and air roared past her ears, whipping her curls into a frenzy until she lowered herself into a chair behind the windscreen. This was the last place on earth she wanted to be, but there weren't any other options.

After securing a last-minute flight to Sun Valley, she'd scoured the feed for intel about the Ranch. Hidden in a remote valley in the Sawtooth Mountains, Lowell's Idaho retreat was a notorious billionaire hideaway, and invitations were highly sought-after among nouveau riche aspirants. It covered three thousand acres of pristine forests and snowcapped peaks, a bastion of private wilderness that was a playground for the rich and famous. Lopez had stopped here while fundraising for his presidential campaign, just as Freeman and all other recent contenders had. It was a place where feed stars cavorted with political brass and business tycoons, where plans were hatched and deals were sealed, where there was no greater sin than innocence.

Diana had insights the gossip columnists could only guess at. Dag had been a regular at the Ranch during Lowell's ascendancy, and his feed archive contained tidbits from dozens of extended visits over the years. She remembered Dag and Lowell standing next to a bloody stag, Lowell grinning like a madman and Dag looking like he was about to vomit. Besides bagging game, they had orchestrated their lobbying and commercial campaigns from here, inviting members of the Arctic Council and an alphabet soup of trade commissions to win favor for offshore bids and preferential tax treatment.

To complement the data she already had, Diana had pulled satellite imagery and sent a handful of drones to buzz the property. But security here was tight, federal tight, and the drones had been jammed or destroyed before they'd captured anything more than kilometer after kilometer of alpine rivers snaking through dense pine forest. Despite her rigorous profiling, Diana knew little more than the obvious, that this was an oligarch's extravagant lair.

She wanted to reach out to every security contractor she knew, assemble a small army of hard-eyed specops vets, splurge on top gear, call in every favor, snatch Helen and Dag and Lowell and whoever else was in on this mess, secret them away in an anonymous warehouse in the middle of an industrial wasteland, pump them for everything she could, and then leave their bodies to disintegrate in an acid vat. But the invitation had precluded such a glorious scenario.

Reaching into her jacket pocket, she ran a finger along the edge of the card. She remembered the gritty wetness of the soil on her fingers, the ache in her knees, the sweaty shirt sticking to her back. Her garden was where she licked her wounds, where she escaped her past, where she found the occasional fleeting glimpse of peace. The void its absence had left behind reminded her that there was no place that was truly safe. The slip of paper in her pocket was a far more dangerous threat than any arsenal Diana could mobilize. They knew where she lived. They knew what she loved. They knew just how to get to her. Helen knew all these things and more.

How did Helen know these things? The answer was obvious. Dag.

He hadn't been her boyfriend, or any kind of friend at all. The tender words, constant affection, even the inevitable friction had been nothing but a front. Dag had succeeded where Haruki had failed.

Starting out green and full of enthusiasm, he'd absorbed her lessons in tradecraft until his subtlety had surpassed her own. He had forged himself into a weapon, and Helen had pointed that weapon at her prodigal protégé, yanking Diana back into her all-encompassing orbit. Diana had lacquered on layer upon layer of protection, wrapped subterfuge around herself like a cloak. Her cottage was a safe house. Every one of her agents was isolated. Each saw only one of many masks that she donned and doffed with ease. She had thought herself unassailable, exiled by her stubborn conscience and sheltered by enforced irrelevance, relegated to scavenge for whatever scraps of intrigue she could access freelance. Yet at the end of the day, all it had taken to break her down was a hot piece of ass and some half-decent pancakes.

Leaning over the gunwale, she spat into the churn of the bow wave. Steep hills rose from the far shore of the lake, their slopes covered with spruce and fir. They were dwarfed by the jagged peak behind them, fingers of snow threading between scree and rocky ridges. Clouds massed above the mountain range, mounds and whorls piling on top of each other, filling the immense sky, front-lit by the setting sun, bearing down on the lake, the coagulated darkness in their midst promising a violent alpine thunderstorm.

Stray pieces fell into place. Sean, Rachel, Lowell, Javier, even Hsu, everyone associated with this job had some connection to Dag. When Dag had left Apex after trading Emily and Javier's exploit for a global carbon tax, he hadn't just puttered around drawing all day long. He'd found new employment immediately, attached himself to Helen, and gone undercover to become Diana's Achilles' heel.

Helen must have pitched him after Diana's root access to Dag's feed had been revoked. That meant after Diana had reported her findings to Dag, revealed that Emily and Javier had been manipulating his digital life just as effectively as any of their other targets'. She clenched her teeth. Dag would have had just enough time to draw that portrait of her, to work up a sappy act that would play off her flirtatious teasing in time for that meeting on Indian Rock. It had been nothing but a show. They must have had a great time laughing at how easily he'd seduced her, how quickly he'd found his way into her bed and her supposedly hidden life. From then on, Helen had held Diana in the palm of her hand.

The whole time, Dag must have secretly despised Diana, seen her as hopelessly naive for believing in him. Diana knew better than anyone how obsessed he'd been with Emily. Why would that obsession wane? Maybe while Diana was off on a mission, Dag had conducted a covert affair, meeting the bitch in some obscure boudoir for carnal celebrations of Diana's credulity.

Pathetic. That's what she was. And now Helen had found a use for her. She whistled, and Diana came running. Just like old times.

The prow cut through the still water of the lake, slicing apart the landscape reflected on its surface. The boat navigated toward a long dock that thrust out from a shoreline fringed with trembling reeds. A pedestrian path led up from the dock through a perfectly manicured lawn and numerous connected patios to what could only be called a palace.

The Ranch was a confection of stone and wood, complete with countless arches, levels, wings, turrets, and balconies that soared and sprawled at the whim of an architect whose only mandate had been excess. A vast boathouse lay on one side and an equestrian center on the other, the lofty crags providing a dramatic backdrop for the estate. It was beautiful and grotesque in its self-aware opulence. And there, standing on the dock, giving her a jaunty wave as the boat piloted itself to a smooth stop, was its master.

CHAPTER 17

"Welcome to my humble abode." Lowell beamed and extended a hand.

Diana ignored the offer of help and stepped onto the dock.

"More like gauche," she said. "Has nobody taught you the virtue of restraint?"

Lowell clapped his hands. "Delightful," he said. "I thought we were off to a strong start, but I was a bit worried the residual alcohol in my system made the memory of your nighttime visit more entertaining than you actually were. Straight off the boat and you've relieved that niggling anxiety. Bravo."

"I came here for answers," she said. "Not to be your dancing monkey."

He raised a finger. "Entertainment and utility aren't mutually exclusive. But fear not, there's no gala this evening. We're dancing in a show far bigger than even my little hideout could contain. Needless to say, you're the star."

Diana considered drilling him with questions but thought better of it. Let Lowell stand there grinning in his tuxedo. Helen was here somewhere. She was the one Diana had to focus on. Lowell was brash, greedy, and daring, but Helen would have him wrapped around her pinkie. Diana would save her energy for the battle that really mattered.

Lowell led Diana up the path toward the mansion, peppering her with small talk, obviously gloating over how their positions had reversed so quickly. Diana responded automatically, reviewing the meager data she'd been able to dredge up about Helen in her feed. Helen was a senior adviser to President Lopez, a position that gave her the perfect excuse to have a hand in everything while never risking the awkward attention of formally running an agency. She had played similar roles in every administration since she'd been elevated from deputy director of the Central Intelligence Agency. Helen was one of DC's few perennial keystones, too well connected for anyone to ignore. Her picture rarely found its way into the feed headlines, but her influence shaped most major decisions.

It was Helen's extreme competence that had drawn Diana to her in the first place, that had made Diana so eager to seek her guidance and ride up the ladder on her coattails. Like capital, power compounded. When Diana last saw Helen a decade earlier, the older woman had just made herself the most powerful person in Washington. Dominance would have accreted in the intervening years, solidifying her hold on the nation's reins.

Diana still felt the echoes of shock from the morning after her last visit to the Oval. President Freeman was in cardiac arrest. The best cardiology experts in the country were treating him. The press corps ran live streams all day, grave doctors delivering meaningless updates, unable or unwilling to elaborate beyond their prepared statements on the president's condition. Early the next morning, he was pronounced dead.

President Freeman hadn't been particularly popular in life, but death deified him. Washington grieved its lost leader. But power abhors a vacuum, and Lopez realized the secret dream and deepest fear of any vice president, taking the office Freeman had vacated. An intelligent young progressive, Lopez desperately needed a guide to help him navigate the DC labyrinth. Helen was right there, ready to take his hand.

At first Diana had beaten back suspicion with outright denial. Helen might have complained bitterly about Freeman shutting her out, but she was a patriot. Patriots understood that the country was bigger than their personal ambitions. Patriots bided their time and waited for the next elected official to woo. But the more Diana tamped down her anxiety, the more it spread. It was a weed that kept coming back, larger and more invasive each time. Soon she was losing sleep over it, staring at the ceiling of her DC apartment and refusing to consider the conspiracy that consumed her thoughts.

For no reason she could fathom, Diana hit the breaking point at an organic market in Georgetown. As she picked up a too-ripe avocado, felt the pebbled skin give under her fingers, she decided that the only way to escape her obsession was to indulge it. She would dig her teeth in and, finding nothing, return to more quotidian cloaks and daggers.

It wasn't nothing. Diana's quiet inquiries revealed that her fears were well founded. The president's toxicology report, autopsy, and reported symptoms were the precise species of nothing promised by the black market biochemist in Buenos Aires. The doctors declared it natural causes, but only because of their ignorance of the new category of synthetic compound that Diana had smuggled into the country, into the White House, in a diplomatic pouch. It was too much to be mere correlation.

"We have an issue." The wide main doors of the manor swung open at their approach, a severe woman in a conservative suit standing immediately inside, arms crossed. "Lito says they're coming up dry."

Lowell rolled his eyes theatrically. "Diana, this is Freja. I believe you've corresponded during previous collaborations. She's the real captain of this ship. Freja, Diana is our guest. We'll have more than enough time to attend to Lito."

Freja gave Diana a perfunctory look. Freja was Lowell's unofficial chief of staff, a consummate operator, and the engine that turned his schemes into reality. Without Freja, Lowell was just a madman. Without Lowell, Freja was just a freakishly compulsive organizer.

"Let's get on with it, then," she said, Danish lilt loaded with disdain. Her heels clicked on the tile floor as she stalked away across the vast atrium.

"Lovely to meet you too," said Diana. "It's a genuine pleasure to experience your vivacious personality face-to-face."

Lowell failed to cover a snort. Freja strode on, impervious.

They walked through a maze of halls and galleries, each parlor dedicated to a particular game. Basketball memorabilia filled one, ivory chessboards the next, *StarCraft* loot the one after that, complete with antique desktop computers and a painfully reconstructed local area network so that visitors could boot up and play the original classic without feed intermediation. There was a sudoku nook, a martial arts dojo, and a beer pong alcove. Lowell's fascination with games clearly went beyond poker and five finger fillet.

Diana half expected to find Dag around every corner, lazily twirling a mini-golf club, grinning like a starved hyena as he surveyed his too-gullible target. But asking Lowell about Dag would show that she cared, thereby reinforcing his advantage. Better to hold her peace, as if his violation of everything she held dear hadn't affected her.

Seeing her look, Lowell shrugged. "What's money for if not to indulge passion?"

"I wish you'd stay focused on the only game that really matters," said Freja over her shoulder. "We have more than enough to handle without these childish distractions."

"We've got a kind of love-hate thing going on," said Lowell impishly. "She hates me. I love her."

"Don't flatter yourself," said Freja. "You're not interesting enough to inspire hatred." She shot a glance back over her shoulder at Diana. "You, on the other hand, have a lot more going on. How did you breach security at the Hay-Adams? We obviously need to update our protocols."

"A magician never reveals her tricks," said Diana.

"Who's working for whom?" Freja glared.

"Don't flatter yourself either," said Diana. "Neither of you are in charge here." She shrugged. "Plus, I don't teach kindergarten." They rounded a corner and came face-to-face with two Secret Service agents flanking a doorway. "Why don't you ask these assholes? They spend their whole careers worrying about attack vectors."

One of the agents leaned over and opened the door. Diana's breath caught in her throat as they stepped through into a dining hall. One entire wall was glass. Beyond it, the vanguard of clouds rolled in over the lake, plunging it into an eerie darkness broken only by angled shafts of dying light from the setting sun. Thunder growled in the distance. At the end of a long wooden table, a woman stood, perfectly relaxed, blonde curls tumbling over her shoulders, hands clasped behind her back, staring out over the wind-whipped water.

CHAPTER 18

"Where are we supposed to sit, then?" asked Lowell, gesturing at the table that could seat thirty but was set for two.

Helen turned to face them. There were crow's-feet around her eyes, and her skin had a papery quality to it, but otherwise she could have stepped right out of Diana's memory.

"Oh, Lowell," she said. "We girls have some catching up to do. Reunions can be so sentimental, and I wouldn't want to bore you and Freja. We'll take dinner alone, and perhaps you two can join us for a drink later. How's that?"

The musical cadence of Helen's Southern accent sent a tremor through Diana. That sweet voice was both the angel and the devil on her shoulder. The honeyed tones, at odds with their realpolitik deployment, had suffused countless briefings, postmortems, and intimate confessions.

"Oh, don't worry about us," said Lowell, with forced levity. "We'd enjoy a trip down memory lane. We'll all get to know each other better that way."

"I'll have Walter lay the extra settings," said Freja flatly.

Helen let her baby-blue eyes fall on Lowell.

"Actually, Freja, don't bother," he said. "Let's leave them to it. We can check in with Lito in the meantime, see if we can get anywhere with his problem."

"Such a gracious host, as ever," said Helen. "Lovely man, am I right?"

"Charming," said Diana.

Lowell offered them a pained smile and a half bow before departing with Freja.

As soon as the door clicked shut behind them, Helen was striding over to Diana, arms wide, a bright smile illuminating her face. Diana stood frozen, hating herself for her impotence, for feeling like an antelope trembling in the presence of a lioness. Helen wrapped her in a tight hug, pressing cheek to cheek, the heady scent of her perfume, magnolia with a hint of musk, setting off a confused rush of nostalgia and panic inside Diana.

"Maria, darling," she said, pulling back to hold Diana at arm's length. "It has been far too long. What a blessing to see you again after all these years."

Maria. Something cracked inside Diana, and visions flooded through the gap. A spoonful of *kiselo mlyako* melting on her tongue. Playing hide-and-seek in the ruined fortress. Neighbors whispering dark tidings. The squeeze of her grandmother's sinewy hand on her shoulder. An ache that never truly went away. No one else called her by her birth name. It felt anomalous even to Diana's innermost self, the name of a little girl lost in the past, the name of a stranger. She could count the people who knew it on one hand. But whenever they were alone, Helen never failed to use it, to reinforce the truism that nothing was beyond her reach.

Diana had to speak, had to say something, had to fend off the awful truth that she was out of her depth. Prying herself away from the tangle of memories, she focused on keeping her voice even and light, devoid of the dread hovering just below the surface.

"I honestly thought the day might never come," said Diana, looking into eyes whose apparent innocence was the greatest lie ever told.

"Every once in a while, fate smiles upon us." Helen squeezed Diana's shoulders. "And when it does, we can't afford to ignore it. Now"—she clapped her hands—"come sit. I've had the chef prepare our *favorite*. It'll be just like old times, even as we're on the brink of new ones."

As they walked down the length of the table, something teased at the edge of Diana's consciousness, something familiar and alien, comforting and sinister. She scanned the room. The table was fashioned from a single cross-sectional cut from the trunk of an old-growth tree, the concentric rings implying untold seasons of drought and plenty. Lightning illuminated the undersides of the clouds outside like a match lit in a cavern. Thunder growled in its wake. Fat raindrops began to fall in an uncoordinated pitter-patter. But it wasn't sight or even sound that was raising Diana's hackles. It was something else, something about Helen's perfume, or some complementary scent playing counterpoint to her perfume, a textured fragrance of grape and banana, so sweet it cooled Diana's breath when she inhaled.

And then she saw it. A vase at the far end of the table where their place settings were laid. Long, wide petals the color of oranges and cream falling loosely into a rough globe. Native to the Himalayan foothills of Southeast Asia. Blooms year-round in tropical and subtropical climates. Minimum temperature tolerance around negative one degree Celsius. A key ingredient in the production of the world's most expensive perfumes. *Michelia champaca*. A bouquet of *Michelia champaca*. A bouquet of *Diana's Michelia champaca*. The notches on the fourth petal of one of the flowers, the arrangement of the broad green leaves, the specific hue and maturity of the flowers. These had been cut from the tree that had once graced her greenhouse.

Helen took her seat and neatly unfolded the napkin on her lap.

Diana, reeling, followed suit, trying not to keel over or knock a stray fork off the table in the process. The sense of personal violation was overwhelming. Far worse than any physical violence she'd suffered. Her body might house her soul, but her garden was its refuge. This was salt in the wound of its loss, another reminder of eternal primacy from the matriarch with a prim smile.

I've killed every plant I've ever tried to grow. Dag's remark over their pancake breakfast hadn't been offhand. It had been a veiled threat. Knowing her as no one else had, he had been able to feed Helen details of the things Diana cared most about. Diana treated her own agents like beloved plants, keeping a close eye on them and offering them sustenance, support, or space as they needed it to thrive. But sometimes, despite all her best efforts, things turned sour. When they did, Diana did what she had to, sifting through everything she knew about the person to unveil the few things they cared about most and then turning those vulnerabilities against them. Carrots and sticks were two sides of the same coin. Love was the truest source of pain.

"Ahh," said Helen, rubbing her hands together. *"Finally."*

A waiter appeared, poured amber ales, and placed enormous burgers in front of each of them, complete with bacon, avocado, and thick beef tallow fries.

"Lowell assures me everything was raised and butchered right here on the Ranch," said Helen. "A step up from Mauricio's, right?"

The rich smell of grilled meat, toasted sourdough, and fried potato had once been a hallmark of coming up under Helen's tutelage. They had frequented Mauricio's hole-in-the-wall, braving the decrepit DC back alley to scarf down the burgers he prepared with a consummate attention he never showed his customers. It was at Mauricio's that Helen had imparted so many of her lessons in espionage, communicated in polished anecdotes and careful euphemisms. Diana had associated those tête-à-têtes with the sense of purpose afforded by public service and accentuated by secret duty. Now the smell made her sick.

Helen ate with enthusiasm, smearing each fry in a pile of ketchup and washing everything down with ale. Blood and grease ran down her hands, and her fingers left dark smudges on the beer glass.

"I know we've had our differences," said Helen, taking another swallow of ale. "And of course, we've grown apart over the years. But if there's one thing I've never doubted, Maria, it's the love we share for this fine country. You were the best case officer I ever had. And that quality, that drive, can only come from the knowledge that you serve something larger than yourself, that there is an entire nation depending on you. It's an honor and a burden."

This woman, who had killed a president, was calling on Diana's patriotism.

Suppressing nausea, Diana hoisted the burger and took a bite, chewing until she could bear to swallow the masticated lump of food. She had to ignore the *Michelia champaca*. She had to act as if Dag's betrayal had left her unscathed. She had to pretend that Helen did not in fact hold Diana's pulsing heart in her manicured hands, lest Diana indicate the thinness of the thread by which her sanity hung. The only way to fight someone who knew your weaknesses was to feign indifference.

"There's a peculiar melancholy specific to fading empire," said Helen. "The Romans, the Mongols, the British, they all knew what it meant to see inherited glory rust away to nothing. America peaked in the final years of the twentieth century, its enemies defeated and its strength uncontested. My rule of thumb is that if a blowjob constitutes a national crisis, then you're at the very top of your game. Ever since, we've been holding on like an athlete who refuses to retire. It's all a little sad, really."

Diana needed to get a handle on this situation. Ever since picking up Helen's note in the empty greenhouse, it had felt like the world was happening to Diana instead of the other way around. *Agency is the agent's first priority.* One of Helen's spitfire maxims delivered in the cramped booth at Mauricio's. The only way to move through intrigue's dominion was like a shark: you either kept swimming, or you died. Another Helen adage rattled home. *Step one of any op is to figure out who the principals are and what they want.* Diana had finally got to the bottom of the first bit. From Haruki to Leviathan to Sean to Lowell and finally to Helen. Helen was the principal. In any operation Helen touched, she was *always* the principal.

That left the second bit. What did Helen want? Why had she dragged Diana out from under her rock, flayed open her life like Dag's stag? Helen didn't fuck around. She wasn't doing this out of some cruel fascination. Sadism was for suckers. Helen always had a plan.

"So you came up with the idea to nationalize Commonwealth," said Diana. "You want to bolster the US government by hijacking its corporate star. Revive economic nationalism."

"You may not believe it," said Helen, "but Lowell was actually the one who came to me with the proposal."

"Take down the people who ruined his oil cartel with a carbon tax."

"Precisely. He was planning to shop it around to whatever government might bite." Helen mock shivered. "He had Sean over at Apex setting up speed dates with high-level officials from South Africa to Singapore. These mercenary types drive me nuts. It's as if they believe money is the only true form of power. So shortsighted. Thank heaven he showed up at my door first. It could have been a disaster otherwise."

"But you're already pulling Washington's strings as a senior adviser to Lopez," said Diana. "Why is hijacking an American conglomerate worth the risk? It would be chaos."

Helen's eyes danced, but all she did was take another sip of beer.

"Commonwealth threatened not just US sovereignty but the sovereignty of every other country with the carbon tax," said Diana, remembering Lowell's confession. "They overstepped. But Wall Street oversteps every decade or so, and all we do is throw on a Band-Aid and hope the wound doesn't fester. Why not just regulate our way out of this one?

Give Rachel a slap on the wrist, toss a few juicy talking points to the press corps, make good on Lopez's recent pronouncements, reassure the international community, and so on?"

Helen rolled her eyes. "Oh, sweetie," she said. "Lopez doesn't know the first thing about this. It's way above his pay grade, if you know what I mean."

Way above the president's pay grade. If Helen wasn't sharing this with Lopez, that meant she might actually be serious about doing it. And if she was serious, that meant there was some prize at stake that was worth risking everything in an unprecedented federal takeover.

A lightning bolt crackled down beyond the glass, forking and writhing as if flung by Zeus himself. The stray thought of Olympian royalty made Diana replay part of the conversation in her head. *The Romans, the Mongols, the British, they all knew what it meant to see inherited glory rust away to nothing.* In framing the problem as she saw it, Helen wasn't referencing constitutional crises, antitrust legislation, or new regulatory regimes. She was talking about *empires.*

Thunder roared and the house shook. Wind churned up whitecaps on the lake. Rain lashed at the window.

It was *obvious.* Why hadn't Diana seen it all along? Probably for the same reason that had handicapped her career before, an enduring faith in the values this country was supposed to stand for.

Diana took a long drink as if ale could wash away the realization. "You don't want to hijack Commonwealth," she said. "You want to hijack the entire world."

CHAPTER 19

Helen wiped the corners of her mouth with her napkin.

Diana continued, picking up momentum as hypothesis compounded into certainty. "Rachel threatened denying feed service to countries who didn't adopt the carbon tax, knowing no government could say no. Without the feed, their economies, their infrastructure, even their militaries would collapse. It works because it's convenient and because it's neutral, the tech stack that powers everything else. But if you seize the feed by nationalizing Commonwealth, you're not going to stop at implementing a carbon tax."

"Shock and awe, baby," said Helen, tracing one of the table's tree rings with a fingertip. "If we move quickly and do things right, we can put Genghis Khan to shame. Governments surrender to us immediately or go feedless and implode, and we send in troops to take over what's left. Their only choice is whether they want to be a prosperous colony of the Stars and Stripes or a pile of rubble. It'll all be over in a week. The first planetary empire." Helen leaned in so close that Diana could smell the meat on her breath. "It's *exquisite*."

Diana sat in stunned silence as the scenario unfolded in her mind. Leveraging their digital dependence, Helen would secure universal political fealty, putting the United States firmly in control of global governance. Foreign countries would be reduced to territories, their national governments abolished or repurposed into regional administrations. Even the Prideful Seven, who didn't run the feed on Commonwealth hard fiber, couldn't survive without the conglomerate's ubiquitous software. It would take years to spin up parallel infrastructure. If Helen struck fast, everyone would be outraged, but no one could refuse.

"It's *insane* is what it is," said Diana. "You'll start a war."

Helen waved a hand. "A war we'll win easily once their equipment stops working," she said. "It'll be no contest. And the best ideas always sound insane until you prove them right."

Diana imagined the opposing drone squadrons refusing to take off, tanks paralyzed on their treads, and assault rifles ignoring their triggers. It would be a rout, not a fight.

"Think about it," said Helen. "So many of the problems we face today only exist because we don't have a global government. Human trafficking, environmental degradation, tax evasion, poverty, immigration, pandemics. All of them would be so much easier to solve if we didn't have two hundred squabbling governments getting in the way. Justice wouldn't be limited by jurisdiction, and opportunity wouldn't be constrained by borders. The feed is already global. The economy is already global. Everything is already global except for our political institutions, and that fundamentally undermines their efficacy. The rest of the world might deny it, but we're doing them a favor. I'm willing to do the right thing even if it makes us unpopular."

"The right thing? That's quite the rationalization from an aspiring colonizer."

"Oh, come on now, Maria. You can claim all the moral high ground you want, but we both know that power is power. We have to make hard choices all the time in order to protect American democracy. Anyone with a weak stomach either loses or outsources. This is a way to renew our country and divert the course of history. We don't have to fade into the geopolitical background like the Brits. We can be better than that. We are better than that."

Despite everything, the plan had an outrageous beauty. Advances in science, technology, and economics had driven global growth and given birth to new powers that challenged American hegemony. The pendulum was swinging away from Washington, and Helen's gambit would reverse the trends everyone had long thought inevitable. Failure would be catastrophic, but success meant DC could dictate a new world order.

"And that's why you needed me," said Diana. "You couldn't risk official channels because you haven't told Lopez."

"There's nothing more sensitive than this," said Helen. "I needed someone with the right skills who isn't an agency asset. I obviously couldn't come to you directly. But having Lowell bring you on with a few cutouts in between provided just enough cover. Or I hope it did, at any rate. Look"—she put a hand on Diana's forearm—"we have a limited window here. Either we make the first move, or someone else will. Other people are going to put the pieces together, and if they strike preemptively, we'll be just as helpless as anyone else. And *that* is the real reason I need you for this mission. Any spook I hire on the open market might turn around and sell the intel. This secret is too valuable to share with someone I don't already trust implicitly."

To Diana's chagrin, she couldn't entirely stifle the budding sense of pride at Helen's words. Knowing that you were being manipulated didn't stop it from working.

"All day today I couldn't get your grandmother's funeral out of my head." Helen's voice dropped an octave. Now it was rougher, confessional. "It was raining almost as hard as this." She indicated the raging storm with a nod. "And what you said, Maria . . . What you said that day reaffirmed everything we do, everything we've devoted our lives to. I can't tell you how many times I've replayed those words. They get me through my darkest moments. That's why I knew that even though you might hate me for Freeman, you would see that this is bigger than our opinions, bigger than our mistakes, bigger than our individual ambitions. This is do or die, and to the victor go the spoils."

Contentment was a condition with which Helen was constitution-ally unfamiliar. She was always reaching, stretching, reinventing herself and her dreams. The relentless metamorphoses could be painful and disturbing, but they also reflected a world in which change was the only constant. That's what had allowed her to remain relevant for so long in a capital populated by upstarts and burnouts. That's what had drawn Diana to her in the first place. That's what made this new web she was weaving so compelling. It was a fantasy, a castle in the sky spun from the dark material of clear-eyed avarice. But could history claim a single visionary who wasn't mad?

Helen was unraveling Diana's life and then offering her a chance at atonement. Maybe she could redeem the people she'd killed, the lives she'd ruined, the treason to which she'd been an ignorant collaborator. Maybe Diana could reenter public service with a gesture of historical grandeur. Maybe she could wipe the slate clean by elevating her adop-tive nation to a prominence no country had ever known.

Thunder pealed.

Helen didn't blink.

"You can't," said Diana. "You can't do this."

When her grandmother had passed away, Diana had been cast adrift. Stoic and pragmatic, her grandmother had possessed a no-nonsense moral compass. Politics had been the last thing on her mind as she ferried information, supplies, and people during Bulgaria's col-lapse. She hadn't acted out of dedication to high-minded principles but out of a concrete sense of fairness. Invaders were trying to dominate her homeland. It only made sense to resist. When resistance became futile, the only option was to escape. So she led the family to a country that prided itself on liberty, where citizens could say and do what they pleased within reasonable bounds, where even the bounds themselves were ultimately amendable by citizens. It was far from perfect. But it was a thousand times better than living under the thumb of an autocrat.

"Oh, I can," said Helen. "And I will. *We* will."

Helen wanted to conquer the world in one fell swoop. Aiding in her effort wouldn't be a glorious atonement, it would be a second betrayal of Diana's personal American dream. This woman had tricked her into helping murder a president. After discovering the truth, Diana hadn't been able to do anything about it for fear of endangering the very institutions she wanted to protect. But she would not make the same mistake twice. Installing Helen as a global dictator would pervert the heartfelt eulogy Diana had delivered at her grandmother's funeral, the very expression of allegiance that Helen was twisting to her own ends.

"Helen, listen," said Diana, trying to keep the frayed edge of desperation out of her voice. "You taught me everything I know about tradecraft. I was just another dumbass recruit. You didn't have to take me under your wing. But you did, and it changed my life." It made Diana sick to admit it given what she had gone on to do, but it was the truth. "I never would have landed Amsterdam without you. I probably would have gotten myself killed, or at the very least ended up sifting data in some bureaucratic dead end. You . . . You've done more for me than almost anyone. Deep down, I know that."

Helen patted her hand. "I know you do, honey. That's why you're here."

Diana made a conscious effort not to let her own hand twitch away. "One of the reasons you invested so much in me, why you trusted me, is because I was always honest with you."

"Speaking truth to power is easier said than done," said Helen, nodding encouragingly. "We want your input on this operation, especially on the tactical side of the false flag we have planned. We need an excuse to justify swooping in on Commonwealth in order to distract the rest of the world from our actual objective. You've already supplied some great initial material from the latest board meeting. I know what we need to achieve, but we need your expertise to figure out exactly how to get there. It goes without saying that you'll be leading the field op."

"Helen," said Diana, repeating her name as if the invocation might aid her plea. "This is a mistake. I know you don't want to hear this, but you need to listen to me. You said you never doubted the love we share for this country, that what I said to honor my grandmother means something to you. Well, the reason that my love runs so deep is because I've experienced what it is to be conquered." Smoke smudging out the sun. Alarms wailing in the distance. Flocks of drones raining death. An uncanny smell that was sweet and acrid all at once. Quiet pride transformed into abject resignation. "If there's one thing I've learned from the stories my grandmother refused to tell, it's that the only way to lead is by example. This country was founded on rebelling against a foreign monarch. We are a symbol of self-determination, of the power of independence. If we become what we once resisted, we lose everything. We achieve so much more as a bastion than we ever could as an empire."

Helen's expression hardened, and Diana spoke faster and faster. "It's not too late. Lopez doesn't even know. We can still scuttle the operation and pretend this conversation never happened. There's already enough evidence to launch a congressional investigation and bring in a special prosecutor. We can lead a global regulatory reform of feed governance, champion it at the UN, show that just as Commonwealth's technology was developed here, so too can we pioneer the effort to make it fair and accountable. Lowell will still get his revenge because we'll rein in Rachel. Washington will be hailed as a paragon instead of a tyrant. You'll win without sacrificing anything."

"Thank you," said Helen, imbuing her gaze with a gratitude Diana wanted desperately to believe. "Thank you, Maria. I really appreciate you sharing that perspective with me. Rest assured, I've spent months wrestling with those exact possibilities." Helen smiled sadly. "And I wish it were that easy. Truly I do. If it were another place, another time, maybe that would be enough. There would be so much less risk, so much less danger. But the world is moving too fast for nuance. Everything is accelerating, and when things start spinning out of control, a strong

117

hand is required. One of the difficult lessons I've had to learn in my own journey is not only to assess risk but to gauge when risks are worth taking. You're right, this puts all our chips on the table. But it's a bet we simply have to make and have to win. There's no other choice."

"There's always a choice," said Diana, despair bleeding through. "You *chose* to kill Freeman. You *chose* to involve me. That wasn't inevitable. It was a bid for power. This is exactly the same, only bigger. But you don't have to make the same choice. You can do what's right, protect the only thing worth protecting."

"I was afraid of this," said Helen, her voice crystalizing into something sharp and brittle. "Your career was so promising until you shied away from doing what needed to be done. Temperance isn't a luxury people in our position can enjoy. Our duty is too sacred. You speak so highly of the international community, but what do you think Taipei, Moscow, or Addis Ababa would do in our place?" She reached out and slapped Diana across the face. "Pull yourself together, Maria. Take off those rose-tinted glasses and wake the fuck up. We either seize this opportunity or surrender to the black hole of history. I won't let that happen. And you won't either. You're going to help, whether you like it or not."

Diana's cheek stung. She remembered working in the greenhouse, knees aching, and discovering that something had been eating the leaves of her milkweed. Leaning in close to inspect the damage, she'd seen a chrysalis hanging from the tattered remains of a leaf, a caterpillar secreted within, midway through metamorphosis. She checked it frequently, hoping to catch the moment when the butterfly finally emerged. But one morning she returned to check, and all that was left was the withered chrysalis hanging from the ruined plant. Betrayed by Dag, trapped by Helen, unable to escape the sins of her past, Diana was as empty as that fragile husk.

"Not going to happen," said Diana, shaking her head. "I've lied, tortured, and killed for you. But this I won't do. We can't go down this road."

Helen sat back in her chair and stared at Diana, who struggled to meet her gaze. The older woman's expression was strangely flat, a forced neutrality that inspired more fear in Diana than outright rage could have. For a moment the only sound was the torrential rain, falling in dark curtains across the lake. Diana focused on the whiff of *Michelia champaca*, as if a scent could transport her away from this place, from this woman.

At long last, Helen sighed. "I didn't want to have to do this," she said. "Really I didn't. But you know the rules. This isn't a game you can bow out of. The fact is, we need you. And that need is greater than the tenderness I hold for you."

Diana's skin tightened as if it had shrunk a size.

Helen dropped a video stream into their shared feed. Diana jerked as audio feedback screeched at earsplitting volume. Instead of settling into any semblance of sense or harmony, the noise skipped and jumped and warped and shrieked in a chaotic melee that defied synthesis, an auditory scalpel that sliced straight through to her brain stem. There were hornets trapped inside her skull. Her heart couldn't find its rhythm. Satan danced on her eardrums. She had to flee, fight, scream. Her hands flew up to cover her ears, but they did little to muffle the cacophony.

That was the first reason it took her a moment to parse the video. The second was that the images were as deranged as the audio, lights flashing and dimming and strobing in a random walk that assaulted her retinas. Like a monster rising from the deep, the scene before her slowly emerged as she pieced together shattered glimpses into something interpretable.

It was Dag.

He was sitting in an armchair. The wall behind him was paneled in dark wood and covered in shelves stacked with books. The room was luxurious but oddly cramped. For a moment Diana thought a visual filter might be imposing pandemonium on an otherwise peaceful tableau. But then she noticed that the angled lights threw shadows a filter couldn't impose. And Dag's eyeballs roved behind his closed eyelids in time with the dazzling bursts, his face and fingers twitching with every crack and howl in the monstrous soundtrack. Tears coursed down his hollowed cheeks, and his body shuddered like a marionette, the inescapable turmoil besieging whatever reserve of control kept him from ripping his hair out and beating bloody fists against the locked door.

As quickly as it had appeared, the nightmare vanished.

Now there was nothing but the murmur of raindrops and distant thunder. Now there was nothing but the soft, warm glow of tasteful dining room illumination. Now there was nobody but Diana, convulsions passing through her in invisible waves, breath coming in ragged gasps, every sense raw and aching. No, not nobody but Diana. Helen was there too, calm and erect, looking at her one-time protégé with pity and disdain.

"This is exactly why we should have done this the easy way," said Helen, as if describing a mislaid restaurant order. "Coercion is so crass. I have faith that you'll come around eventually. If we had more time, I could persuade you on first principles. But time isn't something we can afford to waste at the moment, so we're hosting your boyfriend as an insurance policy. I know it's a little cliché, but classics are classic for a reason, right?" She sighed. "Look, Maria, I'm sorry. But you're forcing my hand here. Your country needs you. I need you. And nothing is going to get in the way of the mission. One day we'll look back on this and laugh. Dag might not, but lovers come and go." She plucked a *Michelia champaca* from the vase. "I will say this though, he still hasn't given up anything on you." With careful deliberation, she pulled off the golden petals one by one, letting them flutter to the floor beside a slim antique briefcase resting against the leg of her chair. "Claims he doesn't know anything about what you're working on, which is obviously horseshit. An ex-Apex operator working under Sean who is blissfully clueless of his significant other's espionage activities? Please. Everyone breaks eventually, but he's holding on longer than most."

Helen held out the naked flower, its bare stamen oddly obscene.

Diana's hand shook as she accepted it.

"Do this for me," said Helen. "Be the woman you were meant to be. Take your place in history. You'll have Dag back in no time at all. I promise we won't physically damage your boy toy. You can return to weeding and fucking and whatever else you fill your time with. You'll be a hero, and you'll have me to thank for it."

Diana crushed the stem in her trembling fingers.

"What would you have me do?" she asked, painfully aware that capitulation deserved nothing but contempt.

CHAPTER 20

Diana couldn't see more than a couple of meters into the darkness surrounding the boat, yet it surged forward from the dock, piloting itself away from the Ranch, Lowell's sparkling fortress receding behind her like a star falling into a black hole. The rocking motion polluted her thoughts with unwanted memories of the smuggler's hold. Fear and curiosity had made the midnight voyage an adventure, until seasickness smothered any other impression. Unwilling to show weakness before the other refugees, Diana had clenched her stomach and swallowed the bile in the back of her throat. Now waves slapped against the hull, rain muddled the windshield, and, reaching for composure honed by years of training, Diana tried to make sense of what had just happened.

Dag hadn't betrayed her. Their relationship wasn't a house of cards constructed to pry Diana's secrets away from her. The pancakes, drawings, and affection were genuine. So were their fights, frustrations, and guilt. He hadn't seduced her, doted on her, shared himself with her only to sell off whatever intel he could glean. In the end, he was exactly what Diana had secretly feared he might be. The real deal. A man driven not to satisfy some ulterior motive but to win her trust.

Dag wasn't Helen's instrument. He was her hostage.

Sitting in that chair, twitching in time to the audiovisual hellscape Helen had woven around him, the sheer fragility of Dag's mental state had been all too obvious. He was doing everything he could to resist, to remove himself from the madness with a continuous act of will. He had that same look when he was working on a sketch, an aura of supreme concentration that drowned out the world around him. But Diana had directed enough interrogations to know that nobody could hold out indefinitely. Everyone broke. The only question was how much they were willing to lose before giving in.

Diana's fingers laced and unlaced atop the briefcase in her lap. Laced. Unlaced. Laced. Unlaced. Laced. Unlaced.

Dag could not give in. They were pressing him for details of what she'd been up to, tidbits that might prove valuable in the effort to coerce her. But the sad fact that she had never trusted him enough to divulge anything meant that he didn't have anything to offer them. His torturers would mistake ignorance for intransigence and wouldn't stop until he was broken beyond repair.

The boat bumped up against the dock. How much simpler the world had been when she had arrived at the lake that afternoon. Opening her umbrella and snatching up the briefcase, Diana disembarked, careful not to slip on the slick wood.

Dag hadn't betrayed her, she had betrayed him. She loved him, but she hadn't shared anything about herself with him, dooming first their relationship and now his sanity. Instead of protecting him, her reticence had disarmed him in a fight against an enemy she hadn't anticipated. And as soon as things went sideways, she had assumed the worst of him, let her paranoia paint him as a collaborator until it turned out he was a victim.

Her first instinct had been revenge, not rescue. Imagining Dag to be an agent of Helen, Diana had lost no time forsaking him.

The rain had turned the path to mud, and Diana lost her footing as she trudged from the dock to the parking lot. Her knee hit the muck, and as she flailed to catch her fall, a gust of wind caught the umbrella, and rain pelted against her, ice-cold rivulets running down her back.

As she knelt there in the mud, a sob tore through her. She had done terrible things. Ripped families apart. Destroyed lives. Ordered interrogations just like the one Dag was suffering through now. Layered deception upon deception until truth itself was suspect. Through it all she had justified her sins as necessary to protect the innocent, to defend this nation she had devoted her life to. And for what? Helen had transformed that nation into a vehicle for the oppression Diana was supposed to be fighting against. If America was to be the next global empire, then Diana's actions were not redeemed by abstract principles enshrined on a piece of parchment fading under glass at the National Archives.

Diana clenched her fist around the slick handle of the briefcase. This country had no special claim on justice. It was as guilty as the rest, and she was its deputy, its assassin, its weapon of choice in the perpetual mission to pursue the only thing its leaders truly cared about. The extension of their own power. Diana was one of the soldiers who had shattered Bulgaria, sanctioned persecution as necessary for the greater good, chased her family into hiding. She was the shadow that haunted her own nightmares, the savvy apologist, the right hand of tyrants. The minute the veil of patriotism fell away, espionage lost its luster. Diana had taken the gift of freedom bestowed by her grandmother's sacrifices, and this was what she had become. An agent like herself was nothing but a murderer, a liar, and a thief. And unlike those common criminals, she'd had the audacity to believe herself superior, to celebrate her atrocities.

Rain rinsing away the tears, she pushed herself to her feet and stalked the rest of the way to the car that had delivered her here from the airport. Helen wanted to domineer Diana, goad her with a stick if a carrot would not suffice. When Diana had helped kill President Freeman, she could at least claim ignorance. This operation offered no such false pretense. She was to be the tip of the spear that would subdue the world.

Wrenching open the door, Diana threw herself into the car and out of the rain. The door clicked shut behind her, muffling the sound of the storm and making the vehicle feel like a hermetically sealed chamber, cut off from the horror of her realizations. For a moment she floated in welcome numbness.

But something lay on the seat beside her, something she hadn't left in the car on arrival. Wiping the water from her eyes in disbelief, she stared.

Helen had left her a final gift.

The ruins of La Jolla came to life before her eyes, Dag's master draftsmanship now complemented by shades of charcoal that gave the drawing a sense of weight and texture that made it feel realer than real life could ever hope to be. The piece hit Diana like a punch to the gut. It impressed a raw power that her glimpse at the semifinal sketch had only hinted at, conveying awe, intimate contamination, and a desperate sense of loss. *You know what I think about when I'm working on a piece? I think about all the ways you might die out there, all the horrible things that could be happening to you, what I would do if you just never came home. It's like some sick fascination.* Diana had never even thought to worry about Dag. She had been too interested in her own problems, a narcissism that now disgusted her. Like a warped reflection in a funhouse mirror, the scenario that had obsessed his thoughts had come to pass, but in reverse. Horrible things were happening to Dag, and she had to figure out what to do.

The wheels finally found traction, and acceleration pressed her back against the seat. Helen had laid the perfect trap. She had collected all the ammunition, reeled Diana in, pitched her on principle, and, when that failed, deployed her leverage with pitiless efficiency and keen attention to detail. Helen's labyrinth had no exits.

There was only one stray thread.

Diana knew exactly where Dag was.

CHAPTER 21

As she sipped her virgin Caesar and adjusted to the abrupt mindfulness brought on by Analog's feedlessness, Diana was all too aware that every passing second was a singularity of torment for Dag. While the dogs snored in front of the fire and patrons murmured to each other over fancy cocktails, he was slowly but inevitably losing his mind. But Diana's only hope of freeing him lay in theater, and theater required production.

The lack of gin robbed the Caesar of its edge, but the presence of her favorite cocktail would help assure her series of guests that this was just another day, that she was in control.

Control was exactly what Helen wanted to exercise over Diana, reattaching a leash to her favorite dog. Diana could feel the weight of the briefcase leaning against her calf under the table. It was a venom no less lethal than the one that had killed President Freeman. This particular concoction was just made of words on paper instead of an array of biochemical compounds.

Budgets, contracts, notes, receipts, accounts, and all the other informational debris that constituted the lifeblood of any corporation, any agreement, any relationship, all doctored by Helen's analytical wizards to be the genuine article, hard evidence that Rachel was using Commonwealth's privileged position to sell state secrets to foreign powers, with the board's knowledge and consent. The software architecture powering America's nuclear arsenal, diplomatic correspondence regarding a secret trade negotiation, target lists for NSA and CIA surveillance—the contents of the briefcase at Diana's feet revealed all these and more to be on the market for the right bidder, Rachel playing matchmaker between first-tier power brokers who had the required discretion and resources.

All that information was connected to the feed in one way or another, after all. Who had more to gain by taking advantage of the situation? Gatekeepers abused their power all the time, and this would be just one more distressing example. Monumental amounts of currency shuttled between a menagerie of offshore accounts, compensating Rachel and the board for their trouble.

But someone as smart as Rachel would never allow clues hinting at her darkest secret to be scattered across the feed itself, so all records of the ploy were kept on old-fashioned paper, as antique and invisible to the digital panopticon as Analog itself.

Diana was to retrace her steps and pay a visit to Commonwealth's next board meeting, ensuring that this briefcase was left behind, its handle covered in the most delicate of oil paintings, expert recreations of Rachel's fingerprints. Diana would then have Sofia discover it and cash in the favor of a lifetime by turning her friend into an unwilling whistleblower. Sofia, ready with a fabricated tale of being the conflicted Good Samaritan, would deliver the evidence to an investigative journalist in Helen's thrall. Supplied with corroborating documentation cooked up within various federal agencies that confirmed the veracity and extent of the corruption, the reporter would author the mother of all exposés. Complemented by the actual testimony Diana had collected at the last board meeting, Helen would have the excuse she needed to launch her coup d'état, sending in the FBI to seize Commonwealth and, with it, the world.

If Diana had not agreed to carry out the plan, she would never have left the Ranch alive. So she had put on a show, her submission made believable by the weakness of the only edge she retained. If she was to make use of that edge, the fiction must be maintained, Helen's inevitable suspicions held in check. Helen must believe that Diana was executing the plan against her will but with the excellence and professionalism necessary to save her lover.

That was why, even though every cell in her body screamed to rush straight to Dag's aid, Diana had returned to the Bay Area to make a few hurried arrangements. Kendrick, attending a conference in San Francisco, had visited her this morning to tacitly confirm a few pesky financial odds and ends that would make the false evidence appear legitimate. When he returned to DC, Helen might have someone confirm the nature of his conversation with Diana, and he would report that things were as they should be. Sofia had arrived shortly after his departure, but confident that Helen wouldn't interfere directly with an agent so sensitive, Diana had simply treated her to lunch. If Helen had Sofia under any kind of surveillance, her visit would imply Diana's continued loyalty.

On her flight back from Idaho, Diana had scribbled fictional updates and added them to an automated queue for scheduled delivery to Helen. She had drafted similar messages to be sent to others, ordered materials delivered to her cottage, even accessed her still-active NSA permissions and created a host of false geotagged activity, digital chaff to throw off pursuers and delay Helen's unavoidable discovery that her new conquest had gone rogue. When Diana became the signal, more noise meant more time.

"Good afternoon."

Haruki called Diana back to the painful present.

"Please, sit."

Virginia emerged from behind the bar to supply them fresh drinks, and they settled in.

"Given that there's nothing in the cache, I'm assuming whatever you've found on Rachel is so sensitive, you had to report back in person," said Haruki, his eyes bright with suppressed anticipation. "I've spoken to our partners, and if the quality of your intel stays high, we'll have plenty more work for you coming down the pipe. This industry report is only one of many projects we have in the works, and it's tough to find reliable people."

Diana had to check herself. Haruki still knew nothing about what was really going on here. She needed his help, but it was going to be delicate. Her timing and delivery had to be perfect.

"You were born just outside of Kamishihoro on Hokkaido," she said, sprightly and playful. "After your older brother committed suicide, your family moved to Toronto, where you spent most of your childhood. When you were a sophomore in high school, you got Brittany Samson pregnant on a backpacking trip and made her promise not to tell anyone about the abortion. You suspect Zara favors you over Willis for the new associate-partner slot, which is why Zara gave you this assignment, but you're also worried it might be a wild-goose chase to distract you while Willis solicits the required votes he needs for the promotion. You've always felt like an outsider, and usually you think that this is a strength that affords you special insight, but once in a while you agonize over whether others see this too and interpret it as arrogance. Oh, and when you're not overworking to prove a zeal you no longer feel, you experiment aggressively with psychedelics and attend bedazzled sex parties. You're a generous lover, and I'm guessing that scar you picked up playing lacrosse is a crowd pleaser. You're a cutout, a fall guy, a disposable messenger with so many layers above you that your boss's boss has no inkling of what this mission is really about or even who the real principals are." Her voice took on a rhetorical, almost musical cadence. "But none of this, *none of this*, is a candle flame to the bonfire that is your desire to know how I know these things about you, how easy it is to peer inside your soul, and whether I am the person who can at last grant you access to that secret world that you've always suspected exists just beneath the surface of things, shaping politics, commerce, culture, and every other human endeavor as easily as a potter molds clay."

Microexpressions flitted across Haruki's face like leaves before a gale. Surprise, anger, discomfort, embarrassment, shock, all of them cascading into that most dangerous of emotions.

Curiosity.

Diana leaned forward and ran the outside of an index finger along Haruki's pale cheek.

"I am that person," she said, the knowledge that the secrets she held would make the world tremble on its foundations lending her words a composed certainty that could not be mistaken for bravado. "You get one shot. Don't fuck it up." She slid a folded slip of paper across the table to him. "Harrison, your pharma guy, fabs drugs outside of FDA restrictions if you act like it's a normal order and pay him triple. Everything else on the list should be fairly straightforward. Deliver it to the drop point at nine fifty-four p.m. tonight. Tell anyone, *anyone*, about this and . . ." She pressed together her fingertips and then blew them apart like a dandelion.

Haruki's lips moved, but no words came out.

"Why are you still here?" Diana asked sharply.

He blinked, jerked up straight, tried and failed to pull himself together. Finally he snatched the slip of paper off the table, slid out of the booth, and scurried toward the exit. A pang of guilt reverberated through Diana as the red satin curtains fell back into place behind him. Poor kid. He had no idea what he was getting into. Then again, Diana had been nothing but a poor kid once.

She left the briefcase with Nell. Where Diana was going, each gram of luggage had to count.

CHAPTER 22

Every millimeter of Diana's body thrummed in tune to the deep vibration of the helicopter's roar. She imagined the view it must command, skimming above the sea that crowned the planet. Black waves churned below, flecked with foam and lashed by frigid wind. Container ships plied the Transpolar Passage, industrial leviathans enjoying a shipping lane newly freed from sea ice by accelerating climate change. Lowell's once lucrative offshore oil platforms, abandoned since the carbon tax had made their operation unprofitable, were now rusting, deserted islands that northern seabirds were colonizing. The sun, pale and engorged, circled low around the horizon instead of arcing across the dome of the azure sky.

Diana could see none of these things, could see nothing at all. The feed algorithms piloting the cargo chopper sated their appetite for data with sensor arrays that pocked the exterior of the bulky aircraft. But even if there had been windows, she could not have enjoyed the vista. She was in the fetal position, curled up around the scarce equipment she had been able to muster on short notice and stuffed into one of many crates scheduled for delivery that afternoon.

Food, booze, medical supplies, fuel—on a rig this remote, everything had to be ferried out by helicopter. The oil reservoirs hidden beneath the undersea Lomonosov Ridge had once inspired a geopolitical race to claim the Arctic as melting sea ice loosened the planet's grip on its petrochemical riches. Dag had helped Lowell win that race and then sabotaged the operation once his conscience caught up with him.

Surrounded by cramped darkness and breathing from an oxygen canister, Diana fought off claustrophobia by reviewing her memories of Dag's feed archive for the hundredth time. He had back-channeled between members of the Arctic Council, financed partisan scientific research, maneuvered through delicate negotiations, run undercover ops to silence opposition, and generally stacked the cards in Lowell's favor. Later, when Lowell tried to solicit more of Dag's aid, the older man had dragged him all the way up here to flaunt their conquest like some Gilded Age robber baron, hosting him in a lavish apartment built into one of the drilling platforms, courtesan included.

Diana pushed away a stab of unexpected jealousy. That courtesan had provided a critical clue when Diana had unraveled Emily and Javier's feed exploit. Knowing Dag's proclivities, Lowell had selected a courtesan who resembled Emily, neither of them realizing his type had been manufactured via careful feed curation. Diana and two maths-guru colleagues had reverse engineered Dag's feed, discovering indisputable evidence of unprecedented remote control.

Helen was ignorant of that secret history. Using one of Lowell's defunct Arctic platforms to hold Dag hostage would have seemed ideal to her. It was outside of US jurisdiction, controlled by a coconspirator, free from prying eyes, and already set up for habitation. All they needed to do was give their private security contractors access to the facility and keep it stocked with supplies. No awkward paperwork, no favors to call in from the Pentagon, no risk of Lopez catching wind of the op before Helen delivered him Commonwealth and a global coup on a golden platter.

Helen had no way to know that Diana had pored through every detail of Dag's feed archive and had immediately recognized the room in which he was now imprisoned.

The shriek of weaponized sound echoed in Diana's memory, aggravating the claustrophobia she was trying to overcome. All new recruits had been subjected to sleep deprivation and every flavor of psychological torment at Langley's disposal. It imbued respect for their methods and gave them practice resisting the opposition. Dag had no such training. The walls of the crate shrank around her as Diana remembered the tenuous, haunted expression on his face. Somewhere down there a professional inquisitor was putting Dag to the question. Interrogators had long since given up physical torture as an inconveniently roundabout way to flay a target's mind. When you could send someone to hell at the press of a button, pulling out their fingernails was just messy.

She took a deep breath, let it out slowly. Freaking out because she was stuck inside a box wouldn't help Dag. Panic was useless. Panic was deadly. Panic was the enemy of operational success. Dag needed her, and for once Diana wasn't going to let him down.

The whine of the whirling blades changed pitch, and Diana's stomach rose into her throat as the chopper descended.

This wasn't how missions were supposed to go. To do this right, she'd need three weeks of prep, an unlimited budget, and a SEAL team. Instead it was just Diana, wrapped up like a rejected Christmas present being returned to Santa's Arctic workshop. She'd collected her meager kit and supplemented it with Haruki's goodies. Her old colleagues would have been horrified by the lack of appropriate resources, but Diana would have to improvise.

The chopper landed with a jolt, sending a flicker of pain up Diana's shins. Muffled voices and footfalls penetrated the confines of her box. Dag's wardens were less than a meter away. She imagined their faces shrouded by the hoods of their parkas, the assault rifles hanging from straps on their shoulders, the frost on their eyelashes. Kidnapping and hostage retention were just another day at the office for private security contractors. They were probably bitching about being assigned to cargo duty.

Inside her camouflaged womb, Diana became hyperaware of every heartbeat. The box was shielded, appearing to be nothing more than the spare parts the label reported. But shielding and sensor technology were in a never-ending arms race with each other, and you never knew when an opponent might pull out a new gadget that rendered your protection obsolete.

The box could burst open at any moment, Diana would collapse out of it, blinded by the weak sun, limbs aching, breath snatched from her by the cutting wind, only to face a circle of gun barrels, the sneering faces behind them an exclamation point in Helen's long line of curveball victories. Perhaps they would throw Diana into the cell next to Dag's and subject her to the same soul-killing regime until she gave up every asset, every source, every angle. They would pillage her stockpile of secrets, diminishing her to nothing more than a series of broken walls, another body to be tossed out of a helicopter to sink, frozen and forgotten, into the uncaring sea, following the once mighty polar bears into extinction.

Without warning, her box was hoisted up, jostled against adjacent crates, and jerked into motion. She was tilted at an angle, then the angle flattened out. Pulling up a recent satellite image in her feed, she pictured an overloaded trolley trundling down the ramp from the cargo hatch and then out across the helipad. Then everything stopped abruptly, and she felt the momentary weightlessness of the cargo elevator plunging down its shaft.

Diana reined in a surge of adrenalized elation. She'd been betting that on a platform this remote, their screening protocols would be lax. The guards would assume that nobody could know they were here except Helen and Lowell and would worry about Dag getting out, not a stowaway sneaking in. If they were moving her to storage, her gamble had paid off.

The elevator came to a stop. More motion, then stillness. Bangs and clicks and distant swearing trickled in. After a few minutes, silence fell.

Diana let her heart rate return to baseline, slowed her breathing, and willed circulation into numb extremities. She gave them half an hour, made all the more excruciating by the knowledge that she had arrived, that despite everything, she was here.

Summoning her feed, she reviewed the extraction plan for what felt like the thousandth time. She had to brand every detail, every step into her subconscious. That was the only way to free enough mental bandwidth to deal with the inevitable moment when the plan fell apart, when some unanticipated factor threw careful choreography into disarray.

The half-hour mark took an eternity to arrive. In the business of subterfuge, patience was the greater part of professionalism. Finally the time came. Diana cinched tight her shemaugh, detached her catheter from the urine pouch, and released the latch.

A brilliant crack formed in the top of the box, a fault line in the geology of her disguise, dazzling light pouring in as it widened to release her like crafty Odysseus into the heart of Troy.

CHAPTER 23

Diana climbed out of the crate and into the fluorescent brightness of the platform's cargo bay. Boxes and equipment were stacked around her haphazardly, the new containers that had come in on her cargo chopper shiny in the midst of the forgotten detritus left over from this facility's days as a producing offshore oil platform.

First things first. She stretched, coaxing blood through cramped muscles and doing her best to regain mobility after spending so many hours stuffed inside a box. Joints popping and toes tingling with pins and needles, she removed the rest of her gear from her crate and closed the top.

As she moved, she felt her mind settling into flow. The moment she had been preparing for had finally arrived, and with it came a sense of mental clarity, like a windshield wiped clean of condensation. The world might be teetering on the edge of disaster, but right here, right now, she knew what she had to do.

Laying a bulky case on the steel floor, she unpacked the drone, slotted components into one another, booted up the processor, ran diagnostics, and double-checked the performance parameters. She tilted it side to side, inspecting it from different angles. It wouldn't hold up to close scrutiny, but the company logo, scratched paint, and dented chassis might convince a casual observer that this was a piece of old equipment gone haywire now that the platform's power and water had been switched back on. Satisfied, she attached the slender cylinders of pressurized paint into their housings and let her bird fly.

It buzzed up and over to the far corner of the cargo area, reoriented, and then opened its nozzles and covered everything in the vicinity with a thin layer of reflective paint that transformed every surface into a mirror.

Diana waited long enough to confirm that it was operating as expected, then summoned her feed and superimposed blueprints of the facility across her vision, a line highlighting her route through the maze. Next she triggered a scripted series of errors in the cargo chopper. By now it was empty and refueled, ready to fly back to the mainland. But just as the blades were starting to spin up, they'd slow back down. That would draw the attention of the guards, whose efforts at troubleshooting the problem would prove worthless as they prompted further technical errors. Gear was always glitchy in extreme environments like this, and veteran security contractors would be painfully familiar with automated equipment failing on them. The incident would keep the chopper grounded until she needed it while distracting anyone who might be paying particularly close attention to Dag.

Drawing her sidearm, she made her way to the door. The hallway beyond was empty, and she set off along it with quick, sure steps that made almost no sound on the rubberized floor. The drone followed at some distance behind her, like an obedient but wary dog. It would make its own way through the facility, playing Picasso until its paint ran out.

At the end of the hallway, she entered the stairwell and froze. Footsteps filtered down from above. Diana needed to ascend three flights, and she didn't have time to waste. Then, gauging her gait to match the echoes, she tightened her grip on the gun and began to climb the diamond-grip steel stairs, keeping her ears pricked. It was a single pattern of footsteps, so only one person, but they were descending toward her, the echoes getting progressively louder. Diana pivoted to cover the line of fire at every landing, finger light on the trigger, adrenaline pumping.

She hadn't killed in years. It never got easier, but eventually she had acclimatized to it, learning to swallow the strange mixture of abhorrence and bloodlust that was so intoxicating and disorienting, compressing the adverse feelings into a hermetic emotional keg. Only later, once it had fermented, would she let the potent brew drain, one drop at a time, drawing out the process to make it manageable, to keep her beyond the reach of angry ghosts.

That would all come later. For now she wouldn't hesitate to double-tap a motherfucker in the face. Her target would see nothing but the open barrel of the gun, the strange black spot hovering like fate's pupil against the slightly warped iris that was her stealth jumpsuit's almost-but-not-quite-perfect projection of the wall behind her.

He was two flights up, the movement of his shadow visible through the diamond kaleidoscope of the stairs above. Diana's palms were wet and her mouth was dry, but her finger was steady on the trigger. She would kill them all if she had to, pay the blood price for Dag's freedom.

With just one flight to go, Diana nestled into the corner of the landing. Just as she raised the gun, the footsteps slowed. Shit. Could he know she was here? Was it possible that she had been found out, that she was walking into a trap instead of laying one? Had she lost the shell game of countersurveillance? Was this another one of Helen's twisted charades? Perhaps she was waiting in what Diana had assumed was Dag's cell to eviscerate her twice-prodigal protégé? But then a metallic squeal sounded from above, unoiled hinges protesting long disuse. He wasn't aware of her presence. He too had been heading to this floor, Dag's floor.

She couldn't afford to let the door swing closed, lest she be trapped on this side of it by the racket opening it would make. Trusting the hinges to cover stray footfalls, Diana dashed up from the landing just in time to slip through the door as it clicked shut.

This hallway was identical to the one below. Fluorescent lights lined the ceiling, some panels no longer functional, so that the illumination was both glaring and irregular. Cream-colored walls gave the industrial facility a strangely lighthearted aesthetic, softer than the pure white of a hospital. The rubberized floor made it easy for Diana to keep her footsteps silent as she closed in on the soldier stalking up the hallway ahead of her. He was alone, assault rifle hanging across his back, and the hallway was otherwise deserted, the defunct oil platform far too large for a team so small.

In her feed, Diana saw that the man was tracing the same path she had laid out for herself. He was heading for Dag's room. Was it time for another interrogation session? Were they going to remove the scalpel from the raw wound of Dag's crumbling mind to challenge him with questions he couldn't answer? Had she somehow miscalculated and they were transferring him somewhere else? No, they had requisitioned the supplies her chopper had delivered. There would be no need for that if they were about to blow this joint.

The man turned to face Dag's door, and this small mystery was solved. On a plastic tray with rounded edges, he carried an MRE and a small cup of water. In any extended interrogation, these small tokens of temporary deliverance, appeals to biological necessity, were the currency that eventually bought the victim's trust.

Acknowledging the guard's credentials, the door hissed open. Keeping her pistol trained on him with one hand, Diana dipped the other into a jumpsuit pocket and pulled out a cylinder the size and shape of a pen. The man stepped through the door, and she followed so close behind him that she caught a hoppy whiff of his deodorant.

As they crossed the threshold, Diana reached up and jabbed the cylinder into his bare neck, the needle within injecting its potent cocktail. A puff of air escaped his lips, not quite a gasp, not quite a grunt, and he shivered as if he had been subjected to a mild electric shock before collapsing onto the floor, deflating as awkwardly as a punctured balloon. The plastic tray clattered down with him, MRE slop and water spilling everywhere.

A powerful sense of déjà vu rippled through Diana. She had never before set foot in this room, but she had analyzed every digital record of it in Dag's feed archive, caressed every memory until they were polished smooth, obsessing ceaselessly since Helen had showed off her hostage like a hunting trophy, careless of the clue that was the very room in which he was imprisoned.

Diana almost couldn't believe it, but there he was, her kidnapped lover, her nemesis, her second half, her Achilles' heel, her best friend.

Dag.

CHAPTER 24

Dag lay on a small couch in the middle of the room. There was no other furniture, and plywood boards covered the doors to the suite's adjoining office, bathroom, and bedroom. The audiovisual deluge had been mercifully paused for the delivery of his meal, although she could see the caged light fixtures that had been bolted around the room. The reek of urine and feces wafted over from a plastic bucket in the corner.

Dag's eyes were wide open and bloodshot, staring straight through Diana into infinity. He was dressed in loose-fitting black pajamas and tucked into a tight ball, knees pulled up to his chest, arms wrapped around them.

A hole opened up inside Diana, resolve draining like water from a leaky vessel. It was one thing to imagine Dag under interrogation. It was another to see him in front of her, gaze vacant, eyes sunken, lost in the maze of a mind rebelling against reality. She had seen prisoners reduced to wrecks before, pushed until they babbled whatever they imagined you wanted to hear, inventing fractured fantasies that held together only long enough to taste a sweet sip of water. Desperation was a blunt weapon. It might eke out a crucial detail at a critical juncture, but it also ate away at truth like corrosive acid. Beyond its questionable utility, using such techniques made intelligence officers believe their actions were justifiable, and the reality of a world in which crises were constant and urgent created a race to the bottom when it came to the circumstantial evidence required to justify torture.

Torture. A word that was anathema to the government doublespeak that buried anything distasteful in acronyms and euphemisms, a broken culture that Diana could no longer ignore now that Helen's power play had ripped the silk glove from the iron fist. This was how Helen guaranteed Diana's compliance.

Self-disgust spurred Diana to action. Now was not the time for wallowing. Besides the man lying unconscious on the floor, there were six more heavily armed killers roaming this platform who would happily dispatch her and Dag if they were caught. She summoned her feed and triggered the next set of distractions. Smoke would begin to pour from the chopper's engine housing, whipped by the Arctic wind, a fake malfunction to call their attention away from the action below. Simultaneously an automated SOS notification would ping every feed in the area, the distress call originating from one of the abandoned oil platforms inhabited by libertarian seasteaders who, in this fictional call for help, were suffering a massive fuel leak. The combination should give Diana and Dag a few minutes of respite before being unveiled as a ruse.

Dismissing her feed, Diana knelt in front of Dag. Belatedly realizing that he could see nothing but an indistinct shimmer, she unwrapped her shemaugh. Her disembodied head appearing before him should have provoked a reaction, but Dag's eyes remained wide and unfocused.

"Dag, honey," her voice cracked. "It's me. I'm gonna get you out of here."

No response.

"Everything's going to be okay," she said with a conviction she didn't feel. "I promise."

She wanted to pull him into her arms, to weep on his shoulder, to apologize for having put him in danger, to confess the awful things she'd done, to tell him this wasn't the person she wanted to be anymore, to comfort him and nurse him back to health. But right now she had to focus on getting them both out alive.

Swinging the backpack off her shoulder, she removed two gas masks and a bandolier of pressurized canisters. She held a mask in front of Dag and employed the calm, firm tone people in shock were most likely to respond to.

"I need you to sit up," she said.

No response.

"Dag, I can't do this on my own. I need you to sit up."

His hands unclasped from around his knees. He let his legs drop off the edge of the couch and slowly raised himself to a sitting position, still staring straight ahead.

"Okay," she said, raising one of the gas masks. "Now I'm going to help you put this on and then put on my own."

Careful to keep her movements slow and precise, she placed the gas mask over his face, tightened the straps, and double-checked the seal against his skin. Then she repeated the process for herself. Shoving the unconscious guard onto his side, she pulled off his jacket and boots and helped Dag slip into them. Standing back, she inspected her handiwork. Almost there. She wrapped the shemaugh around Dag's head, and it vanished against the background. Better.

Who knew how long she had. Maybe they had noticed the guy who delivered Dag's food wasn't responding, maybe they'd seen through the fraudulent SOS alert, maybe they'd realized the chopper's troubleshooting was a sham. She needed to move quickly.

Kneeling down again, she made eye contact with Dag through their visors.

"We're leaving," she said. "It's going to get weird out there, but all you need to do is follow me and do what I say. Understand?"

No response.

"Do you understand?" She hated herself for the command in her tone. It felt like kicking a puppy. But she had no choice.

Dag's head jerked up and down twice.

"Good," she said. She took his hand and helped him to his feet, then turned away and rested his hand on her shoulder. "Keep your hand there, it tells me you're still with me."

She approached the door, Dag shuffling behind her. Pulling one of the canisters from her bandolier, she thumbed the release, heard the hiss of releasing gas, and rolled it out the door and up the hallway. Haruki's pharma supplier didn't have access to lethal compounds, which Diana wasn't after anyway, but he could fabricate aerosolized doses of legal recreational narcotics.

This particular molecule was similar to classic LSD but with faster onset, stronger psychoactive effects, and a longer half-life. A few lung-fuls of the colorless, odorless gas would set off neurotransmitters like Christmas lights. Diana stole a glance around the doorjamb. Excellent. Her pet drone had already come through on its tour of the facility, using thin layers of spray paint to turn the floor, walls, and ceiling of the hallway into mirrors.

"Let's go," she said, leading Dag down the hall.

A door slammed behind them, and Diana looked back to see two men emerge, struggling to orient themselves.

"Hey," one of them bellowed. "What the fuck? Lito?"

She considered turning to shoot, but it was better to use the pre-cious seconds to get to the stairs. Diana was able to parse what she was seeing far better than they would be able to. Coming down to check on their buddy, they had stepped into an underworld where reflections pinballed to infinity in every direction, and retreating into the distance down the center of the prism, a headless man and the disembodied head of a woman bobbed along, mirrored a thousand times over.

And that was before the drug crossed the blood-brain barrier.

Diana crashed through the door to the stairwell, pulling Dag behind her. The drone had come this way too, and descending the stairs felt like careening through a kaleidoscope. At every landing, Diana opened the door to the adjacent hallway and tossed in a canister from her bandolier. Soon enough the air-circulation system would turn the entire oil platform into a psychedelic gas chamber. It would take days for the guards to sober up and even longer for them to figure out what had really happened. In the meantime Helen wouldn't be able to extract anything useful from them, even if they were bold enough to alert her. Better to leave behind confusion than destruction. Conflicting information was much more dangerous than straight-up failure. It didn't just hurt, it paralyzed effective response.

Just as the sounds of footfalls and profanity echoed down from above, Diana and Dag burst out of the stairwell and sprinted down the hall to the cargo bay. Dag tripped and went down, skidding across the floor. Tapping a hidden reserve of strength, Diana hoisted him back up, and they staggered drunkenly forward. Gunshots rang out behind them. Dodging around crates that were now mirror cubes, they made it to the cargo elevator. The pursuers lurched into the bay, assault rifles roaring as they gunned down their own scattered reflections. The doors clanked shut, and Dag gasped as the elevator jerked into motion, a hidden cable screaming from long disuse. Exhausted and overwhelmed, Dag was hyperventilating through the gas mask, hands on his knees.

"It's going to be okay," said Diana, wrapping an arm around his trembling shoulders and giving him a gentle squeeze, not sure whether she was reassuring Dag or herself. "It's going to be okay."

Diana summoned her feed, canceled the chopper's falsified error cascade, confirmed that the loading doors were still open, and initiated the takeoff sequence. Then, sending it a mental thank-you, she triggered the drone's self-destruct. Three seconds later, smoke alarms began to blare. That would attract anyone still above deck.

The doors opened, frigid wind whistled through the growing gap to steal their breath away. Salvation was so close, she could taste it. Soon they would be off this godforsaken platform and hurtling toward friendlier climes. Dag could recover and she could—

145

There was a man standing on the helipad, facing the cargo elevator. The parting doors revealed him to be in his early thirties, a short growth of carrot-colored beard covering a prematurely lined face. Like his compatriots, he was dressed in combat gear, a long beige parka whipping around his legs. His consternation at the elevator's unexpected arrival deepened into confusion and then almost childlike fear as his gaze flickered from Dag's headless body to Diana's bodiless head. He began to raise the assault rifle dangling from a shoulder strap, Diana's feed projecting his line of fire and mapping scenarios and probabilities across her vision.

She pulled the trigger. Once. Twice.

Locking Dag's wrist in a steely grip, Diana yanked him out of the elevator, over the twitching corpse, and across the helipad. The last thing she wanted to do in the world was look down, but she had no willpower left to resist the perverse gravity of slaughter. A single glance was all it took. He lay flat on his back. One shot had hit him straight between the eyes, the other a few inches up on his forehead. His face was surprisingly intact, almost as if the entry wounds were nothing but inexpertly applied bindi. But the bullets had slowed as they tore through his brain, ripping out the back of his skull along with everything inside it, gore spreading out across the deck behind him like a halo, the downdraft from the accelerating helicopter blades sending ripples through the mess even as it crystallized, tendrils of steam rising off hot blood as the Arctic claimed him.

Shoving Dag in front of her, Diana dove into the chopper's open maw. As they slid across the metal floor to thump into the far wall, she pinged the autopilot, and the aircraft leapt off the deck and out across the open sea, engine howling, newly agile thanks to its lightened load.

Never hesitate. He who hesitates, dies.

CHAPTER 25

Diana stroked Dag's hair as he slept on the couch in the small cabin of the charter plane to which they'd transferred from the chopper once it reached the mainland. After administering the sedative, she had stripped Dag down, sponge-bathed every inch of him, and dressed him in clothes she had picked up from the cottage, his chemically induced sleep so deep that nothing could disturb it. After long periods of deprivation, sleep itself began to retreat, like a dog from an abusive stranger. Every cell in Dag's body might have been screaming for rest, but over the course of the past few days, his kidnappers had trained his mind to associate the drift into unconsciousness with violent disturbance, the anticipation of abuse becoming an abuse in itself.

As she stroked, Diana's fingers picked up a thin film of grease. It wasn't just lack of sleep that pushed people to the psychological brink, it was dehumanization. Shitting in a bucket, wearing pajamas, smelling only your own increasingly rank body odor, all these were tactics deployed to weaken resolve and increase dependency. Knowing that Dag was living this particular hell was intended to prod Diana into executing Helen's plan. Nothing, certainly not the fate of a retired lobbyist, would stand in the way of her will to power.

"I've got you now, baby," Diana murmured. "It's over. You're gonna be okay. We're gonna be okay."

Diana began to sing "Izlel je Delyo Hagdutin" under her breath. The words shone through memory's palimpsest, and she could still carry the tune. It brought to mind the strength of her grandmother's wrinkled hands, her funny old-person smell, and the diamond sharpness of her gaze. There was something strangely familiar about this feeling, slipping across international borders, defying the authorities, egged on by fear for those closest to her. Diana was a refugee again, a refugee from the world she'd built, from the life she'd created for herself.

Dag's face had acquired a certain hollowness, and his eyes danced beneath their lids. Diana leaned down and planted a soft kiss on his forehead. She could only hope that he wasn't immersed in some inescapable nightmare, demons pursuing him beyond the bounds of consciousness. As she gazed down at his face, she couldn't help but imagine a halo of gore spread out behind it. She closed her eyes, but that made the vision only more vivid.

It had only been a few hours. The guards must be roving the oil platform, attempting to seek answers even as hallucinations chased them along mirror passageways and into dark spirals of internal reflection. They would doubtless discover their colleague, asleep on the floor of Dag's empty cell, their absent prisoner a ghost who had vanished into the ether, leaving inexplicable traces that added up to . . . what, exactly? The cargo helicopter, miraculously repaired of whatever mysterious dysfunction had maimed it, disappearing over the pastel horizon around which the pale sun circled like a python around prey. The flash-frozen corpse of their colleague awaiting them on the helipad, frost lacing the lashes of still-open eyes that stared into an infinity that even they, in the manic grasp of a most potent psychotropic, could not glimpse.

Diana reached the end of the song, drawing out the last note until her vocal cords matched the vibrato of the jet engine. Between the bizarre state in which they had left Dag's prison and the evidence of false activity Diana had planted, they would have at least a day or two to make their escape before Helen discovered the truth.

"You'll finally get your wish," she said, her voice breaking. "We can leave everything behind, go off-grid, start a new life somewhere." She smelled wet earth, admired the complex pattern of sunlight falling through lush vegetation, tasted the fluffiness of Dag's homemade pancakes. That breakfast felt like a lifetime ago. It was as if she were watching a feed drama instead of remembering something she had actually experienced. If only she could transport herself to a different branch of the quantum multiverse in which every decision forked a new world. Not so long ago, her greatest frustration was Dag's presence in her life, which his absence had clarified as her own insecurity about sharing herself with the person she loved. She had wanted a new mission that could renew her sense of self-worth and secure the fragile dignity tied to her embittered patriotism. Helen had revealed that veil for what it was, a shield with which Diana defended her own long list of sins.

As Dag was so fond of pointing out, history was doomed to repeat itself. Just as her grandmother had resisted until resistance left no option but flight, in rescuing Dag, Diana had doomed them both to live out their lives as fugitives. She grimaced. At least she was practiced at it. Old habits died hard. She rested a palm on Dag's chest, feeling it rise and fall, rise and fall. He would learn. He could handle it. Dag had survived foster home after foster home to make his own way in the world and ended up pulling strings that changed it. She smiled sadly. They would still be able to get their hands on art supplies in whatever backwater they ended up in. He could pursue his passion without the anxiety of her irregular absences. And she could . . . do something. She would cross that bridge when she came to it. For now she needed to get everything in order to make their escape possible.

She dipped into her feed, immersing herself in the vast flow of information like a sea turtle catching a transoceanic current. Messages and notifications vied for her attention alongside headlines decrying a civil war over Congo River water rights, another public appeal for Commonwealth accountability from Javier, and record turnouts for

Comic-Con's annual extravaganza in Kuala Lumpur. She snuffed out these streams like unwanted candles, called up encrypted correspondence with the various contacts she was pressing for all the bits and pieces necessary to establish the false identities they would need to start fresh.

Dag stirred next to her, and Diana dialed back her feed's opacity to look down at him again. If only they could stay here forever, thirty thousand feet above the ground, safe from the depredations of a world gone mad. Was that too much to ask?

Blinking away sleep's cobwebs, Dag opened his eyes.

"I'm sorry, babe," she said. "I'm so, so sorry."

CHAPTER 26

It took an hour for Diana to bring Dag up to speed, an hour during which they hurtled through the rarefied air above Canadian Arctic tundra, its melting permafrost stoking the runaway process of climate change that the carbon tax had only just begun to mitigate. If only there was time to indulge the bleary viscosity endowed by Dag's medicated oversleep. Diana wanted nothing more than to massage his aching limbs, offer him gentle, constant, loving affection that did not flinch when the ghosts of his trial haunted, and promise him that everything was going to be okay, that all bad things had come to an end, that the future was bright and friendly and theirs.

Instead she explained how Haruki had asked her to stalk Rachel, how Diana's suspicions had escalated, how she had burrowed through Leviathan, Sean, and Lowell to find Helen at the conspiracy's rotten core. Then Diana laid out the coup Helen was plotting, why Commonwealth was the key to a new political empire, and why she had kidnapped Dag to ensure Diana's loyalty. Disclosing so many hard-won secrets was a strange feeling, like a mountaineer prying stiff fingers from a trusted ice ax after surviving a harrowing climb. Diana was so used to sealing off her work from her relationship with Dag that her delivery was as halting and awkward as a parent explaining sex to their child for the first time. For his part, Dag listened in silence, his lips pressed into a thin line, his eyes unreadable.

Finally she caught up to the present, telling him about the extraction and presenting the immediate next steps that she was halfway through improvising. They would be stopping off in Vancouver to visit a sake bar whose proprietor doubled as a purveyor of black market identification materials, shuttling resources around to minimize traceability and calling in favors from fixers who could set them up in Chile or Laos. But even as she pitched it, she began to question her assumptions, to recognize that in the rush to rescue Dag, she'd skimped on the follow-through.

Dag raised a hand. "Hold on, what exactly are you proposing we do?"

Diana forced a smile. "It's just like you said to me over breakfast. We'll find a new place, go off-grid, start over. As long as we're smart and we keep our heads down, we should be fine." She reached out to touch Dag's knee, but he flinched and she snatched back her hand.

"No, we won't," he said. "If Helen nationalizes Commonwealth, she'll weaponize the entire feed. There won't be anywhere to hide. We're not talking about fleeing a government by running to a new country. Jurisdiction won't matter. Nothing will matter except that we know too much about what's happening to be left alive."

"I've got people who can keep us hidden. Some of them are even feedless." It sounded weak, even to her. She was walking out onto a frozen lake and only just now seeing the cracks forming beneath her feet. "I've started over before. I can do it again."

"Oh yeah? Were you the high-value target of a megalomaniacal dictator? You're saying that Helen wants to be Alexander the fucking Great and that we'll just sidestep into the wings?"

Just like that Diana's plan evaporated. She wanted to come back with a firm rebuttal, explain how she'd thought through every contingency. But the fact was, she hadn't. Helen wanted Diana to create an excuse for her to take over Commonwealth, but the absence of that excuse wouldn't stop Helen. She would create another one or simply throw due process out the window and call in the troops. Easier to ask the public's forgiveness than its permission, particularly when so much was at stake. With Commonwealth firmly in hand, Helen would set her sights on Diana and Dag.

Even if they went feedless, generated a maze of false data leading to dead ends, and lived out their lives in the middle of a forest, they still wouldn't be safe. With unlimited access to the entire feed, all Helen would need was for a random hiker to stumble on their encampment or a single satellite to recognize the underlying facial structure that even plastic surgery couldn't hide. They would be running not just from Helen but from the feed itself. That was just another way of saying they would be running from the entire world. There was no refuge from civilization.

Diana had been replaying an old pattern in her head. There was a tragic symmetry to following in her grandmother's footsteps that had given the plan false plausibility. But time was inexorable, a cruel vanguard that advanced only forward while its denizens could look only back. This wasn't the dissolution of the European Union. They weren't a family fleeing a battlefield into a friendlier nation's open arms. There was no escape. Not for Diana, not for Dag, not for any of Helen's enemies once she had the feed in hand.

It was over before it had even begun.

"And even if it were possible," said Dag with a sad shake of his head, "what makes you think that I'd want to go with you?"

"Dag," she said, trying to keep her voice steady. She reached out to touch him again.

"*Don't,*" he snapped, and her hand jerked back again. "What? You think that I'm some damsel in distress? That you're winning me over with a dramatic rescue? You're hoping we'll join the mile-high club and jet off into the sunset? Maybe you're about to make one of your cute little jokes, all loaded up with innuendo? Is that it?" Suddenly his fury disappeared, leaving only exhaustion. "Diana, nothing's changed. We're still as trapped as I was in that godforsaken place. You're still living a life in which I'm just a prop, and it turns out even being a prop might be fatal. Fuck." He rubbed his face with his palms. "I could have told you Lowell was planning to turn governments against Commonwealth. He explained it to me the last time I saw him."

"Wait, what do you mean Lowell told you?"

Dag sighed, as if unloading a burden. "Three years ago, the morning after I . . . spent that first night at the cottage, I walked down to the market to get groceries to make you breakfast."

I can make pancakes. She had been so overwhelmed in that moment on Indian Rock, accepting the portrait he'd sketched of her, reevaluating this man whose very sense of identity had been stolen from him yet who had found something deeper, figured out a way forward. *If that's your version of a pickup line, then you're the man for me.*

That was when she had broken protocol and brought Dag back to her cottage. The sex had an intensity she'd never felt before. It wasn't technique or endurance or anything like that. They had simply both been there in that room and nowhere else. Thoughts hadn't strayed, attention hadn't wavered, and every sense, every nerve, had been set alight as if for the first time. The next morning, she'd slept in, waking up to sunlight streaming in through the window and Dag calling her downstairs to eat.

"Lowell was at the market? What was he doing there, picking up milk?"

"He was waiting for me," said Dag. "He had me under surveillance, guessed I was behind Rachel forcing the carbon tax, even though he didn't know how. He had some goon force me into a back room at gunpoint, told me he was excited about Rachel's move, that it gave him an opening to pursue a new opportunity, convincing governments to fight off Commonwealth." Dag let out a humorless chuckle. "He thanked me, even offered me a job helping him do it."

"He had you under surveillance, that's how they knew about the cottage." Diana said this more to herself than to Dag. It fit, and it meant that Helen had had an eye on Diana long enough to actually plan this. She stood and began pacing up and down the cabin. She had seen Dag's entire feed archive, shuffled through his most intimate personal history, assumed she knew all there was to know about him, and yet he still had secrets. "You should have told me."

Dag stared at her in disbelief. "*I* should have told *you*? You spied on Rachel, met Javier, invaded Sean's home, and confronted Lowell. I understand every single one of those people better than you or anyone you know. I've worked with all of them, seen inside their lives. I know what drives them. And you didn't even bother to *mention* it to me, even though we were theoretically in a relationship, even though we *lived* together." He squeezed the edge of the couch, fingers digging into the fabric. "I could have told you a million things. I could have *helped*. Instead"—he spread his arms—"we have this. It's unreal. *You're* unreal."

"I was *protecting* you," said Diana, unable to stop the guilt his words inspired from mutating into righteous anger. "Emily and Javier tore your life apart. You gave up everything to end their exploit. You even managed to trade it to Rachel for something the world needed, a political solution to climate change that governments had failed to achieve for decades. You sacrificed enough, too much. I love you, Dag. I couldn't let you get dragged back into this. You were drawing, building a new life for yourself."

"And how has that worked out? When they came for me, put a bag over my head, drugged me, and took me to that *place*, you know what they were asking me about? They were asking about *you*. What you've been working on, who your contacts are, what your plans are. You think ignorance protected me then?" A tremor ran through him. "Skulking around in the shadows, pretending that I'm some kind of lamb you're guarding from the big bad wolf, that's not about defense or compassion, it's about you wanting to believe that you're some kind of savior, that you're special, that only you can face what this world is really made of."

"I was protecting you." Her whisper was barely audible.

"I never asked for your protection," he said, slumping back against the couch and closing his eyes. "All I've ever asked for is your trust."

Silence rippled through the cabin.

Fuck who you like as long as it doesn't endanger the mission. Love if you can't help it. But trust? Never. Helen had lowered her voice to a confidential growl and held up a french fry as she delivered that advice at Mauricio's. Diana could almost smell sizzling bacon and see the greasy burger drippings pooled on the wax paper covering the red plastic baskets that served as plates. As if to underscore her point, Helen had dipped the fry into the ketchup as swiftly and precisely as a surgical strike, maintaining eye contact while she chewed, breaking it only when she swallowed, satisfied that Diana understood the gravity of this injunction. Helen needn't have been concerned. Diana's experiences as a refugee had long since convinced her of the existential danger of trust.

Diana felt like an overinflated balloon, pressure expanding inside her, forcing its way out from her gut, her mind, her heart. The Dag whom she was protecting, whom she loved, who drove her mad, was nothing more than a figment of her imagination, a manifestation of the purely theoretical innocent public she tasked herself with protecting, a shadow of the flesh-and-blood human collapsed on the couch in front of her. True love meant loving a person for who they actually were, not an imperfect mental construct, just as true protection required empowering people to defend themselves, not pretending that the dark side of human nature didn't exist.

"I've spent my entire life learning to not trust anyone," said Diana, voice cracking with the intensity of the energy built up inside her. Dag had grown up in and out of abusive foster homes. Lowell had used him as a pawn. Hackers had turned his life inside out. How could he trust anyone? How could anyone trust anyone? "I . . . I honestly don't know if I can."

He sighed, eyes still closed, head leaned back against the cabin wall. "We all have to start somewhere. Otherwise what's the point?"

"The point of what?"

"Anything, really."

Diana looked through the long window running down the side of the cabin opposite the couch. Her breath fogged up the Plexiglas. Thousands of feet below, the crags, fjords, and channels of Canada's Northwest Passage slipped past. Countless explorers had lost themselves in the maze of inlets, assaulted by cold and weather, demoralized by dwindling supplies, and driven to mutiny by the bitter anticipation of dreams left unfulfilled. Now pleasure cruisers plied the waters alongside trade vessels, technology and global warming making the impossible accessible. Scientists had declared them extinct long ago, but might there still be a lone polar bear wandering one of these barren islets, ribs visible through uneven patches of yellowing fur, the final thoughts of the last member of a once-proud species consumed only with the pangs of starvation? She could readily visualize Lowell's epitaph: *For a while there, we generated a lot of value for shareholders.*

Helen lived in a world drained of its color by the harsh filter of game theory. When the world was a prize to be won, life became an exercise in tactics. And if someone could find meaning only in victory, then they would stoop to any means necessary to achieve it. By not trusting anyone, Helen endured a spiritual poverty that deserved not hatred but pity. That made Diana pitiable as well, a label that further stoked her self-reproach.

She had lived in Helen's world long enough. It was time to see if other worlds were possible. But if Helen succeeded in conquering the feed, her world would become *the* world. Dag was right, retreat was not an option.

The mounting tension within her was not unlike the ascent to orgasm. She remembered the hot, wet closeness of that last time in the cottage bedroom, the climactic instant when distance, time, and selfhood collapsed into each other, revealing themselves to be nothing but convenient falsehoods, expressions of some deeper, unified truth. But that heightened perception was so fleeting, giving way easily as the onslaught of thought throttled up again, reconstructing the illusions with which it swaddled our waking lives.

Diana pressed her palm against the Plexiglas, the only barrier between the comfort of the cabin and the frigid, howling gales of the upper atmosphere. She imagined the window popping out of its frame, the winds sucking all pressure and warmth from the cabin, throwing off the feed algorithms that piloted them, the plane corkscrewing out of the sky, she and Dag hanging for a transcendent moment in weightless free fall before disintegrating upon impact, their remains to be scraped out of twisted wreckage whose black box would be a rare case study of catastrophe for a generation of aerospace engineers made complacent by years of perfect safety records. But the Plexiglas held firm. Its surface was cool and smooth against her skin.

Sometimes the only way to meet power was with power.

"Dag."

He stirred, perhaps moved by a subtle change in her voice or maybe just responding to the inscrutable touch of providence.

"What is it?"

"I need you to make some calls."

CHAPTER 27

"Hey, girl." Sofia was in the middle of wrapping her hair up in a towel as she accepted Diana's call. Through the feed, her luminous dark eyes were wells of intelligence, and her pale cheeks were flushed from what must have been a scorching-hot shower. "What's cracking?"

"Oh, you know," said Diana, "just jet-setting around the world causing all kinds of mayhem. You know the drill."

Dialing down her feed's opacity, Diana surveyed the Canadian lake country spread out below the charter plane. Innumerable pockets of blue speckled the rugged wilderness, sunlight glittering off them like stars twinkling in the night sky.

"What is it this time?" Sofia held up a slender hand. "Wait, no. I don't want to know."

"Finally you're starting to learn some sense. Dangerous questions have dangerous answers."

"Uh-huh, trouble always seems to stick to you like a magnet."

"How's the training coming along?"

"Just finished a thirty-miler," said Sofia, the American lingo galvanized by her Italian accent.

"You are out of your damned mind," Diana said with feeling.

"You know how sometimes you get in the zone and running feels really good, like you're flying and could go on forever?"

"My experience running with you typically feels like my body is being eaten away by hydrochloric acid while my heart teeters on the verge of cardiac arrest and my soul questions my obvious and pathetic personal and athletic deficiencies."

Sofia tossed her head in a way that made Diana think of a prized mare in an ancient caliph's stable. "And I revel in superiority," said Sofia. "There is no feeling more precious. Why do you think I enjoy running with you?" She winked. "Seriously though, this one was brutal. No fun at all. Grinding, grinding, grinding. Just an exercise in raw willpower. The worst. But I've only got a few weeks before that BC ultra. The elevation chart on it looks like someone gave a toddler an espresso and let them draw it with a crayon."

"Take my word for it," said Diana. "Just quit. You'll thank me later."

"You think I'm intense now? Do you have any idea the person I'd be if I didn't run?"

"On second thought," said Diana, "never quit. You would merge with the machine and transform into a supernatural algorithm that would eat the world and doom everyone to enslaved enlightenment."

Sofia's laugh was throaty and rich. "Me, a techno goddess? Maybe I should consider quitting after all. That sounds appealing."

"Speaking of techno goddesses . . ."

Sofia's eyes narrowed. "I hate it when you use that tone. It means you're about to ask me for something."

Diana batted her eyelashes, affecting exaggerated innocence. "What on earth could you possibly mean?"

Sofia arched an eyebrow.

"All right, all right," said Diana, raising her palms, "I give up. There is something. But you have to admit that my special requests make you feel special too. Try to channel that superiority you revel in while leaving me in the dust."

"Diana"—Sofia shook her head—"it's too soon. I just gave you a big tranche of intel. You want me to lose my job and go to jail? I can't risk that. I'm supporting a family here."

"Don't worry, this isn't something you'll risk jail time for. It's simple."

"If anything comes out, it's not just going to ruin my life, it's going to cost you access to Commonwealth. You know that, right? If you want little birds to keep whispering in your ear, you don't roast them for dinner. Stop pushing me."

Sofia was right, of course. Running agents required managing a delicate balance. Ask for too much, and they'd blow their cover. Ask for too little, and they'd forget what they'd signed up for. Normally Diana would have waited many months before asking Sofia for another favor. In the meantime, Diana would call to chat, supply professional and personal advice, buy her lunch, and send little gifts to her family. That's what she should be doing right now, not milking her for more.

"I wouldn't ask if it wasn't important. I can't share the details, but believe me, there's a lot at stake that affects your work. This is something that matters, not just in general but to you personally."

There was a special kind of emotional dissonance that came to the surface only when Diana forced herself to do something unpleasant but necessary. It made her more tired than upset, submitting to destiny's arc rather than raging against it.

"You know what? No." A lock of long dark hair fell free from Sofia's towel turban. "No, no, no. It's too much, you hear me? Too much. Find another way in, make a new plan, whatever it is you do while you're 'jet-setting around the world.'"

"I'm sorry"—Diana tried to imbue as much genuine remorse as possible into the apology even though she knew it didn't matter—"but I don't have time for that."

"Then make time. Because this conversation is over."

"Wait." Diana closed her eyes and let out a long breath. She didn't want to do this, but she needed to do it anyway. It was time to unlock the vault of secrets she had been hoarding for so long, to start spending some of the political capital she had accrued through years of persistent intrigue. Once spent, those secrets would be gone forever. She could only hope that she was investing them rather than throwing them away. Her bet might have long odds, but there was no reward without risk. "Do this for me, and your debt is paid."

Sofia swept the free lock of hair behind her ear.

"No more requests, no more demands," said Diana. "You'll be free of me, free to dream up new maths and secure your family's future. I can disappear from your life altogether if you want. No surprise calls, no lame running buddy slowing you down, no weirdo sending inappropriate Christmas presents to your nephews. I'll be gone. Poof"—she mimed an explosion—"just like that."

Sofia squinted at her as if negotiating a deal with the devil. Diana couldn't help but think that she wasn't that far off.

"Why should I believe you?" asked Sofia, her voice different now, laced with tension. "What's stopping you from holding this over my head for the rest of our lives?"

A small corner of Diana's heart shuddered as if an earthquake were shaking its foundation. It was selfish, silly really. But she had harbored hope that Sofia would wave away her offer to never contact her again. Certainly Sofia wanted her debt forgiven, but had they not built a relationship that went deeper than quid pro quo? They were friends, or almost friends, anyway. They were connected by their shared history of seeking refuge in America from Europe's ruins.

But that was the crux of it. Diana might have harbored a sense of kinship with Sofia like sheltering a flame from the wind with a cupped hand. But that hardly made it reciprocal. Sofia had been carrying the spy's burden all these years, the weight of lying to those she cared about, of betraying those she respected and admired, of being forced to live a double life. Unlike Diana, she hadn't taken up that burden voluntarily. She had been forced to by Diana herself as recompense for the immigration approvals that were her family's salvation. Diana knew she didn't deserve Sofia's affection. But that knowledge didn't make it hurt any less.

"Your status has been final for years," said Diana. "There's nothing I could do to renege even if I wanted to."

"But you have our correspondence, evidence that I've fed you intel over the years. If that comes out, it's all over for me."

"I'll wipe the logs and you can verify. You know the inner workings of the feed better than anyone."

"You could print out paper copies, hide evidence any number of different ways, and threaten me later unless I help you again."

Diana pinched the bridge of her nose, then looked Sofia in the eye. "Have I ever lied to you?"

"That's hardly—"

"Have I ever lied to you?"

Sofia stopped short at the iron in Diana's tone.

"No."

"And I'm not lying to you now. Do this for me, and your debt is paid."

CHAPTER 28

Diana passed by Dag's seat on her way to the bathroom. He was immersed in his feed, fingers twitching, eyes unfocused as they gazed through the thin veil of physical reality into the digital beyond. As she had hoped, he was recovering quickly from his ordeal. Non sequitur microexpressions of fear or anxiety occasionally flitted across his face, almost too fast to spot, but he wasn't catatonic, and at this stage that was a victory in itself.

She had got him into this mess, and now she had got him into a bigger one that neither of them could escape alone. Was his cooperation predicated on feelings for her that might even survive her recent fuckups? Or was it simply that he saw this new plan as their best chance of making it out alive? Maybe it wasn't even binary. He could be feeling both or neither, her presence in his life a random walk of emotional turmoil.

His presence in her life sometimes felt that way. Every time she thought she had him figured out, something shifted. She used to tune out of conversations, summoning her feed while she put small talk on autopilot. That was an ability she'd developed through years of cultivating agents, but perhaps that subtle distance was perceptible to someone who got close enough to you, even if they knew as little about you as Dag did about Diana. Maybe knowing someone's personal history, knowing their goals, their fears, their dreams, wasn't really knowing them. Maybe there were secrets that ran deeper. Dag claimed that she was inscrutable, but his questions teemed with painful insights she shied away from like a vampire from blistering sunlight.

"I get it, I get it," said Dag, making Diana jump. She had half forgotten he was talking to Javier through the feed. "But I wouldn't be bothering you if this wasn't the real deal."

Dag paused, but Diana couldn't hear the other side of the conversation.

"Remember what you told me right before shutting everything down?" Dag continued. "You said I'd always have a home with you, that even though the back door was closed, you still had a lot of resources and good people to dedicate to building a better world. Well, this is the time to deploy them."

Dag paused again, then said, "Yeah, tomorrow. No, I'm not fucking with you. Be there."

Diana left him to it and squeezed into the tiny airplane bathroom. As she peed, she tried to put herself into Javier's shoes. After escaping a broken family, he had raised his sister and pursued his passion for mathematics and computer science all the way to Commonwealth, where he'd helped design the feed's security architecture before teaming up with Emily to subvert it on behalf of various progressive causes. When Dag extinguished their exploit and Emily had disappeared, Javier had pivoted, devoting the expertise of his team and the billions they'd skimmed off hedge funds to take a major stake in Commonwealth, becoming an activist shareholder and advocating openly for user rights. It made sense. After losing the ability to manipulate the feed to his own ends in secret, he now used his stake in the feed to pursue the same ends under the public eye.

In addition to his duties on Commonwealth's board, Javier traveled the world to give talks, write op-eds, and convince the public that more transparency and accountability were needed at the conglomerate that built and maintained the world's information infrastructure. He wasn't a natural extrovert, and these efforts took everything out of him. Having to force himself into the public eye made him a wiser arbiter of its attention than other feed stars and talking heads addicted to their own celebrity. Nothing would please Javier more than stepping off the world stage, but he wouldn't unless he found a higher-leverage path to effect change. He'd last seen Dag three years earlier, helping Emily to recruit him into their little cabal. Dag might have killed their loophole, but Javier knew he had done so in good faith and didn't fault him for it. Would that be enough to convince him to skip the Electronic Frontier Foundation keynote he was supposed to give and jump on a plane right back to San Francisco?

But Javier was only one piece of this puzzle. Diana summoned her feed and pulled up her research notes for the original report she had sent to Haruki. She skimmed the summaries of board dynamics, voting records, annual letters, stock tiers, analyst reports, cap tables, governance structures, special committees, and executive privileges. On the surface, these might bore anyone but a financial maven, but Diana saw them for what they were. This labyrinth of massaged numbers, sexy charts, and legalese was actually a portrait of how power flowed through Commonwealth. No individual report or ratio was particularly enlightening, but when Diana submerged her consciousness in the boundless material, let the acronyms effervesce through the slipstream of her thoughts, patterns began to emerge, patterns revealing that at the end of the day, only a few people were required to actually make major decisions.

Belatedly Diana realized she was still on the toilet. Dismissing her feed, she stood, the sound of the vacuum flush harsh in the cramped space. Pins and needles prickled her legs. She'd been sitting long enough to cut off blood flow. She washed her hands, threw water on her face, and looked in the mirror above the sink.

Unlike Diana's consummately plain features, Sofia made a striking impression with her strong Italian jaw, high cheekbones, and large brown eyes. She had been effortlessly beautiful with her hair wrapped in that towel, a genius who was gorgeous to boot. It was her mathematical brilliance that had allowed her to overcome even the misfortune of being born European to earn a position with the privileged few who maintained, improved, and ran the feed. She would be freaking out right now, trying to find a way to fulfill Diana's request without endangering the job she so identified with. Ironically this final favor broke no laws or confidentiality agreements but required Sofia to take an overt social risk that was even less palatable to her than private betrayal.

Diana leaned forward, examining the flecks and whorls of her irises, staring until she became less and less recognizable to herself.

Maria.

Helen had invoked Diana's birth name with the cruel nonchalance of a fickle god. Those three syllables were still rippling through Diana's psyche, reincarnating entombed memories, displacing the stories she told herself about herself. Dag, Helen, Rachel, Lowell, Freja, Hsu, Javier, Haruki, Kendrick, Sofia, Emily, Sean, Lopez, Nell. Did names hold some secret power, or were they nothing but random phonemes, convenient tags for easy reference? Sometimes a name was so banal as to be unmentionable, and sometimes it was a key that opened doors into forbidden realms.

Looking into the mirror, Diana wondered whether it was simply her reflection that stared back or whether the mirror was actually a window into one of those forbidden realms, a parallel universe where everything was different except for the fact that she and her doppelgänger showed up in front of the mirror at precisely the same time with precisely the same backdrop and made precisely the same movements. She contorted her face, and doppelgänger Diana did the same. There was no way to trick your doppelgänger into revealing themselves because the shared bond ran far deeper than causality. Your every intention stemmed from the same source. Maybe the woman staring back at her was a kindergarten teacher, not a spy. Maybe she was surrounded by loving friends, was morbidly embarrassed by farting, or, horror of horrors, preferred country music to hip hop. Maybe she still went by Maria, enjoying the ultimate privilege of never having had a reason to hide who she really was.

Diana lowered her head, letting brown curls fall in front of her face. Enough delving into imagination's fever dream. She was acting as if she'd inhaled some of the concoction Haruki had supplied. Let the kidnappers wander their hall of mirrors, she had work to do.

CHAPTER 29

Dag was still immersed in his feed when Diana came out of the bathroom, but his tone and body language had changed subtly.

"This isn't Yushan, Baihan," he said with distinct coolness. "I'm not following you on a wild-goose chase again. I need to talk to Mr. Hsu directly, and I need to do it now." A pause as Hsu's assistant replied. "Given what happened last time, I think that even you can agree that he owes me a conversation. Maybe things will play out differently."

Diana walked to the front of the cabin and surveyed the mountain ranges that spread out below like crumpled wrapping paper. When she had crossed the lake to make good on Helen's invitation, a storm had been brewing in the alpine heights behind the Ranch. She had that same sense now, tension building beneath the surface, static threatening to electrify every touch. But there would be no clouds to release a downpour, no thunder to roll through the heavens. This was a uniquely human tempest—personalities, philosophies, and technologies all coalescing in the melee we call politics.

She summoned her feed.

"Haruki?"

"I'm here."

"Good," she said. "Because I have a new assignment for you."

"Look," he said. "About that—"

"Hey," she said. "No second-guessing. Believe me, you're not going to want to miss this meeting, and I need you to be there."

"Meeting?"

"Tomor—"

Diana frowned. Another call was coming in. It was tagged "Urgent," her feed bleating harshly.

"Look, whatever it—"

"Sorry, Haruki," she said. "But I need to take this. I'll call you right back."

She ended one call and accepted the other.

"What's wrong?"

Fear creased Kendrick's face, his lips pursed, his eyes wide and a little wild.

"Diana," he said. "I love you, girl, but I don't know what you've gotten yourself into."

"What are you talking about?"

"Do you know how rare it is for me to get called to the White House? I mean, it's happened more often over the years of course. The higher you rise in this behemoth of a government, the fancier the company." He was racing, talking too fast. "But still, it's not normal, *not normal*, for me to get called into the Oval fucking Office. I'm a regulator for heaven's sake. I crunch numbers, slap wrists, do my best to champion the public interest and all that good stuff. I didn't work on the Hill for a reason. Policy over politics. Stay out of the snake pit."

"Kendrick," she said. "Calm down."

"I should never have gotten involved with any of this. What was I thinking? I love you. I said that already. But I never should have fed you intel. That's wrong. Those weren't my calls, they're not part of my purview. And when this happens, when all of it goes down, I'm gonna be under the microscope. Any discrepancy will be blown a mile wide. It's crazy, *crazy*. This isn't why I became a public servant. See? It's even in the name: *public servant*. It's not supposed to be the other way around."

"Kendrick," Diana snapped. He startled, and through the semitransparent feed projection, she saw Dag startle too, head snapping around to check on her even as he continued his own call from the couch. "Take a deep breath, buddy. Remember that golden retriever you were telling me about? Think about him and his dumb, cute face. Imagine his gross slobber and how he goes crazy when his ball gets stuck under the couch. He's a big stupid dog, and you love him, right? Take another breath. Inhale, that's it. Exhale. Again, slower this time. That's it."

Kendrick tried to get himself back under control.

"It'll be okay," she said, channeling all the composure she could muster. "Whatever it is. We can handle it. We always have. We always will. It'll be okay."

"Diana, please—"

"Shh, take a minute. Settle down. My whole job is dealing with crises. The best way to speed up is to slow down. Panic doesn't help. There we go. Inhale. Exhale. All right, that's it."

"Diana, I-I don't know what to do." He was sobbing quietly now, shoulders shuddering. That was better than a breakdown, though. Rationality could shine through tears. "It doesn't make sense. I don't want it to happen, but I can't stop it. And I keep asking myself, 'Is this happening because of what I told Diana?' but I know you would never want such a thing, but then I don't know if I even know you well enough after all these years to know what you would want and then—"

"Start from the beginning, Kendrick," she said, keeping her voice steady even though her mind was already racing like wildfire. "You said that you were called into the White House."

"Yeah, yeah," he said, clinging like a drowning man to the chronological life raft she offered. "It was just a few hours ago. I mean, I'd had requests over the last few months for various reports on Commonwealth. All the datasets we hold, transcripts from executive interviews, correspondence with auditors, all that stuff. It's like I told you, you're not the only one asking questions. But this is way off the charts, an unprecedented amount of activity. I mean, they're America's most valuable company, so there's always a lot of scrutiny, but this was crazy."

"So you were called into the White House," she repeated like a mantra.

"Uh-huh." He hiccupped. "And I walk in there, and President Lopez is right there, sitting at his desk."

"Yes," she said. "Well, it is his office after all."

"Yeah," he said. "Anyway, there are a bunch of other people too. I recognized the attorney general, the national security adviser, Senator Watkins, and then there were a few others I'd never seen before." He paused for a moment, trying to gather his thoughts. "This woman, Helen, took over the meeting and gave a presentation. She introduced herself as some kind of senior adviser, but I don't remember the title. She said that Rachel, Commonwealth's senior executive team, and the company's board were all guilty of treason, that she had evidence that they had been funneling state secrets and selling illegal feed access to foreign intelligence agencies for billions, that she was heading to San Francisco to oversee the strike team that would bring them in. Given the situation and how critical a piece of national infrastructure the feed is, she said that the only option was to nationalize Commonwealth and seize control of its assets, at least until we can verify that the perpetrators have been caught, the problem has been fixed, and that we can implement a foolproof safeguard on their operations."

Kendrick pressed his fingers to his temples. "It's *insane*. I don't know what to think. I mean, I've been studying Commonwealth for years, and it doesn't make sense. Why sell classified intel when you're already a dominant monopoly? They make legitimate money hand over fist. It seems ridiculous to risk everything for a few big personal payouts. I mean, she was talking big money, but these people are already billionaires. Diana, Helen quoted some of what I told you about Commonwealth's financials. Those weren't confirmed numbers, that was just the idle speculation on what we might be able to read between the lines of their official reporting. It's nothing that could stand up in court or even under analyst scrutiny. Does Helen think those numbers are real? But why would she think they constitute proof? Is this what you were working on the whole time, drumming up evidence for this operation?"

Diana felt as if she had just been dunked into an ice bath. Somewhere, somehow, Helen had discovered that Diana was not, in fact, executing her mission of planting false evidence. She could have had a physical surveillance team disprove one of the fake reports Diana had been automatically delivering, or maybe one of the security contractors had called in Dag's escape. It didn't matter how. What mattered was that the avalanche was starting, and far faster than Diana could have imagined. Diana going rogue meant that Helen had, at best, fabricated circumstantial evidence to work with. But she was pulling the trigger now, forcing things through while she still had the element of surprise rather than risking that Diana might spread the word and ruin her ambush. She would backfill whatever evidence she wanted after the raid.

"What did POTUS say?" It had to be asked, but she knew it was a foregone conclusion. Her mind was already braiding new contingencies like glossy strands of spun sugar.

Kendrick frowned. "He was shocked. I thought he was going to have a stroke. He challenged her, questioned the evidence, said that even if this was true, the solution wasn't to attack Commonwealth head-on. They should run a full investigation, share the results with friendly nations at the UN, lead a joint intelligence committee that brings the guilty parties to heel." He sucked in a shaky breath. "Helen said that was a good point and that maybe they should change their tactics. But then the national security adviser freaked out, said they couldn't guarantee the nation's defenses if the feed was compromised. They had to act now, and unilaterally, or every American could be at risk. Watkins chimed in too, and suddenly the whole room was pushing for Helen's original plan. I didn't know what to do. I just stood there, mute. Helen called me forward when she was talking about Commonwealth's financials, but it felt like some kind of staged play where I was just there as a prop. After two hours of debate, POTUS rubber-stamped the operation. He looked like hell."

"Where are you now?"

"Still at the White House. Helen just flew out to supervise the field team in California. None of us can leave until the operation is wrapped. There's an impossible amount of work to be done. They've called in everyone they can who has a security clearance. It's a circus. I don't even know what to think. Is this all true and we've somehow missed the biggest cover-up in history? Could it be some huge mistake? But why would all those people believe it? How could they be wrong?"

"When did Helen take off?"

Kendrick shook his head. "It's time for you to start answering some of *my* questions. Is this why you were asking about Commonwealth? Are you working for Helen?"

"Look, time is a critical factor," said Diana. "Believe me, I'll fill you in later, but for now I need as much information as possible. You signed up to serve your country, and this is the definition of a national emergency."

He stared at her for a long moment, crow's-feet forming around his eyes.

"No," he said, his tone firming like wet concrete under a summer sun.

"Kendrick."

"No, this isn't sharing the contents of a report a couple months before we publish it. It's not the same. I'm getting called in to see POTUS and people are fudging my data and the world is spinning out of control and I don't know a goddamn thing. Tell me what the hell is going on. Why is this happening? Who do you *actually* work for, Diana? Come on, you owe me the truth after all these years."

Diana appraised her longtime agent, remembering the cheap beers they'd shared at Freaky Pete's, his genuine if credulous commitment to public service, the relish with which he'd tasted that artisanal joint as they walked along the Potomac. He had already given her all the information she needed at this point. She should sever the connection and scramble to update their plans now that Helen was launching her offensive. Even if Kendrick was holding something back, which she doubted, Diana ought to deploy one of the ready lies she always had on hand. She should lead him down a path that reaffirmed their relationship and his dependence on her. She could even bully him, dredge up a compromising detail from his past to assert her dominance. That's what Helen would do in this situation, and that's how Helen had coached Diana to manage her agents, an unending stream of misdirection with unpredictable applications of prizes and rebukes.

Diana dialed down the opacity on her feed and looked at Dag, who was just nodding quietly, listening intently to whatever apparition haunted his feed. *We all have to start somewhere. Otherwise what's the point?* She refocused on Kendrick, his burgeoning conviction as delicate as a seedling. At their core, infosec protocols balanced security against efficacy. If you never told anyone anything, you could keep your secrets safe, but you'd never get anything done. Helen was building an empire with her keen intuition for sniffing out veiled fear, using intimidation to inflame it, and playing people against each other in a deadly, recursive dance. Diana didn't have to run her agents, or her life, the same way.

"Kendrick, you're right," she said. "I owe you answers. The truth is that I used to work for Helen. I was investigating Rachel on her orders. But in the course of the investigation I discovered that Helen was using the intel to fabricate evidence justifying a bid to seize Commonwealth." She had expected that sharing the truth would feel like laying down a burden, but it was more like loading a gun. "That's why she's citing your unconfirmed reports and using your numbers to drum up proof of treason. Your gut is correct, this is a conspiracy to take over the feed.

The other people at that meeting were either already in Helen's pocket or innocent but convinced to acquiesce by her false claims and political pressure. But we can't let this happen. You can imagine what will happen if she overthrows Rachel. That's why I need you now more than ever. I'm assembling a team to fight back, but we need someone who knows what's really going on at the White House."

Blood drained from Kendrick's face. "Diana." He stumbled, tried again, faltered again. Finally he found his voice. "Diana, I've got a family. Rob and the baby. I can't do this. I can't."

"For now all I need you to do is stay put and pretend to do whatever they tell you to do," she said. "They can't fault you for that, right?"

His expression pleaded with her to assure him that this was all some twisted joke or hyper-realistic nightmare. Truth was a bitter antidote.

"I will do everything in my power to protect you and your family, even the dog," she said, hoping for a bleak smile that didn't rise. "In the meantime, I need you to hang tight and trust me."

Trust. Diana felt naked exposing so much for so little. She could only hope that showing vulnerability might inspire loyalty, not just illustrate weakness.

CHAPTER 30

Haruki was waiting for them at the hole-in-the-wall coffee shop, macchiato sitting untouched in front of him as he nervously scanned passersby. Here in downtown San Francisco, he might be just another budding entrepreneur anxiously awaiting his chance to pitch a new piece of world-changing tech to savvy venture-capital investors. But Diana knew that the briefcase on his lap didn't hold a prototype. She remembered her first real-world op, the knowledge that it wasn't a training exercise heightening the senses, turning every detail into a highlight.

"Dag, Haruki," she said. "Haruki, Dag."

They shook hands, eyeing each other suspiciously.

"You chaps can get to know each other later," she continued. "For now we need to get a move on."

Haruki passed her the briefcase. "Everything's arranged."

"Thanks," she said.

Dag's gaze flickered in and out of focus as he tapped into his feed. "Hsu just arrived."

"Time to strap on our little space boots and get this show on the road," said Diana.

Wanting to stay, to press pause, but unable to avoid the necessity of haste, she led them out of the coffee shop. Cars sped along the streets, the feed navigating them in smooth curves that avoided pedestrians and minimized congestion. Sunlight slanted through the dizzying sky-scrapers towering over them, artifacts hinting at the human aspiration to apotheosis.

Diana still remembered the childlike sense of wonder inspired by her arrival in the United States. Manhattan's towers dwarfed the squat, utilitarian construction so common in Bulgaria. Waterworks held back the rising Atlantic as if issuing a challenge to nature itself. The smells of sauerkraut, urine, leather, fish, and stale coffee assaulted her nostrils. But the people made the biggest impression. Hordes of them crowded the sidewalks, individuals striding in all directions but always *forward*, driven by indefatigable purpose and buoyed by the inborn confidence that they were participants in a shared destiny, that freedom itself was a right, not just a privilege.

Still just a kid, she hadn't been able to articulate it, but she felt the tug of this ideology of confidence, of denying that anything was impossible, of knowing that she was doing her part to advance the cause of progress in an uncertain world. Unlike the crumbling castles of what had once been her home, this strange new country was zealously focused on the future. For its citizens, the always-vanishing present was not an inheritance but an opportunity. History was as mutable as the waves that hurled themselves against the seawalls. Like religion, the future belonged to those who believed in it.

Diana cultivated that faith. From that day forward, the unfamiliar glimmer of hope was inextricably linked to her new identity as an American. The future was a real place, a land, a people. Her metaphysics was bounded by geography, and every step she took into the shadowy world of espionage reinforced the sanctity of national borders. Spymasters, generals, and security experts acknowledged "nonstate actors" as exceptions that proved the rule that countries were the units that really mattered when it came to shaping the course of future history. The political boundaries on a map yielded more insight than its topography.

The doors slid open, and they stepped across the threshold into the hushed redwood forest of the atrium. The trees were silent sentinels, their highest branches lost in artificial mist. Diana's heart skipped a beat as she waited for the inevitable alarm to sound, their feeds blaring notifications that they weren't authorized to enter Commonwealth headquarters, that security was already on its way. That was how delicate their desperate plan was, how easily it might be torn apart. But Sofia had done at least part of her job, tagging Diana, Dag, and Haruki as legitimate guests. Proud Sofia, who had played the spy in order to nurture her own seed of hope, suffering the psychological torment of double-crossing friends and colleagues in order to earn the privilege of mere participation.

Perhaps that was why she had harnessed herself to this particular behemoth, eschewing Diana's Beltway lair to seek her fortune in California, where the future wore a different costume and history was shaped by the agricultural, industrial, and information revolutions more than the French variety. Sofia helped construct Commonwealth algorithm by algorithm, fiber by fiber, turning life into data and data into insight until the feed was a digital mirror reflecting the universe of human experience. That was a dream no less ambitious and no less flawed than that of nation states themselves, whose borders proved irrelevant to the digital infinity of the feed, parallel worlds with different rules whose collision spelled catastrophe.

Diana glanced over at the bench hidden in the thickest part of the grove, but Rachel was not there today. Just as Diana had latched on to Helen, soaked up her life lessons and worldview like a sponge, eager for a guide to the promise and contradiction of her new home, so had Sofia found a role model in Rachel, an avatar of providence who deigned to offer her a first-class ticket to board the techno-utopian ark.

Dag's arm grazed Diana's shoulder as they entered the elevator, their stomachs dropping and spines compressing as it whooshed them silently upward. His kidnapping had been a wake-up call of sorts, ripping away the blinders of patriotism and forcing her to look with fresh eyes on the people she'd manipulated, betrayed, and killed in the name of national security. She was a monster. That's what it came down to at the end of the day. Monsters hid in the shadows, stalked their prey, and imagined their misdeeds cleansed by ideology. Diana had thrown off the mantle of personal responsibility, deferred her own moral judgment, replacing it with loyalty to a woman whose ambitions had finally exceeded Diana's limits, her conscience snapping like an old rubber band spread between the fingers of an inquisitive child.

The elevator deposited them into the sculpture garden. Abstract shapes, mythical beasts, and impressionist fantasies leered at the three intruders as they traipsed through the exquisite jungle of blown glass, forged iron, and hewn marble. Diana let her fingertips brush the copper coat of the penny bear, half wishing for a miraculous return to that simpler time when her objective had been nothing more than good old surveillance, harvesting secrets instead of deploying them to build a bridge to nowhere.

Her grip was tight and slick with sweat around the handle of the briefcase, its lightness at odds with the gravity of the evidence it contained. By rights she should have to drag it in behind a locomotive, wheels screeching as they searched for traction on rusty rails and engine straining to pull a load that no one should have to bear. Rescuing Dag could be shrugged off as bucking under the yoke of duress. This, though. This was treason through and through.

Diana could only hope that even treason might serve a higher purpose.

CHAPTER 31

The striated granite boulder still held the giant cut-glass table like Atlas shouldering the earth, but this time the vase at its center held tulips, not sunflowers. Some were a purple so deep as to be almost black, while others were scarlet rimmed with fiery orange, and a few were pure white, all sprouting from bright-green stems like inverted bells ready to toll this world's demise and ring in the next one. Street vendors had hawked tulips near Amsterdam's train stations while Diana had been deployed there, wrapping them in brown paper for hopeful lovers and happy tourists. Diana had ignored the colorful bouquets, preferring stands offering buttery, raw herring or dry cappuccinos. There was a part of her that saw cut flowers as fresh corpses.

Despite his advanced age, Hsu was anything but a corpse. His eyes had a mischievous vivaciousness as he surveyed the newcomers, and his crooked fingers drummed on the surface of the table as if his old bones couldn't quite contain the abiding energy that had fueled his lifelong campaign to assure the ascent of Taiwan's geopolitical fortunes.

"Dag," he said, gripping the knob of the cane that rested against his chair and rising to his feet. "These aren't the circumstances I imagined for our reunion."

Diana touched Dag's lower back lightly. He might flinch, but she wanted him to know he wasn't alone. Even if he hated her with a zeal she deserved, she was here for him.

Dag summoned poise from some unknown reserve, perhaps replenished by hours of sleeping on the plane. He was still gaunt and shaggy, but he was here, not lost in daymares of an Arctic cell. "You made me climb a mountain to meet you last time. I figured the least I could do was make you cross an ocean."

The corner of Hsu's lip quirked. "I lost a substantial amount betting against you. Baihan made every effort to convince me to ignore you. What made you think I would come?"

"You never struck me as the kind of man keen to repeat mistakes."

"And who are your charming companions?" Hsu looked Diana and Haruki up and down.

Dag inclined his head to Diana. "She's the one in charge here. I'm just a sidekick."

But Diana's eyes were on the other person in the room. Javier stood before the far wall, the tips of his slender fingers on the glass, gazing out across the gleaming spines of Commonwealth skyscrapers to the flocks of seagulls floating above the ruffled silver of the San Francisco Bay. He was tall, skinny, and dressed in his customary black leather, as if channeling an aesthetic that was half-flaneur, half-ascetic. He might as easily have just returned from robbing an ancient tomb as from dashing off a philosophical treatise.

"It's good to hear your voice," he said. "It's been too long, Dag. We've missed you."

His large dark eyes sought Dag and then flicked back to Diana. His expression of wanting to say more than he could turned to consternation.

"Yeah," said Diana, giving him a wink. "We've met."

"I—"

"Excuse us." Relief flooded through Diana at the brisk tone of Sofia's words. She had come through after all.

Diana, Dag, and Haruki made way for Sofia, Rachel, and a small entourage of high-level Commonwealth executives. From her initial investigations of their corporate governance, Diana recognized the general counsel and chief financial officer. They filed into the room, flanking Rachel as she took her seat at the head of the table.

Sofia looked at Diana, and they held each other's gaze for a long moment. Diana could see smoke in the skies of Italy, feel the pangs of a homesickness for a place that no longer existed, and smell the instant ramen Sofia had subsisted on while supporting her family as she tried to make her way in this strange new country. A wave of affection washed over Diana, a sense of kinship, a desire to offer support that was unconditional, not tied to a quid pro quo that cheapened what might otherwise have grown into an authentic connection. There was only one thing she could offer Sofia now, a parting gift to bless the journey she had embarked on so many years ago.

Freedom.

Diana nodded once.

Sofia nodded back, her straight face somehow both solemn and elated. Then she turned and left. The door slid silently shut behind her.

The debt was forgiven.

Everyone followed Rachel's lead and took their seats. Everyone except Diana.

Within these walls, America is our only soul mate. Helen's words echoed inside Diana's head, simultaneously inspiring a resurgence of conditioned guilt for what she was about to do, no matter how necessary it was, and a sudden awareness of how ludicrous those hollow words were. What Helen had really been saying was that Diana should owe nobody else loyalty, should reserve her trust for Helen alone. And what did Helen offer in return for such devotion? Special attention that affirmed Diana's secret wish that she was unique, that she had a place in this universe, that her life meant something, that her actions were important.

Diana laid the briefcase flat on the table. The well-worn grooves of habit told her to run, to lie, to spin a web of misdirection that would ensnare these power brokers and make them hers, and through her, Helen's. Diana felt the leash of years of training tugging at her neck, urging her to reverse course, to return to the comforting structure of obedience. She looked from person to person, marshaling her thoughts. They stared back with curiosity, impatience, and skepticism. This time it was different. She was on the verge of something new, launching into the void of true autonomy.

Diana's gaze finally met Rachel's. That single purple eye shone out from its nest of wrinkles like a beacon. Diana had observed Rachel from afar, watched her interact with colleagues, swim laps at the local pool, and head up to bed with her husband and their lover. But they had never seen each other face-to-face, and Rachel was not looking at her but *through* her, piercing the many veils Diana had wrapped around herself, not attacking or invading but *seeking* what might lie beneath, what could possibly have inspired this young woman she had never heard of to orchestrate a secret meeting with her senior team and two most prominent board members. A lesser CEO might have demanded an explanation posthaste, blood rising to her cheeks, voice straining under the weight of countless responsibilities, the ragged edges of her words colored by rage at time's implacability in the face of a singular purpose that opened so many other doors. But Rachel just waited, quiet, calm, composed, comfortable in the knowledge that simply being present was in fact the rarest strength one could muster in the face of fate.

"You're all wondering why you're here," said Diana. "Each and every one of you has been screwed over in the past. You wouldn't be at this table if you hadn't figured out how to turn adversity into opportunity. Well, I'm here to tell you that no matter how badly you think you've been fucked before, no matter how badly your heart has been broken, your plans have been thrashed, your fortunes have been sacked, or your spirit has been shattered, it's the smallest slice of nothing compared to the shitstorm that is currently bearing down on Commonwealth. Now I'm no history buff, but Dag here has a special penchant for the past, and I think that even he would agree that this is a clusterfuck of historical proportions and that what you decide to do with the information I'm about to share will shape the future all of us are going to live through or die for."

CHAPTER 32

Silence reigned as Diana delivered her presentation. There were no interruptions, no questions, just the gradual draining of blood from cheeks and a general shortening of breath. She found a rhythm as she laid out the situation, feeling like a World War I–era artilleryman loading high-explosive shells into a mortar again and again and again as the enemy huddled in their trenches under the barrage. The secrets in her arsenal were more incendiary than even the most advanced weaponry at the Pentagon's disposal, and she would need every last one of them plus a mountain of luck. Standing in front of these people, offering up hard-earned intel for expert inspection, she felt naked. But rather than the crushing social anxiety of a dream in which nudity becomes apparent only after taking the stage, this nakedness was exhilarating, a bold first step into a new world.

"Now that you know what's going on," said Diana, her tone signaling the end of the pitch, "we need to get all of you to a safe house where we can discuss next steps. With Helen preparing to raid Commonwealth, we can't risk having the only people able to decide how to respond getting swept up in the initial arrests. A satisfactory place has already been arranged." She signaled Haruki, who stood up. "If you'll all collect your things, we have cars waiting below."

"Whoa, whoa, whoa," said Commonwealth's general counsel. "We aren't going anywhere. There won't be any arrests. Our executive team and board of directors have done nothing wrong, and we have more than sufficient legal resources to tear apart any drummed-up charges. If even half of what you're saying is true, and I'm sure I'm not the only one who's harboring doubts about your story"—she looked around for support—"then we'll have it thrown out by a federal judge faster than you can say *bullshit*. Hell, I *hope* they try something like this. We'll be able to milk the blowback from the false accusations and government overreach to weaken any regulations the feds try to throw at us for the next few *years*. Journalists will have a field day. I doubt we'll be so lucky, though. No offense, Ms. . . ." She waited in vain for Diana to supply a surname. "But this plot of yours is really quite far fetched. I'll have my analysts look into your claims, and we can have our government-affairs people make some calls on the Hill. If there's anything actually here, we'll nail it down and circumvent."

Hsu tapped his cane on the floor. "I've heard nothing about this from my contacts in Washington. If the White House was planning an operation of this magnitude, it would be hard to keep under wraps. Furthermore, if the US government were to make such a move based on falsified evidence, it will create an international incident. The rest of the world won't acquiesce when they see the Lopez administration try to seize power over the feed. At the very least, trade sanctions will be issued, and countries will start divesting from infrastructure that's dependent on Commonwealth. It will weaken the feed and America's standing at the same time. I know Lopez. He's a moderate, reasonable man whose priority is stability and incremental social progress. He would never do something like this." He glanced at Dag. "I'm surprised, Mr. Calhoun. I would not have expected you to rush me over from Taiwan just to listen to some conspiracy theory."

Javier had been staring at Diana quizzically throughout the conversation. She could see him putting the pieces together, trying to figure out who she was and where he had seen her before.

"I wish it were just a theory," said Dag. "But unfortunately for all of us, what Diana's saying is true. Hard to believe, certainly, but true. I was kidnapped by a black ops team last week because Helen suspected I knew something about her plans and might provide her with additional leverage over Diana."

Everyone looked at Dag.

"Wait, what?" asked Javier. "Kidnapped? What are you talking about?"

The chief financial officer threw up his hands. "Okay, enough already," he said. "We have a company to run. I'm not wasting an entire afternoon on some crackpot circus. Go live out your soap opera somewhere else. This is a monumental waste of time."

"Amen," said the general counsel, rising to her feet. "I don't know how this got onto our calendars, but we can all pretend this meeting never happened and just get on with the day."

Diana saw her own failings in the group's predictable objections. When faced with an uncomfortable truth, people's first instinct was to ignore it, justifying denial with the same assumptions that girded their obsolete mental model. If she had only thought bigger, been more skeptical, asked harder questions, she might have unraveled what was going on far earlier and been able to avert disaster. She wouldn't have helped lay the groundwork for the impending raid. She would have demanded more background before picking up that fateful vial of synthetic venom amid the flowering jacarandas of Buenos Aires so many years ago. Now her only option was to do what she could with the time she had.

Summoning a shared feed, Diana dropped in a video clip from the recorded board meeting. That they were sitting in the very same room at this very moment made the footage feel both intimate and surreal, as if every word spoken in the past, every action taken, did not fade into time's relentless current but lived on in karma's ghostly inventory.

"Look," said Hsu. "What we really need to do is organize back-channel conversations with governments and their UN representatives, assure them that the carbon tax was a . . . one-time thing. We're not a threat to their authority. We're not encroaching on their sovereignty. We're a partner. We're here to make it easier for them to run their own countries. This Lopez interview was a shot across the bow. If we don't convince world leaders that we're friendly and obedient, they're going to ram new regulations down our throats."

"That's the absolute last thing we should do," Javier snapped. "Open your eyes. Nation states are dying. The economy, the environment, the feed, everything is global now. Governments are so focused on ensuring their institutional survival that they're failing the people they claim to serve. Even if they tried, they don't have the tools to deal with global problems."

Diana paused the replay, the expressions of her current audience as frozen as the recorded phantoms overlaid on their vision.

"Helen had me running surveillance on Commonwealth leadership to give her the material necessary to orchestrate this raid," said Diana. "I didn't know what her ultimate goals were at that time. My orders were to sniff out weaknesses, map out key relationships, and build an extensive personal file on Rachel. Haruki here was a cutout hired to relay those orders to me to protect the identity of the principals."

Haruki nodded confirmation.

"I recorded the board meeting with cameras hidden in the flower arrangement and submitted the footage back up through the chain of command along with the rest of the data I collected. From there—"

Javier slapped the table and everyone jumped. "I saw you," he said. "I saw you as I was heading to the elevators. I knew I recognized you."

Diana inclined her head. "That's right."

She called up images of Rachel working in the atrium's redwood grove, climbing out of the pool, water cascading off wrinkled skin that concealed sinewy strength, and chopping heirloom tomatoes in her kitchen. A tangible hush descended. In the minimalist elegance of the corporate conference room, these candid personal shots of Commonwealth's founder were incongruent and disturbing.

"When you're looking to frame someone, particularly people as powerful as the folks around this table, you go the distance," said Diana. "Trade secrets, financial shenanigans, and strategic priorities can sometimes pale in comparison to knowledge of the principals' personal lives, proclivities, and motivations. That information wouldn't be relevant in a legitimate investigation of suspected malfeasance. That I was tasked to assemble a full take on Rachel is what initially tipped me off that this operation went far deeper than I thought." She dropped the rest of her reports into the shared feed. "And that's just the tip of the iceberg. In these files you'll find extensive documentation of every bit of questionable behavior, competitive intelligence, and organizational weakness I discovered over the course of the investigation."

The lawyer spoke up again. "We are going to sue the *shit* out of them."

"This is certainly troubling," said Hsu, "but the fact is that nobody here has actually done anything that would justify the raid you claim is imminent. Certainly nothing that could be used to 'nationalize' Commonwealth. That's an entirely different league of abuse of power."

Diana unclasped the briefcase, opened it, and spun it around to face the table. As she did so, Haruki handed out paper packets to each person. Everyone frowned, flipping through the pages and trying to skim for the gist. Everyone but Rachel, whose eye remained steady on Diana, a spotlight that held her in its lilac thrall.

"You're right," said Diana. "My investigation yielded results that would serve you going after the US government rather than the other way around. But my investigation was only step one of a larger operation. Helen isn't trying to *find* skeletons in your closet, she wants to plant them there. She used details gleaned from my reports to fabricate this physical evidence of treason, padding it with legitimate classified intel from within the American intelligence community. In these papers you'll find documentation of sales of state secrets to foreign governments. They claim you accessed CIA, NSA, and White House feed databases, pulled critical intel, and auctioned it off to Mr. Hsu's personal connections using Javier's frequent speaking trips as cover. All of you were rewarded handsomely with transactions hidden within matryoshka-like layers of fake accounts created and linked to you by Helen's analysts. The paperwork you're holding is the intelligence equivalent of a nuclear weapon. Its discovery would yield a scandal large enough to justify a draconian response, at least temporarily. Seizing control of Commonwealth might even be welcomed by an international community that suddenly realizes that their own secrets might be at risk."

Diana rested her hands on top of the open briefcase. "That was stage two of my mission. Plant this in Rachel's office and then have someone inside deliver it to a journalist who would break the story, justifying Helen's raid as necessary and appropriate. As soon as her people took the helm, she could use root access to the feed to acquire precisely the kind of state secrets she claimed you stole, leveraging them to bring every world leader into her personal sphere of influence. That was going to be stage three."

"But you brought the evidence to us instead," said Javier.

"That's right," said Diana.

"So her plan fails," said Hsu. "Without the evidence, she can't justify the raid."

"It makes it harder to justify to the public or the international community," said Diana. "But Helen knows I flipped, and she's going for broke. She has enough to convince Lopez to sign off on the raid itself. But stage three changes. Instead of going slow, she has to throttle up. Otherwise other countries will realize it's foul play, especially given that any 'evidence' presented would be ex post facto. So as soon as she takes Commonwealth, she will use feed blackouts to subdue an unsuspecting world. Physical conquest is trivial when the other side can't use any equipment or infrastructure and their entire country shuts down." Diana could almost smell the cloying scent of *Michelia champaca*. *If we move quickly and do things right, we can put Genghis Khan to shame.* "It's old-fashioned empire building."

"Damn," Javier murmured to himself.

Hsu rubbed the knob of his cane, lost in thought.

"Seriously? *Seriously?*" asked the CFO, directing his disbelief at the rest of the room, not Diana. "This isn't Star Wars. Crazy conspiracies like this are great for feed dramas, but they just don't happen in the real world. There is no fucking way that the US government is just going to take over the world via the feed. Helen, whoever she is, most definitely *isn't* Alexander the Great. We all just need to calm down, take a step back, and see what parts of this story we can actually confirm. Once we have enough information, we can decide on appropriate next steps, the first of which, as Liane says"—he motioned to the general counsel—"is likely to be a lawsuit."

Liane nodded. "It's just not credible. I'll have our legal team get to work on due diligence right away and we can go from there."

But even as Diana prepared to launch into a rebuttal, blaring feed notifications declared an urgent incoming call. It was Kendrick. Her chest tightened.

"Even if there's a small chance that what Diana says is true," said Hsu, "I can't afford to wait for confirmation. I need to get in touch with the Taiwanese defense minister and the UN Security Council right away."

"There's no way I can allow that," said Liane. "We need to keep this as contained as possible until we know what's really going on."

"Given the circumstances, that's not a call you get to make," said Hsu, anger rising. "It's your damn country that's going Machiavelli on the rest of us."

Letting the debate gain steam, Diana accepted Kendrick's call. His face appeared in front of her on an encrypted stream, dark smudges below his eyes and stress lines turning his expression into a topography of fear.

"It's happening," he said, his voice high and reedy. His eyes flicked back and forth. "Diana, I don't know what to do. There's no more time. It's *happening*."

Her heart froze, blood moving through her veins like glaciers carving out mountainsides.

"What's happening, Kendrick?"

His head twitched to the side. "Shit," he said. "I gotta go. They think I'm in the bathroom."

"Kendrick," she hissed.

But he was gone, his image vanishing into the roiling vortex of the feed, Rachel's eye boring through where it had been superimposed to skewer Diana as she tried to regain her composure.

Diana placed a palm on the cool, smooth glass of the tabletop, steadying herself. Then she stepped around the table, behind Hsu, to stare out over the angular skyscrapers of downtown San Francisco. Clouds scudded across the sky like an advancing army. The bay was covered in whitecaps, as if an invisible baker were smearing frosting onto the crest of every wave. Diana's tongue was thick in her dry mouth. Something burgeoned inside her, a conviction that burned hot in her gut.

There.

Sunlight glinting off something. No, not something. Some*things*.

Off to the southwest, a flock of drones was launching from a skyscraper around Civic Center, spiraling up and schooling around five helicopters lifting off the roof. The armada rose, arranged itself in formation, and then angled for downtown, engines screaming. Looking down, Diana caught glimpses of a parallel squadron of matte-black trucks roaring through the grid of streets far below, lights flashing, sirens wailing, civilian cars parting automatically before them like wheat before a falling scythe.

"That's the federal building," Liane's voice came out in a harsh whisper.

"Fuck me," said the CFO, choking on the words.

"Niitakayama nobore," said Dag.

"Niitakayama nobore," Hsu echoed softly. "A new Pearl Harbor."

Everyone had joined Diana at the window, looking out over this metropolis that had inspired so many dreams of riches and conquest, from colonizing conquistadors, to gold-obsessed forty-niners, to Silicon Valley moguls eager to put their dent in the universe. They all watched, transfixed, as fate approached in a tempest of whirling blades and burning rubber.

Helen was taking her place in history.

CHAPTER 33

Diana appraised Rachel. The chairwoman stood erect, outwardly calm but brimming with barely concealed tension in the face of the coming storm. She had spent her life building Commonwealth. Doing so had required laying new fiber across every corner of the planet, defeating competitors, gobbling up new entrants, orchestrating a cybersecurity program to rival the ambition of the Manhattan Project, cultivating relationships with countless political leaders and corporate partners, challenging every assumption, managing a cantankerous board, overcoming the fear of attempting the impossible on a daily basis, optimizing an unprecedented business model, and leading an army of technologists to apply the feed's algorithms to every conceivable application and embed them in every manufactured object.

Anyone who pushed themselves to such extremes suffered greatly. Rachel had sacrificed everything on the altar of the feed and had stopped at nothing to defend it. She had entered the geopolitical arena to implement a carbon tax when Dag demanded it in return for Javier and Emily's exploit. An exploit that would have destroyed public trust in the feed, and Commonwealth with it. An exploit that Rachel still had no idea had been the handiwork of Javier, her brilliant software architect who had helped secure the feed's digital ramparts before deciding to help breach them in the name of social justice. They were witnessing the child of Rachel's ambition being harnessed to Helen's chariot on its fiery ride to global annexation.

Diana's dream was dying alongside Rachel's. It was too late. Helen had won. Diana had done everything she could to stop the avalanche she'd helped start. But sometimes doing everything you could just wasn't enough. Time was cruelly finite, and she simply hadn't had enough of it to orchestrate an effective resistance. Diana had dared to hope that if she unlocked her vault of hard-won secrets, called in every favor, and used every trick she'd learned over the years, she could defeat, or at least deflect, Helen's inexorable ambitions. She remembered the smell of Helen's perfume, the bounce of her blonde curls, the cold calculation at the heart of every maxim.

Who was Diana to challenge such a matriarch? What was she thinking, trying to organize a last-ditch effort to avert such a well-prepared campaign? David had defeated Goliath with technology, a sling that had rendered the giant's bulging muscles obsolete. Diana held no such trump card. She was David, unarmed, about to be pummeled senseless by Goliath's massive fists. She was a failure as a spy and now a failure as a defector. She was a failure as a friend—she had none. A failure as a partner—Dag despised her. And a failure as a moral being—she had lied, killed, and betrayed more times than she cared to count, all for a cause she no longer believed in. She was, in short, a failure.

Whatever Helen's wrath held in store for double agents, Diana deserved it, many times over. The halo of flash-freezing blood materialized in her mind's eye, tiny ice crystals forming as steam billowed up from the scattered gore. She wouldn't receive the mercy of a quick death, and she had dealt out far worse. Ruining lives was often crueler than ending them.

But staring death in the face wasn't what drew a searing line of pain through her soul like the red-hot steel of a half-forged katana. Death was inevitable, and an early, painful death was a professional hazard in her line of work. What hurt was knowing that everyone whose life she'd touched, every agent she'd cultivated, every relationship she'd built, every person in this very room had been doomed by her efforts. Helen would squeeze every last contact from Diana's broken mind before letting the grim reaper exact his toll. Helen would co-opt Diana's network and put them to work establishing her empire. And whatever Helen had been planning to do with the people in this room, the revelations Diana had just shared with them would seal their fate. Nobody who knew the truth could live. They would be a threat to the new regime, and a regime whose jurisdiction included the whole of the digital and physical world would harbor no such threats.

That regime would be the legacy of Diana's failure. She had fled persecution only to enable it. Life was nothing but a vicious circle that transformed you into the object of your deepest fears.

We'll go off-grid, start over. A sad smile teased at the corners of Diana's lips. If only she had listened to Dag over breakfast that day, actually listened instead of putting the conversation on autopilot as she tapped her feed like a junkie. She had wanted a mission so badly. But what was a mission, really? An adventure? An opportunity to help forge a better world? Maybe that was the case for someone somewhere, but Diana had to admit that for her, a mission was an excuse to feel important, to expand her hoard of precious secrets, to polish her ego, to distract her from the miserable reality that a lifetime of missions had added up to.

For a shimmering moment, Diana indulged the fantasy of paths not taken. She and Dag sipped fresh coconuts under the shade of palms on a West African beach, or they tilled a hobby farm in the French countryside, taught chess to orphans, chased the sunset at music festival after music festival, raised a brood of spoiled children, trekked the Himalayas, debated the relative merits of history's greatest horticulturalists, or piloted boats along Amsterdam's canals. *We'll go off-grid, start over.* If only.

Something clicked inside her, like a boiler switching on in a forgotten subbasement.

Finally sensing Diana's gaze, Rachel met her eyes.

"Turn it off," said Diana.

Rachel stared back, unblinking.

"Turn it all off," said Diana. "It's the only way."

CHAPTER 34

Staring into someone else's eyes was far rarer than people assumed. In conversation most people let their gaze hover at a socially neutral point in space, flicking around to take in body language or facial expressions, letting peripheral vision do most of the work, maybe dipping in for a brief second of eye contact to accentuate a point. Lovers occasionally transgressed this norm in moments of intimacy, but even that was unusual. Even if you did look into someone's eyes, doing so meant shifting your focus back and forth between them.

This was different.

Rachel's single eye was a stained-glass window, lavender panels stitched together with flecks of green the exact shade of weathered bronze. Behind that luminescent partition raged a silent inferno whose flames Diana could glimpse only in the interstices through which Rachel's soul shone.

Turn it off.

The implications were unfathomable, the scenarios impossible to anticipate, the contingencies infinitely recursive. Efficacy bred dependency. The feed was the information infrastructure that empowered nearly every human activity and on which nearly every human activity relied. A talisman that lent mere mortals the power of demigods.

Doctors used it for diagnosis. Brokers used it to place bets. Physicists used it to explore the mysteries of quantum entanglement. Farmers used it to grow food. Kindergarteners used it to learn the alphabet. The feed was power, water, transportation, communication, entertainment, public services, relationships, industry, media, government, security, finance, and education. Without it the churning torrent of human civilization would cease. The feed was lightning captured in grains of sand, a miracle of science, engineering, and culture that wove the entire world into a single digital tapestry of unparalleled beauty and complexity.

Turning it off was madness. But leaving it on meant surrendering the feed, the world, to Helen. It was an impossible choice.

Rachel closed her eye. As the eyelid shut, Diana suddenly became aware of Rachel's age. The decades had inscribed deep lines across every centimeter of her face until it resembled a satellite image of eroded, rocky foothills, an archetypal example of the ravages of time. Chlorine had leached her silver hair, leaving her ponytail dry and stiff. Her simple, elegant suit made her thinness appear slender, but exercise, stress, and elderliness had taken a toll, leaving too little meat on fragile bones.

Rachel exhaled slowly through her nose, and her posture shifted subtly, as if she had been holding that particular breath for half her life. Then her eye opened again, but she was no longer looking at Diana. She was gazing out across the city.

The lights in the conference room clicked off. The gentle background hum of the building's internal processes died. Diana's files vanished from the shared feed. No, not just her files. The feed itself was gone. It was as if Diana had just stepped through the red satin curtains, Nell's sure grip leading her into the exotic feedlessness of Analog.

But this wasn't Analog. This was Commonwealth headquarters, the nerve center of the feed. Just a moment before, Diana had been playing in the final match of the World Cup, a key node in the deluge of global attention, and now she was standing in the middle of an empty stadium, her teammates vanished, the crowd abruptly absent, the cameras off, nothing but the frantic beating of her terrified heart and a distant ball rolling to a stop in the grass. The millions of voices that were her constant companion, always there, murmuring just below the threshold of hearing, had been silenced. The humble drinking cup that she constantly dipped into the font of all human knowledge had been slapped away. Her access to the vast prosthetic mind whose presence she had long since taken for granted had been severed.

The lights in every window in every skyscraper around them shut off, rippling out across the city, the state, the country, the world, as feed-enabled electric grids failed. Every car in sight, from the streets of downtown to distant vehicles crossing the Bay Bridge, froze as if captured in a still photograph. The container ships and yachts plying the bay coasted to a stop, their bow waves dissipating and their wakes catching up to make them bob where they sat marooned on the open water.

The ominous swarm of drones and helicopters converging on them came to a halt in midair and then descended to land on the nearest patch of clear ground they could find, per their emergency backup protocols. The convoy of trucks died along with all the civilian cars, their lights going dark and their sirens quiet.

Diana imagined transoceanic flights automatically detouring to make emergency landings, surgeons whose equipment failed midcraniotomy, a feed soap opera dissolving at the moment of a transcendent plot twist, control panels winking out before terrified astronauts, newsrooms descending into an unprecedented hush, nuclear power plants shutting down, a vocal track evaporating to reveal a pop star was lip-synching to a packed arena, a trail map fading from an endurance runner's vision, ovens shutting off before the lasagna was ready, students cursing as their research papers melted away, Wall Street's algorithmic ballet extinguished right in front of traders' eyes, a hidden sniper pulling the trigger to no effect, factories grinding to a halt, pumps ceasing to push wastewater through treatment facilities, and tourists at the Louvre being thrown into utter darkness. The world was a windup toy that had unexpectedly exhausted its clockwork motor.

The feed was gone.

Silence reigned.

"Ladies and gentlemen," said Diana. "Please follow me."

CHAPTER 35

The sculpture garden was dim, the only illumination coming from sunlight filtering through exterior windows. Carrying the briefcase in one hand, Diana led the group through a dreamscape populated by monsters that darkness had enlivened. The rich shadows playing across the avant-garde pieces made solid marble appear to shift and react as they passed, incarnate imagination trying to throw off its physical shackles as reality frayed around the edges.

Other Commonwealth employees stumbled out of offices and into the space, murmuring to each other in confusion as they tried to wrap their minds around the impossible absence of the feed. Diana navigated by the layouts she'd memorized in preparation for tapping the board meeting. The others followed her, overlarge egos deflated by shock and fear. For the moment at least, they were happy to follow someone who had a plan, any plan.

Instead of paralysis, crisis conjured practiced clarity within Diana. This was an op, and running an op required clear thinking, rationality untainted by the deadly panic to which civilians so often succumbed. Panic, uncertainty, confusion, these were Diana's allies, moats to hold back the opposition as she struggled to make it to higher ground. She had used spray paint and psychedelics to distract and confound the guards while spiriting Dag away from the abandoned Arctic oil platform. She needed to use this ruse to even greater effect.

Data wasn't insight. Helen and her confederates would be trying to figure out what was going on. Given the sensitivity of the raid, Helen would have shared the strategy behind it on a need-to-know basis. Now her sound infosec would work against her as ignorant field commanders improvised with incomplete information, unable to solicit mission-critical updates and new orders.

Helen herself could only speculate. Even though she had initiated the raid after noticing Dag's escape and deducing Diana's defection, she didn't know what they'd done after escaping the Arctic. She'd have to assume that Diana had been able to pass along some kind of warning to Rachel, but her plan to sack the quarterback required that the quarterback actually be there. Diana almost pitied whatever adjacent officers were suffering her wrath at this precise moment, made guilty by their presence at the undoing of her long-laid plan.

The steel door was right where it was supposed to be. She shouldered it open.

"Single file," she called back. "Hold hands."

Diana reached back to take Rachel's hand.

The emergency stairwell was pitch black. Diana ran the briefcase along the wall until it hit a railing. Feeling ahead with her foot, she found the edge of the first step and began to descend, instructing the group as she went. They followed, obedient, robbed of their vision, their neighbors' sweaty palms and Diana's curt orders their only companions as they forged ahead into darkness.

Stairs became landings became stairs became landings until flight after flight merged into a single extended journey through a special level of hell characterized by burning thighs, blindness, crippling doubt, and heavy breathing. Diana watched her thoughts coalesce and dissipate like sediment-laden eddies in a mountain stream. Mental acuity was most valuable when it was least accessible, and the best way to retain it was to treat every movement, every breath, every heartbeat, as a meditation. Either your monkey mind controlled you, or you controlled your monkey mind. Perceiving the formation of her own emotions, reactions, and lines of thinking freed her from their constraints, allowing her to see the world simply as it was instead of the convenient illusion her brain constructed from it.

Feeling Rachel beginning to lag, Diana slowed the pace. This long descent would be a physical challenge for anyone. It was a lucky break that Hsu climbed mountains as often as Rachel swam laps—otherwise they would have been trapped in the skies above San Francisco by elevators that no longer worked. At least the supporting hands would help steady them.

Hsu had survived enough geopolitical firestorms to weather this one. He had initiated some of his own as he navigated Taiwan's rise through the world order and bulwarked the institutional power of the UN. He was a man who saw opportunity in chaos and was pragmatic to a fault in shepherding his little nation. That's what had driven him to side with Lowell three years ago and then divest as soon as the tide turned against the oil magnate. He would pursue whatever path offered the most advantages for Taiwan.

Javier was a different story. He was an idealist, and idealists were difficult to work with. You couldn't buy them or even threaten them. Because they focused on abstract goals above all else, you had to actually win them over if you wanted them to change course. The direction Javier took out of this crisis would need to align with the better future he obsessively pursued.

And then there was the issue of Emily, Javier's partner and the group's original ringleader who seemed to have vanished off the face of the earth. Was Javier still in contact with her? Was she yet another principal directing events from behind the scenes, a bitter dropout licking her wounds in a Kathmandu tenement, or something else entirely?

Diana's stomach tightened at the thought, remembering Dag's utter, custom-built fascination with her.

But Rachel would be the hardest nut to crack. Even now Diana could feel the echo of the woman's gaze as surely as the knobby knuckles clasped in her sweaty grip. Those hands had built the feed. It was her empire, her baby, that was under threat. Rachel's path out of this labyrinth would depend entirely on *why* she had dedicated her life to constructing the digital fascia that stitched the world together. Was it wealth? Fame? Pride? Power? The simple joy of solving a riddle? The satisfaction of touching billions of lives? Whatever it was that had driven her so hard for so long, it would find its ultimate expression in her response to Helen's attack. Liane and the CFO were just along for the ride.

Time acquired a warped quality in the endless darkness of the emergency stairwell. It stretched out, languid and thick, and then snapped back as Diana's silent floor count finally reached its end and she pushed open the door to the atrium.

With only ambient natural light, the redwood grove might appear to be a haunted forest shrouded in mist, but for the pilgrims stumbling out from the black abyss of the stairwell, it was like reaching the promised land. Diana was Orpheus, leading them out of the underworld. Confident that there was no Eurydice to banish with a glance, Diana looked back over her shoulder. Haruki had thrown an arm around Hsu and was helping him along. The CFO was wheezing, and his shirt was soaked with sweat. Rachel was pale and shaky but fierce. Dag was bringing up the rear, making sure they didn't lose anyone. He caught her eye and smiled, the first unguarded smile she'd seen from him in ages, and something unexpected and solid and warm welled up inside her, and she bit her lip and smiled back.

Then they were out on the street, blinking in the direct sunlight, looking around at the crowds of confused pedestrians, Commonwealth employees emerging from their office blocks, frustrated passengers disembarking from stopped cars, everyone as helpless as they were incredulous at the sudden disappearance of something as pervasive, vital, and taken for granted as the very air they breathed.

"Wait here."

After pressing the briefcase into Haruki's hands, Diana crossed the street and dashed up to the corner, leaving the rest of the group to catch their breath and dodging around groups of people asking each other the same questions over and over again.

There. Nine or ten blocks up the street, helicopter blades drooped above the intervening cars. That's where the convoy had been stopped in its tracks. But it wouldn't take them too long—

Shit.

FBI agents were jogging between the cars in formation, announcing their presence to the scared civilians who scattered out of their way. The strike team was advancing on foot, and Helen wouldn't be far behind. Diana spun and ran back toward the group.

If they were caught right here and now, it would be even worse than before. The feed blackout would give Helen all the justification she needed to take emergency action to subdue Commonwealth, and she could simply leave the feed off in every country that didn't immediately surrender on her terms. Diana needed to get her people clear of the raid, but the FBI agents were only a block away and closing fast. Hsu and Rachel might be in good shape for octogenarians, but they would never be able to outrun trained combat operatives. They would somehow need to blend into the crowd of civilians, keep their faces hidden, work their way slowly around the adjacent buildings until they were free of the search perimeter.

"Stop! FBI! You're under arrest."

Fuck. The vanguard had turned the corner and spotted her sprinting down the sidewalk. No better way to draw attention. Her old teachers at the Farm would have been horrified at her clumsy tradecraft.

"Freeze or I'll blow your fucking head off!"

There was nothing for it. She accelerated, legs pumping, lungs burning. At least she knew they were bluffing. Even if they were willing to fire in the middle of a crowded street, their guns were as useless as any other feed-connected device. The high-powered targeting software that made their weapons so deadly now rendered them useless. She wanted to shout back, *Go ahead and pull the trigger, assholes,* but couldn't spare the breath. Her defiance would be short-lived anyway. Fists would do where guns wouldn't.

"Come on." Dag was waving to her.

There was one final car between her and the group. Over the roof she could see they were all standing . . . strangely. Torsos bent slightly forward. Not running and scattering into the crowd as they should be, dispersing into whatever open doors they could find. Again she wanted to yell, to tell them to get out however they could, to figure things out on their own, that she would cause a scene, distract the invaders while they made their escape. But she was gasping as she sprinted the last few steps, unable to force out the words.

"All of you, on the ground," someone screamed from behind, voice hoarse with rage.

"Come *on*," Dag repeated.

Almost there. She leapt, sliding across the hood of the car instead of detouring around it. And then she understood. They were all mounted on bicycles. Dag shoved one at her.

"No feed, no locks," he said, shrugging. "And Hsu's a sneaky one. He slashed the tires on the rest."

Diana could see the adolescent boy shining through the old man's grin.

"Let's go," said Dag.

Diana didn't need to be told twice. She hopped on the proffered bike and pedaled with all her might, leading the little gang down the street, through the cars, and away from the frustrated pursuers. She cut around the first corner, and then another, and the shouted threats began to fade. A few more turns and they were free, flying along the streets of San Francisco, weaving through frozen cars, adrenaline surging, sunlight pouring down on them like honey, feedless and present as never before, and then Diana realized she was laughing, that they were all laughing and whooping like a bunch of maniacs, these people who hardly knew each other and yet were bound by the deepest secret that had ever graced her collection.

As their energy bubbled down to a simmer, Diana noted the next intersection and placed them in her mental map of the city. She led them down block after block, under freeway overpasses, through public parks, and past condos and warehouses and hole-in-the-wall food joints until they finally reached the right street in the right postindustrial neighborhood.

"Yo, D!"

Diana met Gerald's fist bump as she dismounted.

"I know you like to be fashionably late," the enormous bouncer continued gruffly, "but Sam here was starting to get real worried. For the sake of his cuticles, you should really make more of an effort to be timely."

"I don't bite my nails," said Sam indignantly.

"Of course you don't." Gerald rolled his eyes at Diana. "Seriously, though, even Nell was starting to lose her cool a little bit after you had that Haruki kid arrange everything and then didn't show up, and then the feed just went poof and—"

Diana raised her palms. "Better late than never, right?"

Gerald jerked his head toward the imposing oak doors.

"Go on, then," he said, and Diana felt the latent strain, the forced professionalism, the fear lathered in playful banter.

Sam opened the doors for them, and Diana led the group into the anteroom where Nell waited, radiant as ever behind her polished podium.

"Welcome to Analog," she said with a lustrous smile.

"Of course this is your safe house." These were the first words Rachel had spoken in Diana's presence. "Every disaster seems to lead me back to this place."

"Well, I hope our hospitality makes up for it," said Nell, unasked questions circling like hammerheads behind her pale-gray eyes. "Normally I'd warn you that the . . . *transition* . . . can be disorienting. But we seem to be ahead of the game in that regard. If you'd just follow me."

The fire roared in the enormous hearth, bottles glittered on the wall above the bar, and oil lamps guttered overhead. Virginia was polishing glasses, holding them up to check for imperfections. Everything was entirely normal inside Analog, except that there were no other patrons and a large circular table had been set in front of the fire. As the red satin curtains fell closed behind them, the feedless world beyond seemed less a victim of their desperate escape attempt than the result of a simple expansion of Analog's borders to include the entire planet in its anachronistic embrace.

CHAPTER 36

"First step is to find out what they're actually charging us with and tear it apart." Liane gained steam as she leaned into her argument. "We'll bury the Justice Department in suits, appeal all the way to the Supreme Court if we have to. We can have a technical team analyze every molecule of the material in that briefcase. If we get a single skin cell with DNA matching one of Helen's team, it'll corroborate Diana's version of events. At the same time, we'll vet every claim made in the documentation and refute it with time-stamped data. Meanwhile we'll have PR launch a counteroffensive, the most important campaign they've ever touched. We need to control the narrative here, in the courtroom *and* in the press. That'll be particularly important for the appellate courts. We can frame the current shutdown as an emergency measure against criminal USG overreach. We'll have every headline. It's going to dominate the news cycle for months anyway, so we can get ahead of the game and stack the deck before a judge even sees a brief. Might be best to start with international press. They'll be primed to spin things as a nationalist coup. Our government-relations people will storm every office in Washington, and we can rest assured that every vendor on the feed is going to demand answers too. That's just the start. We can use the momentum from the overall effort to push forward our current policy priorities and end up stronger than we started."

The shared moment of hysterical celebration of their temporary escape faded as quickly as vapor boiling off hot blood spilled on an Arctic helipad. Diana's gaze wandered up above the heads of the others to take in the tapestries hung on Analog's walls. Medieval armies rode into battle, pennants flying, horses rearing, the sky dark with arrows. Some artist had invoked this violent vision, painstakingly selected a palette and materials, translated it into thousands upon thousands of stitches. Time emasculated the raw brutality of the scene, the modern eye so absorbed in the hubris of the present that chain mail and lances appeared almost romantic, evoking the nostalgia of half-forgotten children's stories instead of bloodshed's horror.

"Helen's not stupid," said Dag. "Do you really think she'll let this go to the courts?"

"*We'll* take it to the courts."

Diana's fingertips began to itch. Sofia would know. Sofia would understand. But Sofia wasn't here. War. No one else at this table had experienced it. To them, war was statistics, Pulitzer award–winning photos that made destruction glamorously tragic, political debates over the defense budget, a crazy vet uncle, occasional donations to charity, and watching a feed documentary that made the skin crawl even as it filled that strange need to play voyeur to the suffering of others. Helen hadn't even experienced it, not really. She'd directed a long list of black ops, but always from afar, always from the safety of her DC office. Like an eager archaeological intern stumbling upon a tome of necromancy in a pharaoh's dusty tomb, Helen was invoking a demon with which she was utterly unfamiliar, as damnably innocent as the artist who had dreamed up that tapestry.

"When I was working deep cover in Amsterdam," said Diana, "I discovered an assassination plot targeting a member of parliament. Helen decided we should let it happen because the minister was opposing a new bilateral trade deal we wanted passed. After he was killed and the deal was signed, we assisted Dutch intelligence in the 'search' for the assassin, whose identity we already knew. When we brought them in, the US was hailed as a stalwart ally in the press, and the Pentagon was able to deepen our ties to their security agencies." Diana paused, making eye contact with every person seated around the table. "If Helen's sending in the FBI, she's willing to risk everything. The Pentagon will already be scrambling troops to support her feed sanctions and takeover bid. She's not going to let due process get in the way of winning. They'll wait for us to surface, take control of the feed, and then questions like jurisdiction and rights won't matter anymore. I forced Helen's hand by coming to you. Our escape forces her hand even more. She can't afford to be subtle, so she'll go for shock and awe instead. Liane's points prove it. Given time, the fact that you're being framed will come out. So Helen won't give it any time at all."

The fire hissed and popped in the hearth, fracturing the silence that followed Diana's words. She could feel the specter of war gathering in the world beyond, sliding soft tendrils into hidden corners like fog fingering through San Francisco's hills. Déjà vu transported Diana to a time long past and a place that no longer existed. Adults whispered while she lay awake, eyes closed. Other children intensified their bullying, displacing aggression and anxiety they felt but couldn't understand. Grocers ran out of canned food. Even the street dogs had a harried, nervous look about them. Years later, in combat training on the Farm, Diana's instructor had choked her out on the mat. Black spots that she couldn't blink away danced at the corners of her vision until the world receded into a pinprick that winked out of its own accord. That was how the engine of war advanced, quietly, relentlessly, throwing shadows in the forms of premonitions you couldn't quite dispel.

"You *really* think she's prepared to bulldoze her way into a dictatorship?" asked Liane.

"Are you willing to bet that she isn't after what you've seen today?" asked Diana. The lengths to which people were willing to go to live in denial always amazed Diana. But she couldn't really blame Liane. When you grew up in a world where rules were respected, where institutions mattered, where justice might arrive late but always came, how could you internalize the reality of impending chaos? "Knowing Helen, she won't claim any titles for herself. She'll deliver the empire to Lopez. There's no need to upset American political structures when she's already subverted them."

"Lopez won't want this," Hsu said sharply.

"No," said Diana. "He won't." Lopez was a moderate progressive, and this would be the last thing he wanted. Helen had never much cared about the desires of her many pets. "But he won't have a choice. Lopez didn't want to approve this raid in the first place, but Helen fabricated evidence and then used people she holds sway over to twist his arm. She's run in the highest DC circles for longer than almost anyone. She'll make this happen and then hand Lopez an empire before he can even figure out what's going on. Once other countries surrender, Lopez won't be able to renege. Doing so would destabilize everything and risk the rest of the world launching a devastating counterattack."

Dag nodded. "Helen's thinking in historical terms. She's not limiting herself to the current sociopolitical system, and she knows that nobody else can catch up. They'll be constrained by the assumptions baked into the system because it's what they've always known. She's using the feed as a catalyst to set off a phase change in global politics and consolidate control. It's like Rome establishing their base around the Mediterranean or Qin Shi Huang uniting the Chinese states into an empire. Only this time it'll be much, much faster."

Hsu raised a hand. "Hold on," he said thoughtfully. "The solution here might be simpler than we think. What gives Helen the ability to take down Commonwealth all in one go?" He paused, then spun his index finger in a tight circle. "Because Commonwealth headquarters is here in California along with the majority of key personnel. 'Seizing the feed' really means kidnapping and coercing the people around this table to yield root access and operational control to Helen and her team. So . . . we relocate. I can arrange for us to move Commonwealth headquarters to Taipei. The government will extend every benefit they can: land, housing, freedom to operate, tax incentives, the works. Between Taiwan and its allies, there will be more than enough military resources to defend against any physical attacks from aggressors, even the United States. Given the feed's global presence, it would make sense for Commonwealth and United Nations headquarters to be colocated anyway. We can get ourselves onto a private plane, turn the feed back on, and be the first ones off the ground and out of US jurisdiction. Then we can evacuate the staff and fight Helen in court without ever letting anyone with command-level access touch US soil."

"Ahh," said Javier darkly. "Hoping to button up an empire for yourself? What you just described is basically the same except with you in control instead of Helen."

Hsu's eyes flashed. "That's not at all what I'm proposing. This is an offer of refuge in a time of crisis. And Taiwan has the resources to actually serve as a base for the feed, along with the political structure to legitimate it."

The arguments Diana and Dag had anticipated on their flight back from the Arctic were falling into place. Negotiations were a dance, and this one had to be exquisitely choreographed, stepping and twirling and gaining momentum before culminating in a resolution that was at once surprising and inevitable so that conflicting interests could be synthesized into a fresh system of incentives. But there was one enigma that still eluded Diana, one solo she'd have to improvise, one purple eye that never wavered.

"Sounds to me like this particular 'refuge' could evolve pretty quickly into a hostage situation," said Javier. "As soon as Commonwealth moves in, you can make its protection contingent on whatever you want. That's hardly fair for feed users. You're offering a plush cell, nothing more."

"How dare—"

"I'm not questioning your intentions," said Javier. "I'm just pointing out that the help you're offering won't solve the underlying problem."

"And what, pray tell, is the *underlying problem?*"

Javier shrugged. "The feed has transcended its role as a consumer product to become a global public good. The fact that we can do this"—he sliced a finger across his throat to indicate the shutdown—"proves it. Commonwealth has always operated at the mercy of the US government because it's headquartered in US jurisdiction. It makes no sense for Washington to hold so much sway over a piece of global infrastructure, and so far it's worked, largely because nobody had the guts to try what Helen's attempting to do. But that era is over. Even if she fails, the minute other governments discover what happened, they'll all dream of copycatting. Everyone will start building up backup infrastructure as a defense against another shutdown even as they try to figure out how to capture the feed, and the world, for themselves. Moving our headquarters to a new country just means putting ourselves at risk of their particular flavor of coup."

Something pressed down on Diana's thigh. One of the vizslas had stirred itself from napping by the fire and was standing under the table, resting its head on her leg, blinking its golden eyes up at her in a shameless appeal for attention. She scratched behind its ears and felt the vibrations of a below-audible growl of satisfaction. Even the sweetest pets had their secrets. Vizslas were hunting dogs, bred to kill and jealously guarded by the warlords and barons who had ruled Hungary for centuries. She imagined this trio loping through a shattered San Francisco, long-forgotten instincts kicking in, splintered shards of bombed-out towers rising above them, smoke thick on the wind, snarling over the glistening entrails of a rotting corpse.

"Enough." Rachel's voice cut off the debate like a guillotine. She leaned her head back and looked at the ceiling for a long moment. Then her gaze descended to move from person to person around the table. "Patients are dying in ICUs all over the world. Children are stranded.

Assault victims are trying to call the police but can't get through. Planes are making emergency landings. Markets are hemorrhaging capital. Generals are executing contingencies. Trust is evaporating. All of this, *all of this*, is happening just to buy us a little time. Every minute the feed is down condemns people to death and pushes civilization closer to the brink." The overt calm in her voice was brittle with tension. "There is no room for petty grievances, no room for ulterior motives, and no room for error. So the next time any of you thinks of saying anything, anything at all, I want you to first ask yourself, 'Are these words worth thousands of lives and trillions of dollars? Are these words worthy of being my last?'" Her eye finally landed on Diana. "I assume you didn't break faith with your masters and invite us here without something in mind. Why are you here, and what exactly do you propose we do?"

Diana nearly faltered under the scorching clarity of Rachel's full attention. Forcing herself to take a few breaths, Diana returned the stare as if it were a gateway through which she could slip inside the older woman's skin.

Rachel didn't care about wealth. She swam at a public pool and lived in a modest home. By her age, mortality must be a familiar companion, not a distant thought experiment. However many billions she collected, she couldn't ferry them beyond the pale. Fame wasn't what she was after either. She rarely made public appearances and eschewed the limelight the media was so eager to throw in her direction. She was powerful, but not particularly power hungry, at least in any traditional sense. Helen tried to gather all the strings in her fist, while Rachel seemed to halfway resent the responsibilities she was saddled with.

Diana remembered the sweat stinging her eyes as she'd installed greenhouse panels under the hot summer sun. She'd brought in contractors to help with a few things she couldn't manage on her own, but she'd built most of it with her own two hands. When she'd first walked through the cottage and stuck her head through the back door, extending the structure into a greenhouse had been obvious. Not an intricate architectural dream she'd spent months designing but an immediate, straightforward vision for what *should be there*. The rest had been nothing more than the application of effort, time, and money to make that vision a reality.

There was something about Rachel, her poise, her focus, her propensity for listening instead of jumping to conclusions, that reminded Diana of the mind-set she'd been in while building the greenhouse. Whether she was negotiating with the electrician or making decisions about soil chemistry, her absolute belief in the project, her confidence that the greenhouse would be built one way or the other, had been a supremely useful filter for decision-making.

The feed was Rachel's greenhouse. Connecting the world, weaving every human, satellite, database, widget, and transistor into a throbbing, cohesive whole. That was her refuge, her obsession. It wasn't the intricate result of marathon brainstorming sessions with legions of experts. It was Rachel's obvious thing that *should exist*. She was just assembling the pieces until reality reflected her imagination. She was a mogul, a power broker, a force of nature. But more than any of those, she was a builder.

Espionage had instilled in Diana an instinct for collecting as many cards as possible, holding them close to her chest, and letting other players run the table while she observed from the sidelines, seeking the thrill of omniscience over victory. It was that instinct she now repressed. She couldn't let the world slip into madness without doing everything she could to avert it.

"I was born in Bulgaria," said Diana. "Right before the occupation. My grandmother used to tell me this story all the time. I think most grandparents there did. She told me how when NASA launched the *Voyager* in 1977, they included a Golden Record, a gold-plated copper disc loaded with the most glorious things humanity and Earth had to offer the universe, a precious snapshot of civilization. There were images of tropical islands, Olympic sprinters, and breastfeeding babies. There were recordings of thunder, hyenas, and blacksmithing. There were greetings in fifty-five languages. There was music by Bach, Beethoven, and Louis Armstrong. And there was *Izlel je Delyo Hagdutin*, a Bulgarian folk song about suffering and hope in the face of oppression. This humble ballad that peasants sang for centuries as they labored under the yoke of the Ottoman Empire was now arcing toward the stars."

A lump rose in Diana's throat. "My family was lucky enough to escape the occupation. But I was six, and I threw a tantrum on one of the many smugglers' boats that carried us away. I can't remember what it was about. I was probably hungry, or tired, or missed my friends. Anyway, my grandmother dragged me up to the deck, and we looked up at the night sky glittering overhead. She told me the story for the thousandth time. Then she knelt down and poked me hard on the chest. 'You,' she said. 'You are the Golden Record now.'"

Diana stifled a sob, shocked at her sudden failure of self-control. "I've come back to that night again and again over the years. What did she mean? Was the Bulgarian diaspora meant to carry forth some essential ingredient of our national spirit? Was I supposed to live out that folk song? Was this inheritance a gift or a burden?" Diana looked at her lap, the dog's head still resting there contentedly. Rachel didn't want to be some dictator's pet. She wanted her creation to enjoy an autonomy no protector would allow. Diana raised her eyes to meet the chairwoman's.

"The feed is a Golden Record," said Diana. "It's a reflection, an embodiment of civilization. It must go on. Letting someone like Helen weaponize it doesn't just transform it into a tool of oppression, it shatters the promise it was built on." She looked around the table. "Javier, Hsu, Liane, everyone here is right. We can't let Helen take control. We can't let any other country take control. And we can't do nothing, however much we'd like to turn back the clock. So far you've kept the feed nominally independent of overt political control by pretending to be neutral as often as you can. Implementing the carbon tax changed that and woke up people like Lowell and Helen to the feed's potential as a superweapon. With neutrality off the table, the only way to maintain independence is to establish it on your own terms. It's too late to play by anyone else's rules."

Diana let her eyes settle on Rachel's once again. "Buy back all of Commonwealth's shares. Take it off the public stock market. Establish coequal offices on every continent. Declare sovereignty." Without breaking eye contact with Rachel, Diana nodded toward Hsu. "Send ambassadors to every capital and the UN to negotiate treaties with special dispensations for early signatories." She nodded toward Javier. "Offer algorithmic, individualized benefits that turn users into constituents: social support programs, educational opportunities, health care, welfare, legal protection, the works. Do all that, and a thousand more things I'm missing, and you'll transform Commonwealth into a political institution that can wrestle with national governments on equal footing, except you're bound by users, not geography. It's the only way to give the feed the autonomy it deserves as a piece of global infrastructure."

"Almost like the Vatican in medieval Europe," Dag cut in. "Commonwealth will be a horizontal and distributed geopolitical player instead of a nation state."

"Fuckin' A," murmured Javier.

"But this is all *impossible*," spluttered the CFO.

"It's not impossible, it's unprecedented," said Diana. "Those are two very different things." She returned her focus to Rachel. "Between you, Hsu, and Javier, you have the votes and the capital to do it. By taking all shares off the market and declaring Commonwealth sovereign, your money will be locked up permanently, so pretty much worthless. But you get true autonomy, Javier gets the transparency he's been lobbying so hard for, and Hsu gets major concessions for Taiwan, the UN, and any other governments he can rope in to make the first deals. Lay what groundwork you can tonight. Tomorrow morning, turn the feed back on and make the announcement. Launch a major public relations campaign explaining why the feed went down, what's changing, and framing the narrative so that Helen can't. It wouldn't hurt to take Hsu's offer of temporary asylum as you ramp up. It'll make it that much harder for Helen to arrange a convenient accident. Speaking of, you need to spin up a real security service. Add all this up, throw in enough luck to bankrupt a casino, and we might just have a chance."

Silence coiled around them. The world might hang in the balance, but Diana was spent. Fate, that deadliest of snakes, would do what it liked with her.

"Does anyone else have a better idea?" asked Rachel.

Crickets.

"Do it," she said. "Let's keep this Golden Record spinning."

CHAPTER 37

Do it.

Those two simple words were the infinitesimal low-pressure pocket thrown off the trailing edge of a single flap of a butterfly's wing, the perturbation growing and picking up momentum as it zigzagged through weather systems, urged on by the secret prayers of chaos theorists, until the resulting tornado spun open the door to Oz.

The discussion turned tactical. What fiduciary hurdles would they need to clear to execute the buyback? What legal loopholes could they take advantage of to legitimate the process? Whom did they need to bring in, and when would they be able to reach them? What talking points did they need to prepare for the inevitable press briefing? How could the feed's back-end architecture be adjusted to adapt to the new governance framework? What new data pools would they need to collect, and what new algorithms would they need to design in order to automatically evaluate, balance, and deploy individual direct benefits across the global feed? What promises could they make to users, and in what order? What was the best way to evacuate Commonwealth staff or otherwise guarantee their safety? How would other governments react to the news, and how would Helen spin a response? How could they continue to stay a step ahead once the feed was back on?

The list of problems was endless, each proposed answer generating a dozen more questions. But even as arguments ebbed and flowed, coalescing into decisions before dispersing again into fraught deliberation, Diana couldn't fully engage. Like a child released unsupervised into a zoo, her attention wandered.

The flames in the hearth took on mesmerizing, phantasmagoric shapes that flickered in and out of being faster than Diana could register them. The peppery smell of the oil lamps made Analog feel warmer and more intimate than it otherwise might have. A sickle of hair fell across Nell's eye as she leaned in to pour another round of steaming coffee. Nell had been a lifesaver. If she hadn't had Nell and Analog to rely on, Diana didn't know what she would have done. This was precisely the safe house they needed, real security, professional staff, and probably the only building still functional with the feed down.

Something tickled the back of Diana's mind. She wasn't failing to participate in the planning process because she was exhausted or overwhelmed. She was both of those things and more, of course, but that wasn't why she couldn't focus. Instead it was that she didn't have anything to add. No, that wasn't right either. She had thought more deeply about this situation, and had had more time to prepare, than anyone else around this table. Rather Diana felt that this conversation was itself a distraction. That, having initiated it, she could be more useful elsewhere.

But if not here, where? The people around this table were making scores of decisions, and surely scores of mistakes, that would ripple out into the world, generating cascades of side effects that might persist for decades to come. Outside Analog, people were flailing. When you were always connected, disconnection was the ultimate disorientation. At least with any other crisis, no matter how major, you could tap the feed for context, updates, and guidance. But without the feed, how could you find out why the power was out, the water wasn't running, the cars didn't work, and the world had gone quiet? Helen would know the score of course. Her team would have scoured Commonwealth headquarters by now, and having failed to capture the principals, she'd be scheming with her key lieutenants, identifying new search parameters, and planning for the moment when the feed finally came back on.

Back in Washington, President Lopez would be panicking. He had just approved a raid on Commonwealth and was probably watching a live stream from the strike team when the feed went out with the FBI still a few blocks from the target. No communications. No intel. No idea what the hell was going on in the middle of an operation that would define his presidency, an operation guaranteed to upset the world economy, an operation he never wanted to approve in the first place.

"Diana, what do you think?" Diana snapped back as Dag's voice cut through her reverie. She ran back her short-term memory, trying to catch up to Dag's question. They were talking about what each of their immediate priorities should be as soon as the feed came back on, working backward from shared goals to individual tasks.

"We need to assure the world that turning off the feed was self-defense, not an act of war," said Hsu. "Given how integral it is to every country's national security infrastructure, that'll be the worst-case scenario everyone will be paranoid about and preparing for. I'll reach out through my people at the UN and cycle through as many heads of state as I can to give them personal briefings. Hopefully that'll be enough to hold them back from calling in the cavalry immediately."

Diana knew better than anyone how quickly national intelligence services would reach the same conclusion. With everyone scrambling to get ready for what might be an imminent invasion, a single mistake could spark a world war. Rebooting the feed would be the starting pistol in an Olympic sprint of game theory, intel-starved analysts, repressed generals, and Machiavellian strategists trying to outdo each other in a desperate and convoluted bid to cross the finish line. It was a race she had no choice but to win. Something stirred inside Diana, dark omens whispering violence and an inkling of the kind of gambit required to avert it.

"Washington is going to be the biggest problem," said Diana. "Other leaders had no warning and still have no context for what's happening. Their ignorance is dangerous, but at least they'll try to assess the situation before making a big move. But Lopéz is operating under the assumption that Helen's intel was genuine. If he believes that Commonwealth's leadership has already committed treason, then he'll have to assume that we somehow figured out the raid was coming and initiated the shutdown. In his eyes, that confirms our guilt. And if we're guilty, then he'll have no option but to order a preemptive strike. In fact, he'll see it as reactive, not preemptive. It won't be the FBI this time, it'll be the Pentagon. That means mobilizing SEALs, Rangers, and a few other specops units."

Fear curdled in her gut as Diana realized the truth in her own words. "They'll send drones to intercept us if they figure out what plane we've taken, use all their feed surveillance privileges to find us if we hide, and have everyone from local cops to the CIA trying to pin us down."

"We should be able to revoke those privileges, right?" asked Dag. "Can't we turn the feed back on and then carve out whatever capacities they're using to track us? Their drones don't work, their spy satellites don't work, their weapons don't work, but everything else goes back to normal?"

Javier was shaking his head. "That's theoretically possible, but we'll never be able to pull it off. The problem is time. If we had a week or so, we could have an engineering team figure out exactly how to specify and revoke those individual access privileges without screwing up a host of connected systems. It would be breaking a thousand laws and contracts, but it could work. But if they're going to swarm us the minute we flip the switch, they'll catch us before we can figure out how to turn off *only* their gear. We'd have to turn the whole feed off again."

"No." Rachel's statement was solid granite.

Javier grimaced. "Right, so . . ."

"Whatever we try to tell the world, Helen will undercut it with spin," said Diana, her underarms suddenly damp. Facts might be facts, but truth was relative. "If the feed is all or nothing, then we have to fight her on an even playing field. She isn't omnipotent, but she has people in most major institutions. That includes Commonwealth. She had me cultivating inside sources, and she must have some of her own that she's grooming to take over after you take the fall. That's enough of a coalition to obscure our message while she solidifies her position. It'll be a hot mess, and the confusion benefits her, not us." The fire popped and she flinched. "With allegations this severe, she'll find a way to step in until they're cleared, and once she does, it's over. She'll lose the element of surprise once we tell the world what's going on, but if I know one thing about Helen, she's in it for the long game."

The CFO ran his hands through his thinning hair. "So first you tell us we have to pull this crazy maneuver. And *now* you're telling us we're fucked either way."

He was right. They were fucked either way. She should have seen this coming from the beginning, but some part of her must have never quite believed they would get this far to begin with. Bile rose in her throat.

Hsu frowned. "I can back-channel Helen's ulterior motives so that other governments will be prepared, whatever the news reports say."

"How long will those channels survive a smear campaign?" asked Dag. "And even if they do, how many governments will invest the billions necessary in developing parallel infrastructure to reduce their feed dependency?"

None of them. They'd all politely thank Hsu for his warning and proceed to ignore it. And with all of them painted as traitors, claiming they were being framed would come across as blatantly self-serving. Diana could already see the sneer hidden within Helen's too-sweet smile, could already hear the whiplash of passive aggression in the heart-felt apology she would doubtless offer after the tribunal condemned Diana. At least that was if she didn't play things simple and just make sure Diana disappeared.

"This is politics." Hsu shrugged. "There are never any clear-cut answers. No matter what we come up with around this table, Helen is still going to do everything she can to get her way. We just have to be smarter and work harder."

Diana remembered long nights spent poring over plans in Helen's office, the scent of her perfume and stale coffee mixing into a strange olfactory cocktail that Diana would forever associate with preoperation anxiety. That anxiety always seemed to evaporate once Diana's boots hit the ground, but it could appear out of nowhere to ambush her at the most inopportune times. The instant panic professionals had to antici-pate and mitigate if they were going to survive to work another job.

Now that the physical exertion was over, Hsu looked relaxed, almost as if he were enjoying himself. This was his milieu after all, the court intrigue that coalesced around power's choke points. Diana took a deep breath, trying to channel his composure. Right now, after the adrenaline of the chase had ebbed, was the time when panic was most insidious. It leaked into your head as the clarity of action faded, poisoned your thoughts, and sapped your strength. She needed to calm down. Nobody ever held all the cards.

Not even Helen.

Even if she were to establish an empire, it would be far from perfect. Ironically, poorer nations were less at risk than richer ones. Those with the least advanced tech were least dependent on the feed. Their lack of modern infrastructure was a strength if modern infrastructure could be remotely hijacked. And rich countries might be hit the hardest, but they also had the resources and expertise to mount an opposition, whether that meant building independent infrastructure to compete with the feed or ousting Helen. She might conquer the world, but could she keep it? The harder she pressed for concessions or tribute, the hotter the flame of rebellion would burn.

Every tyrant and every revolutionary dreamed of an end to history, a defining triumph that would forever fix a broken world. But reality was far messier than any manifesto could capture. History didn't end. It swung on its axis and came back to bite you in the ass.

That said, even an incomplete or passing victory was a death sentence for those in this room and would send ripples of suffering far beyond it. In the very big picture, it might not matter. But in the very big picture, a city reduced to rubble, a nation torn apart, a family broken, a life snuffed out, none of those things mattered. Which was why Diana didn't hold much stock in such bullshit generalities. Life mattered because *life* mattered. If she wasn't helping to stop the kinds of things she'd had to suffer, then she was the failure she feared herself to be.

She raised her eyes.

"I need to get to DC," she said. "I need to talk to the president before Helen can."

"What?" The palpable concern in Dag's voice was almost more than she could take. "Why?"

"If I can convince Lopez that Helen is playing him, it'll wreak havoc on her ability to get anything done," she said. "Even if I can just plant a seed of doubt, she'll be thrown way off her game. It'll give all of us the advantage we need to actually execute this plan."

Hsu nodded slowly.

"What are you going to do?" asked Liane. "Just walk up to the White House?"

"I'll figure something out," said Diana. "It's hard to keep me from getting where I want to go."

"You could cycle down to SFO," said Javier. "We can get you on a private jet, turn the feed on, and have you in the air and over to Washington before anyone else can make the trip."

Diana grimaced. "That means Helen will have hours to conference with him over feed and kick off whatever she's planning before I arrive."

Rachel narrowed her eye. "Once we turn the feed back on, I can open a direct line to the president. You can talk to him over feed, do whatever convincing you need to do right away."

"Helen will call him the minute the feed comes back on," said Diana. Every turn led to a dead end. "There's no way we'll get him to pay attention to me, especially when he finds out I'm helping presumed traitors. Helen will burn my credibility in a heartbeat, and we'll be back to square one."

Javier held up his hands. "Which poison do you prefer? You can't sprint from here to Washington."

Diana restrained the urge to punch him in the face. If she physically flew there, she'd arrive late but might have a better chance of getting heard. If she called in via feed, there wouldn't be a delay, but it would be easy to shut her up. Both were bad options. But she'd have to choose one and start prepping her pitch. At least it might give Lopez pause and buy them some time.

Nell leaned in to fill Diana's coffee. "Did you say you need to get to DC before the feed comes back on?"

"That's right."

Nell placed the jug of coffee on the table, produced a pen from a hidden pocket, and began scribbling on Diana's napkin, mumbling under her breath. As she flipped the napkin over to use the reverse side, Diana saw complex calculations scrawled across the flimsy paper.

Nell chewed on the end of the pen, unfolded the napkin so she could see both sides, and waggled her head back and forth. Then she looked up, and Diana couldn't tell if the fire dancing in her eyes was a reflection of the hearth or blazed forth from some internal source.

"Did whatever training they gave you for your, ahh, *professional development* involve aviation?" she asked, arching an impossibly elegant eyebrow.

"Oh, I'm aces in a cockpit," said Diana, wondering how much Nell knew about her background. "Top gun. Flygirl. The whole nine yards."

"I can get you there," said Nell matter-of-factly.

CHAPTER 38

It was Diana's second bicycle ride of the day. She pedaled along behind Nell, weaving through the dead cars that filled the streets of San Francisco, making the city look like a giant diorama. Scared faces stared down from dark windows, but many residents had taken to the streets, trading rumors with neighbors they'd rarely had cause to interact with before. In front of a squat apartment building, someone had set up a charcoal barbecue, and the mouthwatering smell of grilled meat was attracting people like moths to a lamp. A street performer played violin on a corner, earning what must have been the largest crowd of her career. It took Diana a moment to register what was odd about the crowds, but finally it clicked. They were weirdly heterogeneous. Bankers, kindergarteners, lawyers, house husbands, artists, teachers, courtesans, engineers, therapists, county clerks, doctors, and baristas united in common confusion at the miraculous and frightening lack of feed.

The thick scent of brine enveloped them as they reached the bay. A small private harbor was tucked between two of the piers, pleasure yachts and speedboats rocking gently in their berths. More boats. Diana was sick and tired of boats. If only there was solid ground to stand on anymore.

Nell pulled up and tried the gate.

"Damn," she said. "Looks like this one defaulted to stay locked without the feed. Give me a hand?"

Diana dismounted and boosted Nell up and over the fence. Diana collected the briefcase from the basket, passed it over to Nell, and then followed her over the fence, chain links cold against her fingers. Seals barked up at them as they walked out along the dock, the animals' slick hides and blubbery bulk reminding Diana of some of the old sketches Dag had shown her, split panels featuring spectacularly diverse marine life under the waves while the land above was a ravaged waste.

She had always found the fantasy a little odd. If anything, ocean biodiversity had plummeted faster than its terrestrial equivalent with acidification and dead reefs pushing ecosystems over the edge. Apex predators like sharks were all but extinct. Seals were doing okay, especially the ones near urban centers that supplemented fish with human scraps. Maybe he had been depicting one of the marine protected areas where sea life was reestablishing itself faster than anyone had expected. More likely she was taking the whole thing far too literally, and the juxtaposition said more about the subsurface motivations that drove people to destructive acts than about actual fish.

How strange a person Dag was. Brokering secret deals, undergoing commando training in Namibia, and now finding his sensibility as an artist, weaving together disparate ideas, conflicting themes, and a wide palette of styles into a counterintuitively cohesive whole that created more of an emotional impact than an intellectual one. He was so damn weird and marvelous all at once. That look he'd given her when they made it out of the emergency stairwell. The concern in his voice when she'd stated her intention to go straight into the belly of the beast and seek out Lopez. In their hours of planning on the flight down from the Arctic, everything had been coldly professional, two fugitives orchestrating a last-ditch maneuver where teamwork was a matter of survival. She'd assumed that he hated her, that any relationship they once shared would end with their gambit. But if they somehow made it out of this mess, might something more be possible?

"This is she," said Nell, kneeling to untie the lines of a thirty-foot sailboat. They hopped on board, and Nell adjusted various knots, checked the rigging, and raised the sails. "We're lucky, it usually calms down at this point in the day, but we've still got a good west wind blowing."

With Nell at the helm, the little boat zigzagged out of the docks and into the open bay, tilting at an angle as it picked up speed. Afternoon sunlight turned the water to liquid amber, the dark hulks of frozen container ships throwing shadows across the waves lapping at their gargantuan hulls.

"They're almost like islands, aren't they?" asked Nell. "Going from state of the art to derelict in the blink of an eye. There's a certain beauty there. Like those colored sand mandalas Buddhist monks create and wipe away. A reminder of impermanence."

Diana looked back at Nell. Wind whipped at her hair, white water of the cresting waves matched her light-gray eyes, and the sun made her umber skin appear to glow from within. She was comfortable here on this boat, self-possessed, unconcerned, or at least not terrified by the crisis that had short-circuited the entire planet.

"How did you know I could fly?" asked Diana.

Those beautiful gray eyes settled on her.

"Duck," said Nell.

"What?"

"Duck, we're jibing."

Diana ducked just in time for the boom to swing across above her head. The boat settled into its new line.

"It took me more than fifteen years to earn my place as Analog's receptionist," said Nell. "I knew I wanted it from the beginning. There were others that did too, but they dropped off along the way, got distracted, moved on to other adventures. Receptionist. One who receives.

Not usually a particularly sought-after position, right? Not a career most people dream of? That's why Analog's current owner always serves as its receptionist, passing the role along to whoever takes over when they retire. You can tell a lot about a person by how they treat the receptionist, how they act when they don't think they're performing. Duck."

Diana was quicker this time.

"We're a club, not a bar," said Nell. "Everything depends on our community of members. That means we need to keep that community strong and healthy and vibrant and diverse and a little off kilter. Otherwise things go sideways. The rolls are deeper than you might have heard. Over the years we've had members who were heads of state, subversive poets, public intellectuals, Olympic athletes, leading technologists, business moguls, graffiti artists, and Nobel Prize winners. We've hosted everyone from Mara Winkel to Huian Li. There are a lot of . . . personalities. You learn to read people pretty quickly. Duck."

Across came the boom.

"So one day you wander in, so unassuming you made it a kind of art form. The thing that initially piqued my interest was just how *little* I could actually remember about you. It was hard to remember what you looked like, how you spoke, or why you were there. So I started paying more attention. You met with all different sorts of people. Hackers, lawyers, government officials, pianists, a much broader social array than most folks, except maybe journalists. But you weren't a journalist. And you weren't anything else either. And in all the little conversations we've shared, it's incredible how few personal details you've let slip. Never in an awkward way, everything just seemed to move around you like you were the center of gravity in a dance that you were observing but not participating in. I talked to the retired owner about it, but I already knew. We've had spies as members before. Duck."

Another jibe.

"I saw how good you were," said Nell. "That's why I guessed you might have trained as a pilot. But that's the wrong question."

Diana let out a long breath she didn't realize she'd been holding. It was as if Nell were undressing her, clothing peeled away with tender care and then tossed crumpled on the floor.

"Why are you helping me?"

Nell released the helm and clapped her hands.

"Much better!" She reached over and squeezed Diana's thigh. "I'm helping you because you're a good person, Diana. People in your position"—she shook her head sadly—"you put yourselves through a lot, put others through a lot. When you transform yourself into so many people for so many people, it must be easy to lose yourself, to forget what it means to just be you, to believe that you have anything real left inside."

"It's because of the *Akira* reprints, isn't it?" Diana twisted her mouth into a smile to cover her inner turmoil.

Nell laughed. "Jorani is so *obsessed* with those comic books. I don't think we're ever going to be able to rescue her from them."

"I'm telling you," said Diana. "You should give them a try yourself. They're really good."

"I'm worried I'd like them too much," said Nell. "That's what keeps me away."

She gave Diana's thigh one more squeeze. The pressure transmitted a frisson of empathy that Diana was at once terrified and fascinated by, a hint of kinship that bled all the way through the growing network of cracks in her layers of burnished armor.

Then Nell's eyes flicked up with a soft "Oh."

A peregrine falcon rocketed down slantwise through the golden air, descending in a murderous dive toward a pigeon that was attempting to flee across the open water. The falcon went in for the kill. Missed. Raised its wings in powerful flaps to regain altitude. Dove again. Missed again. Ascended again and finally struck true, then soared off to devour the prize held fast in its talons.

You were the center of gravity in a dance that you were observing but not participating in. The bloody aerial ballet sucked Diana in. She wanted to be able to look down on everything from a safe vantage, to catch thermals as she noted every nuance and detail of the creatures cavorting below, to be a watcher who could strike with deadly precision. Peregrines were a particularly good example of raptors' resilience. Unlike the sharks in Dag's drawings, these graceful airborne assassins thrived in an anthropogenic world where skyscrapers were their cliffs and street pigeons their quarry. Peregrine populations were higher in urban centers than they had ever been in the wild. Cities were a counterintuitively ideal habitat. Diana realized that deep inside she was still a little girl wishing she could rise above the fray of a failing state.

A heavy plopping sound brought her back to earth.

"We're here." Nell stretched and then ducked into the cabin. "I just dropped anchor."

"Here" turned out to be fifteen meters offshore. Instead of a beach or a dock, waves broke against barnacle-encrusted boulders. Peeking over the tops of them was the air traffic control tower of Oakland International Airport.

Nell emerged from the cabin carrying a bright-yellow dry-bag. Then, in one smooth motion, she pulled off her dress.

"Take off your clothes," she said. "You're not going to want to be damp for the flight."

Diana did as she was told, and Nell stuffed the clothes and briefcase into the dry-bag and strapped it shut. They climbed on the gunwale.

"On three," said Nell. "One, two, three."

The water was shockingly cold, driving the air from Diana's lungs. They both came up gasping and laughing at the silliness of it. Needing to bike and sail and swim to the airport because the world had stopped working altogether. It was ridiculous. But it was also real. They reached the rocks in a few strokes and scaled them with extreme care, trying not to cut bare hands or feet on the vicious barnacles. Then they climbed over the fence at the top, and finally they were standing on the grass, runway after runway spread out before them, planes parked in place where the feed had left them.

Nell slung the bag off her shoulder and shook the hair out of her eyes. Her nipples stood erect atop bell-shaped breasts, and sunlight turned the droplets clinging to her trimmed pubic hair into rainbow prisms.

"Damn, girl," said Diana. "You *sexy*."

Nell chuckled. "Right back at you."

Diana shrugged. "This bod might be tight, but it ain't hot."

Nell gave her a look. "That's only because you've spent your life trying not to be noticed."

Nell tossed her a towel from the dry-bag, and they dressed quickly before jogging off, shoes squeaking on the tarmac. It took them a while to get to their destination. Airports were big when you were a pedestrian. No planes took off or landed. No lights blinked from the towers. There was no real activity at all, though there must have been people holed up in the terminals. Soon they were past the terminals and in an area reserved for private hangars.

Nell pulled up in front of one. Panting, she pulled a physical key from her pocket and approached the human-size door next to the airplane-size hangar doors.

"You use an old-fashioned padlock?" asked Diana.

"Nobody knows how to pick mechanical locks anymore," said Nell. "It's better security today than it was when they were in common use."

Inside it was dark, but the hushed echoes of their footsteps indicated a cavernous interior. Nell unbarred the hangar doors, and they pushed them open, straining against the weight, hinges squealing. Sunlight fell through the gaping opening, illuminating the treasure within.

"Lockheed P-38 Lightning," said Nell in a reverential tone. Propellers tipped the ends of twin booms. Between them was a central nacelle with a cockpit under a bubble of glass. "It was the primary

American long-range fighter during World War II. They used it for bombing, ground attack, and interception across every theater, but primarily in the Pacific. With the drop-tanks, you should have just enough fuel to make it to DC."

The fighter gleamed in the angled light like a sleeping predator.

"This one was built in Burbank," said Nell. "It's a reconnaissance model. No armaments, but a much longer range because there isn't as much weight. They put cameras on these things, used them to map out enemy movements." She ran her fingertips along the fuselage, which was painted in what looked like thick black-and-white racing stripes. "These are the invasion stripes they used for the Normandy campaign." The American World War II insignia was painted on each boom, and near one end of the wing, a white star in a midnight-blue roundel with white bars coming off either side. Belatedly Diana realized it matched the small pin Nell sometimes wore. "The commander of the Eighth Air Force personally piloted one over Normandy so he could watch the offensive. 'Sweetest-flying plane in the sky,' he said. He's right. She's stable, forgiving, and quiet thanks to those turbo-superchargers. I've replaced, repaired, and maintained every flap, bolt, and wire. That's the only way to know she'll fly like a dream."

Nell scrambled up a ladder onto the wing and then gave Diana a hand up.

Diana squatted and placed a hand on one boom, imagining the engine roaring to life, the propeller blurring into motion, this manufactured bird of prey charging hungrily up the runway and into the empty sky it was engineered to dominate.

"Here," said Nell, leaning into the open cockpit and tossing something to Diana.

Diana caught it. It was a battered leather flight jacket, complete with squadron patches and an elaborate tiger stitched across the back, rampant and glorious. She shrugged it on and looked up at Nell.

"You really think of everything, don't you?"

Nell squatted in front of her, a delicate frown creasing her forehead. "Lots of people think Analog is nothing but a fetish, a way to put the past on a pedestal. But I wouldn't be so devoted to something that was just a shrine to anachronism. That's not what Analog's about at all. It's about using technology with *intention*. It's about recognizing and respecting the hidden powers of the tools we use and how we choose to use them." She placed a hand on the boom next to Diana's as if checking the P-38 for a heartbeat. "How we do things shapes what we do."

Diana zipped up the jacket. "I'll take good care of her," she said. "I promise."

Nell sighed. "You wouldn't be here if I didn't know that already. Now let's get you airborne, sister."

CHAPTER 39

The yoke thrummed under Diana's hands as the P-38 clawed into the sky. Her eyes danced across pressure gauges and dashboard indicators, tiny diagnostic windows into the workings of this antique marvel. She mentally cycled through every button, lever, dial, and switch, silently repeating Nell's instructions, thinking through scenarios where she might need them, branding everything into memory.

Diana had proved herself a decent pilot during training. Even though nearly all aircraft were feed driven, Langley wanted its field officers equipped to handle as many situations as they possibly could. That included manual flight training for a wide variety of models. But that had been years ago, and she'd never flown anything remotely close to this venerable specimen. They hadn't anticipated the possibility of escape from an aviation museum. Shame on them.

Takeoff had been hairy. After finding a stretch of empty runway, people pouring out of the terminals to gawk at the strange spectacle and Nell giving her two thumbs-up, the twin engines had howled like banshees as Diana opened up the throttle. She had got off the ground just in time to make it over the tail of a passenger jet sitting frozen on the tarmac farther down the runway.

Now she was airborne, curving around in a long arc over the bay to soar east over Oakland. The city shrank beneath her, and cumulus clouds towered above, their bulbous protuberances shaded in hot pink and saffron by the sun setting behind the Golden Gate Bridge.

Everything went white as she entered the belly of a cloud. The feedless P-38 became a microcosm of the feedless world, blinded by the hand of a fearful goddess. The cramped cockpit turned suddenly claustrophobic, the domed glass shrinking to entomb her in this aerial coffin that she should never have acceded to climb into. Having so far survived this day's many dangers, it was suicidal to have boarded this death trap. Was she really after a solution? Or was she seeking annihilation instead of redemption?

But then the propellers shredded through the far side of the cloud, and the world opened up around her again, spires and arches and cliffs of colored fluff forming a vast celestial palace beyond even the intricate fantasias detailed in Dag's notebooks. Even this world devoid of justice was occasionally blessed by beauty. Diana drank in the view, dousing the flames of anxiety with wonder.

This was the peregrine's vantage she had envied. It was a relief to leave Dag, Nell, Rachel, Javier, Hsu, and the rest behind to debate their options and make their plans. She had convened them, offered them a new path forward, and now she had a mission.

Missions had always been handed down to her. That they came from above lent them an authority that confirmed Diana's confidence. The job must be important because it came from Helen. The job came from Helen because it must be important. Whatever the specs, whatever it demanded of Diana, it was necessary and therefore undeniable. That was what *chain of command* meant, and chain of command was sacred. There was no need, no opportunity, to question. Diana could perform the most vicious acts safe in the knowledge that her conscience could remain clear. She had outsourced her moral compass to a higher power,

Helen. Even as a freelancer, moguls and robber barons had set Diana's agenda, dubbing her a pawn in their convoluted intrigues.

The second Diana had rescued Dag, that house of cards came tumbling down. This new mission bore no seal of approval but Diana's own, and the prospect was scary and intoxicating. This was her life, and she would choose how to spend it, come what may.

The P-38 reached cruising altitude, and Diana double-checked the heading, matching it against the charts she and Nell had pored over in the safety of the hangar, mapping out her route to the nation's capital.

Glimpses of farmland were visible through gaps in the clouds below. California's Central Valley provided fresh produce to much of the country, massive industrial farms in a battle of attrition with drought, pests, and climate change where the prize was keeping millions of pantries full. Despite their apparent verdancy, Diana hated these vast tracts of monoculture. They were precisely the opposite of what she had tried to achieve in her greenhouse. They were a green desert, a poor, brittle ecosystem whose lack of biodiversity increased short-term yield at the expense of everything else.

Over the last few centuries, the world had become a monoculture of polities, every scrap of land divided by borders into countries where the nation state ruled. But the feed had no borders, and its digital fascia might support novel social institutions. Tomorrow's announcement would inject new dynamism into the system, rebalancing incentives, freeing things up so that maybe, if they were very lucky, one day the world's political ecosystem might resemble the wild perennial grasses she and Sofia had admired on the slopes of Mount Tam, diverse, messy, and resilient.

The Sierra Nevada mountain range emerged from the clouds ahead, the last rays of sunlight igniting the peaks like a menorah. Each candle snuffed out as the sun dropped below the horizon behind her.

How we do things shapes what we do. Diana remembered the enforced calm with which Rachel had taken the day's devastating news. The old woman was an enigma that Diana was only starting to crack. The intensity with which she listened. The facility with which she let others lay out the arguments that were doubtless raging in her head. The conviction with which she confronted impossible decisions.

Commonwealth was everything to Rachel, and yet she had killed the feed in an instant once she realized it was necessary. Hours later she was risking everything, *everything*, yet again to sidestep Helen's coup and challenge the entire geopolitical status quo on first principles. *Do it.* Diana had never expected her to say yes. It was a last-ditch effort, a sliver of hope in a bleak situation. It was too much to ask, too much to even internalize. And yet it was happening. All because Rachel was so ruthless in pruning her assumptions that she faced every obstacle as if it were unique. Despite her age, she didn't live in the past, hobbled by the constraints of experience even as she harvested its benefits. It was awe inspiring.

It was full dark now. Peering down through the cabin window of a normal flight, Diana was used to seeing webs of lights spread out below. Sprinkled thinly across rural stretches, they amassed into sparkling terrestrial nebulae around urban centers. Not tonight. There was nothing but darkness below as stars began to wink to life overhead.

While there was still so much to do, she didn't have time to dwell on the events of the day. Reflection would come later. For now, she had to prepare to meet the president of the United States. Diana marshaled her thoughts, calling to mind every detail she could remember about Lopez. There was the public stuff of course. When you ran for office, your PR people tried to buff up your reputation just as the opposition smeared it. One way or another, your life was on public display. But Diana knew more than what a civilian could find on the feed. She'd heard chatter about Lopez from staffers in Beltway bars, reviewed his government file when he'd become vice president, and kept her ear to the ground for rumors from her agent network.

Hours passed, and the stars wheeled above her.

The important thing wasn't winning a trivia contest about Lopez's background. It was figuring out what made him tick and how he made decisions. She compiled a mental model of his personality, dropped him into imaginary scenarios, and played out how he would respond, always ready to defend his theoretical actions with anecdotes from his past. Logic was important, but people put rationality on a pedestal. You didn't change someone's mind with a frontal assault, lobbing facts at them with an intellectual trebuchet. That was how you started a fight at a family Thanksgiving dinner. If you truly wanted to sway someone, you had to understand them first, figure out how they felt and why they felt it. Then you worked your way up from emotions and values to beliefs and points of view. The long route to decision-making was the only accurate one.

Diana yawned and took her body's hint, popped the stimulants Nell had supplied, and washed them down with a swig from the water bottle at her side. This was a long flight, pushing the very limits of what the P-38 could handle. Exhaustion could kill.

She focused on the rumble of the engines, feeling the vibrations travel up and down her spine and numb her hands on the yoke. This was a beautiful machine, an angel of death built by the leading aerospace experts of its time to rain destruction from the skies. That Nell had offered her such a treasure was an extraordinary act of trust. That Nell had inferred Diana's profession was an indication that her own security protocols needed to be improved and that Nell was even more dangerous and useful than Diana had come to assume over the years. Then again, the very fact that Nell knew more than she ought to was in many ways the truest reason why she'd offered to help. She knew Diana as few others did, even though her evidence was slim. The only place where Nell's intuition had gone awry was in dubbing Diana a good person. Nell's incomplete estimation won Diana a pass she didn't deserve. She had done horrible things to good people all in the name of patriotism. When you owned your own decisions, you owned your own sins.

The moon rose above the horizon, yellow and fat, throwing its buttery light over the miles of country spinning past below. Diana checked her course. She was on track. Hour after hour after hour. The engines purred. The fuel gauge edged toward empty. The moon arced across the sky, painting the ragged clouds chrome, obscuring the stars with its brightness.

And then the radio squeaked and Diana nearly had a heart attack.

"This is Captain Lisa Woodward of the United States Air Force." A burst of static. "Identify yourself and divert course to these coordinates." A string of numbers. "I repeat, this is Captain Lisa . . ."

Diana craned her neck around to peer through the glass bubble of the cockpit. There, up and off her tail, were two sets of running lights. Shocked, she instinctively tried to summon the feed, but nothing came. Squinting back at them, she could make out their wedged shapes. Antique F-16s. Late-twentieth-century fighter jets. The military must have started to scramble whatever prefeed equipment they could find. They both rocked their wings and flashed their running lights. She looked down. That must be Cherrydale. She was so, so close.

For a mad moment, she imagined peeling off into a spin and trying to ditch her tail before coming into the city under the radar. But she was in a P-38, and they were in F-16s. They were air force jocks, and she was someone who had once gone through flight training years ago.

". . . yourself and divert—"

Diana rocked her wings in response and clicked through. "Hi, Lisa, this is Special Agent Valerie Daniels from the San Francisco bureau of the FBI. I am on an emergency mission with critical intel about the feed disruption to deliver to POTUS. Thank you for your escort. Never thought I'd fly a relic."

"Please divert course, and we will bring you down at Reagan."

"Roger that."

They must have cleared the runways. Reagan wasn't far from the White House. It would do just fine.

The left engine coughed, and Diana's eyes flew to the fuel gauge. Empty. The engine sputtered, quit, came back to life for a moment, sputtered, and died. The left propeller began to slow, the individual blades becoming visible as if emerging from a heavy mist.

"So, Lisa, this is a little awkward, but my left engine just died, and I don't know if I have the juice to make it to Reagan."

The Potomac appeared ahead, an inky serpent slithering through the capital.

"If you cannot make it to Reagan, eject and ditch the plane in the river. We'll have someone come pick you up."

The right engine coughed.

"I really, really can't do that," said Diana, thinking of the gentle way Nell had run her fingers along the underside of the wing. "I'm going to bring her down on the Mall."

"We cannot let you fly any closer to the capital. Follow my instructions, or we'll be forced to shoot you down."

The Potomac was approaching fast. There was the Arlington Memorial Bridge. On the far side would be the Lincoln Memorial and the Reflecting Pool behind it. To the right was West Potomac Park, where she'd smoked a joint with Kendrick and explained watcher, sleeper, and dreamer dikes. That meant—

"Oh, come on, Lisa, you don't want to get pushed in front of a tribunal to explain why you shot the messenger during a national emergency, do you?" There was the Washington Monument, the needle polished silver in the moonlight. "It won't be just a reprimand. You'll be court-martialed."

"Divert your course immediately, or we *will* fire."

"They won't let you fly all the nice, shiny toys anymore." Keep talking, even hardened pros rarely shot people midsentence. "It would be such a shame, a flygirl with your skills never getting to go up again." The right engine died. "They'll throw you away to rot in some military prison." She was over the water, gliding now. "On the other hand, all you need to do is pull up and you're a hero." There. Just past the Lincoln Memorial was the JFK Hockey Fields, a long stretch of empty grass running parallel to the Reflecting Pool. "See that stretch of open grass? That's where I'm headed. I'm out of fuel. No way I can even go—"

"Do it *now*, or we will—"

"I mean, you already have quite a story to tell given that you're the one they sent up in an antique when the feed went down." She was coming in low, tree branches almost brushing the belly of the P-38. "And this'll make the story that much better. You can tell your grand-kids you met Valerie fucking Daniels." Her knuckles were white on the yoke. She was going too fast, had too little control. "Totally worth it, if you ask me. Then again, I'm biased. I really—"

Impact.

It was all Diana could do to keep the yoke from leaping out of her hands. Sparklers exploded in her vision. The P-38 leapt and jolted and squealed as it plowed across the field. It was going to flip. She was going to die. At least it would all be over. And then the plane slowed and slowed and slowed and came to a sudden stop. She was alive. The P-38 wasn't at the bottom of the Potomac. Nell wouldn't hate her forever. Probably.

The F-16s screamed overhead.

"Lisa," Diana called into the radio as she popped open the canopy. "You're a goddamn saint."

Blood pounding in her ears, Diana grabbed the briefcase, pushed herself out onto the wing, and dropped to the ground. Her legs turned to jelly when she landed, and she collapsed onto the grass. The world spun. Taking a deep breath, she stood, knees trembling, and stumbled toward the squad of marines jogging up from Independence Avenue.

"Oy," she called. "A little help over here, please?"

CHAPTER 40

Diana had practice bluffing her way through complex bureaucratic hierarchies. An agent who couldn't talk her way out of an arrest wasn't much of a spy at all. There was the time she had got into the VIP soiree at the World Economic Forum without a ticket and made it all the way to a UN undersecretary's suite. Once she had to cross from Malaysia to Singapore without papers and with a refrigerated pack of wildly illegal biosamples. Cadence was important. Bureaucracy had a certain rhythm to it, a steady drone punctuated by authoritative emphases not unlike a didgeridoo. Body language was another piece of it. She had to emote confidence that everything was guaranteed to work out in her favor and that she was happy to wait as long as necessary for it to do so. Social dominance was key. No matter what their rank, they were lucky to be helping her. But the real trick was empathy. Being the agent of a massive bureaucracy was tough. The organization behind you gave you power, but it could also crush you for the smallest of mistakes. If you wanted folks to do something, you needed to offer them a path forward that appeared to minimize their chances of backlash from their bosses. If their ass was covered, they'd help you out.

The marines were easy. Diana was used to operating in foreign countries where she might not know the intricacies of rank, internal organizational dynamics, and social cues. But this was America, and she'd known enough marines to know how to talk to them. Soon they were all jogging up Seventeenth Street, saving her from harassment by the other street patrols who had effectively put this part of the capital under martial law.

Secret Service stopped them at the gate.

"I'm Special Agent Valerie Daniels, FBI," she said. "I've got time-critical intel for POTUS about the feed disruption. Please let Kendrick LaGrange know I'm here. He should be with the president right now." Without the feed they could neither vet her credentials nor contact the FBI for confirmation.

"Ma'am, we have the whole area on lockdown. Nobody's allowed in or out."

"This is a national security emergency, and I've just flown across the damn country to deliver a message. Work with me here."

"I'm sorry, ma'am, orders are orders."

She stepped right up to the man's thick besuited chest, dialed up her intensity, and lowered her voice.

"I'm not asking you to let me in, I'm asking you to send for LaGrange. Tell him it's related to Operation Diana. Don't worry, he'll come running and relieve you of the need to make this call yourself."

The agent stared down at her for a moment and then raised a battered old walkie-talkie. Kendrick was there ten minutes later, shepherding her through the gate and waving off the escort. Tension suffused his large frame like static electricity. They set off across the South Lawn.

As soon as they were out of earshot of the Secret Service agents, he hissed, "What the *fuck*, Diana? What's going on? How are you here?"

She squeezed his shoulder. "Don't worry, I'll fill you in on all the details. For now the important thing is Helen's raid failed. The feed will come back on in the morning. As long as I can speak to POTUS, everything should be okay. Or at least as okay as we can hope for. Can you get me in?"

"To talk to Lopez? Jesus, Diana, you never stop."

"Kendrick, I need this. Can you get me in to see him?"

He grimaced. "Yeah, I can manage it. But no promises as to whether he'll listen."

"Let me handle that."

And then she looked away from Kendrick's face to the building waiting across the grass. They must have managed to get a feedless generator working because lights were shining from the windows. The streets the marines had marched her through were dark, and the electric glow elevated the White House into a sacred hall where fickle gods might sit to bicker over the fate of humanity. Suddenly Diana was once again that veteran spook returning from Buenos Aires with a special delivery in a diplomatic pouch. She was an agent fresh off the Farm approaching the White House for the first time, trying to absorb some of the confidence that Helen exuded at her side. She was a little girl entering the first-grade classroom in Arlington, enduring the stares of the other kids and failing to understand a single word of this strange new language that nobody spoke in the home she had never wanted to leave in the first place. But she had paid the price, earned herself a place in this new reality, etched its principles into her identity, and lived to see them broken.

Diana was a refugee from the state of being a refugee, and she was going to turn everything upside down.

CHAPTER 41

The Oval Office was crammed. The Joint Chiefs, the attorney general, Senator Watkins, the director of the NSA, and other key advisers Diana didn't recognize. Hard faces. Then there was Sean representing a broad array of private-sector interests. He had flinched when she walked through the door at Kendrick's side, and she remembered coconut water splashing across his kitchen floor. Lowell was there too, game face firmly in place as if he had been expecting Diana's arrival. Lopez sat brooding behind his desk, leveling an unreadable gaze at Diana as she made her presentation.

She explained Helen's plans. The fabricated evidence. The subsequent phases that would turn a simple raid into a global empire. As if reliving the scene earlier that same day, Diana opened the briefcase and passed around its contents. Then she moved on to why the feed was down and what Commonwealth would do when it came back on.

There were questions, arguments and counterarguments, and a lot of profanity. Diana was surprised to find herself weathering it with the calm of someone who knew she'd already won. Warning Commonwealth about Helen had been a start. Convincing Rachel to transform Commonwealth into a new species of geopolitical player had been a victory. Against all odds, Diana had even beaten Helen to Lopez. This was the coup de grâce.

Ragnarok. World peace. Rapture. Humans loved to dream of endgames. Nothing was more alluring than a decisive victory, a moment after which the world would be forever changed. Except the world was forever changing. Victory was always temporary. The only prize was the opportunity to fight another day. And that meant that this briefing couldn't *only* be a coup de grâce. It must also be the preface to what came next.

So Diana left things out. She never mentioned Kendrick's clandestine involvement. She didn't name Sean or Apex. And she painted Lowell as an unwitting ally of Helen rather than the man who had inspired the entire scheme. The lies of omission began to pay off even as she spun them. Kendrick bolstered her position, pointing out how Helen had misrepresented his team's financial analyses. Sean stayed silent. And Lowell. Oh, Lowell. Diana remembered the burgeoning resentment in his eyes when Helen had dismissed him and Freja at the Ranch. The firebrand opportunist struck again, feigning shock at the suggestion that Helen's evidence might be fake, backpedaling with all his might even as he searched for an orthogonal strategy to latch on to. So much for loyalty. He was a man in perennial search of the next game, and Diana had just handed him a ticket.

Helen could still undo much of the damage. She was a master of spinning up counternarratives and applying just the right kind of personal and political pressure. But in order to save herself, she'd need to apply all her time, effort, and focus to defense. She couldn't build an empire if her coalitions crumbled, her reputation tarnished, and her influence waned. And her influence over one man in particular was crucial to Helen's grasp on the reins of power.

"Mr. President," said Diana. "There is a related matter that I think you ought to know about."

"You've gone this far," he said in that famous gravelly baritone. "Why stop now?"

"This is extremely sensitive."

He raised his hands, and Diana noticed calluses on his thick fingers. "More sensitive than what you've just described?"

"Mr. President, I think you'll want us to be alone to discuss this particular item."

"Oh, come *on*," said the attorney general in disbelief.

Lopez silenced her with a gesture. "These are my most trusted advisers. All of them have the highest level of security clearance. Anything you want to say to me, you can say to them."

Diana looked at him for a long moment. The craggy face, the thick black mustache, the dark-brown eyes that made you wish he was your grandfather. He was a fair, thoughtful, optimistic leader. A far better president than Freeman had ever been. The United States had thrived under Lopez's split administrations, and his patient, diplomatic style had run counter to the divisiveness that had suffused American politics.

"May I?" She leaned over his desk, plucked a pen from its case, tore off a strip of paper from the pad, and wrote a short note. Then she folded it and handed it to Lopez. He opened it, frowning, and then descended into some kind of fugue state as he read. He just sat there, staring down at the slip of paper in his hands.

Ten seconds passed. Twenty. Thirty.

"Sir?" asked the chairman of the Joint Chiefs.

Lopez emerged, looking up at them as if through the veils of a higher dimension obscured by the vicissitudes of space-time.

"Out," he said in a tone that brooked no argument. "All of you."

Without his retinue and robbed of his composure, Lopez was suddenly just a person. The weight of office still rested on his shoulders, but Diana saw only the earnest, tired, haunted man beneath.

"What *is* this?" he asked, beseeching her to make it all go away as easily as the note he crumpled and slammed onto the desk.

But Diana didn't make it all go away. Like a banker leading a prized client to the most secure vault, she reached inside herself and unlocked the darkest secret ferreted away in her psyche. She told him about how

Helen had recruited her, trained her, cultivated her refugee's overdeveloped patriotism, made Diana her protégé, dispatched her on missions of increasing importance until she became the most trusted of lieutenants. And then there had been that most sensitive of mandates, orders straight from this very office, so delicate that nobody else at the agency could know. The jacarandas had been so beautiful, turning Buenos Aires into a whimsical paradise of fluffy purple and green. But Diana had eyes only for her black market biochemist. With his concoction safely stowed in her diplomatic pouch and after running a twelve-hour surveillance-detection route through fallen flowers, she had retraced her steps to Washington, to this very building.

"I saw you that day," she said. "We passed each other in the hall. You were in a gray suit and seemed upset about something. You'd have no reason to remember it, though."

But remembering fleeting faces and names was a critical skill for a politician like Lopez. He was constantly forcing himself to recall this or that donor and the niece or nephew of whichever congressperson was holding up his latest initiative. With an archaeologist's care, he excavated the memory, and she saw the flash of recognition in his eyes.

"That was the day," she said. She told him how she'd delivered the package to Helen. How shocked and appalled Diana had been at the announcement of Freeman's death. How suspicion had curdled into certainty as she obsessively matched every detail she could gather from the autopsy with the symptoms of the engineered poison she had clandestinely delivered. Diana had left no stone unturned looking for an exculpatory explanation, something that could leave her conscience, her sanity, her loyalty to Helen intact. But when she returned to Buenos Aires, the biochemist had vanished like a Borgesian knife fighter, his lab stripped, every detail of his existence corroded away. So it was with every other lead. The operation had been so tightly planned, so perfectly executed, that its very competence confirmed Helen's guilt. Then Diana's years in exile, the painful silence borne in the knowledge that revelation would do more harm than good to her beloved adoptive country.

By the end they were both crying.

"I still have the files from my personal investigation in a secure cache," said Diana, swiping away tears. "I'll forward you them as soon as the feed comes back on, and you can corroborate them with whatever you have access to that I don't."

"All vice presidents dream that they might step up to take the president's place in a time of crisis," said Lopez, blowing his nose into a tissue. "But it turned out to be a nightmare. I wasn't ready. I didn't want it. That's why it took me so long to run for a second term."

"Helen didn't care about what you wanted," said Diana. "She couldn't have Freeman locking her out. He hated her, never could stand women in positions of power, from what I heard. Sexist asshole. Helen knew you'd be a better president, even if you didn't want it. The best leaders are unwilling."

"This can't come out," said Lopez. "Not now. Not with everything else."

"I know," said Diana. "You're the first person I've ever told about any of this."

"What would you have me do?"

Diana shrugged. "Just be yourself. I didn't fly all the way out here to tell you what to do. I did it because you're an honorable, decent man and the kind of president this country deserves. You need to know about Helen, about Freeman, about Commonwealth. Now you do. It's up to you to decide what to do about it."

"How about you?"

"I'm Commonwealth's new chief intelligence officer." The thought occurred to Diana as she formed the words. The only way to stay safe was to stay powerful. Anyway, Rachel wouldn't have much of a choice. "I'm going to build them an independent security service. Can't play the game without messing around in the shadows."

"You know I have to fight it," said Lopez. "We can't have a private firm challenging American sovereignty."

"Of course you do," said Diana. "I'm not asking you not to fight it. But whatever you do, make it slow and deliberate. With Hsu in hand, we'll have provisional backing from Taiwan and the UN. The faster the US gets behind it, the better provisions you'll be able to negotiate for Americans. So denounce it at a press conference, let the SEC and DOJ file their suits, but use that as leverage to get the deal you want instead of trying to undermine a process you won't be able to stop anyway. Don't waste billions building shitty parallel infrastructure. We're happy to paint Helen a rogue, give you a chance to save face and make nice. If you play your cards right, you'll keep a lot of Commonwealth jobs and benefits onshore and get access intransigent countries won't. That alone will secure a substantial American advantage for at least the next decade. A better legacy than sour grapes and a recession."

"Hijo de puta."

"That about sums it up."

Lopez narrowed his eyes.

"Anything comes up," he said, voice regaining some of its steel, "I want to deal with you. Directly. No proxies. No bullshit."

"Mr. President," said Diana, extending a hand. "It would be my honor."

Diana wasn't just loosening Helen's leash by opening Lopez's eyes to her conspiracies. In confiding in him, Diana had begun to forge a new bond. Secrets shared could be more valuable than secrets held.

CHAPTER 42

Her message delivered, the storm of White House politics passed Diana by. Lopez was back with his advisers, struggling to work out a way forward and get ready for the inevitable moment when the feed came back and they would have no choice but to make a move. Diana wandered the halls, hands buried in the pockets of her flight jacket, half-formed thoughts and emotions she couldn't name surging through her. She needed space. She needed to get out of this suffocating building.

Outside, the brisk night air refreshed her. She stepped off the path and onto the grass, relishing the feel of springy turf under her feet. She moved along the south side of the East Colonnade. There was a rectangular lawn here, surrounded by garden. Just enough light spilled out from the windows above for her to examine the horticulture. She reached out and rubbed the small leaves of the low line of sculpted bushes. Boxwood with some ageratum behind it. Magnolia and littleleaf lindens enjoying pride of place. A smattering of perennial flowers. Many of the same plants were massed together, with foliage plants filling the gaps. The organic structure reminded Diana of Beatrix Farrand's seminal gardens. The overall impression it left was of something designed but not engineered, a marriage of botanical growth and human imagination.

Diana yawned. Her adrenaline was receding and the stims with it. A migraine threatened. She lay in the middle of the lawn and looked at the sky. Only then did she realize how exhausted her body was. The cockpit of the P-38 had left her stiff and cramped everywhere, and she hadn't even sat down since. Everything ached. But spinning above her tender flesh were thousands of stars.

Besides the White House itself and a few other critical buildings, Washington was dark. The moon had set, and the absence of city glow left the Milky Way to shine in all its glory, stretching across the sky from horizon to horizon. She let her tired eyes follow the pinpricks of glittering light and the smudged nebulae that seemed so solid, so close that she could reach up and singe her hand on the cascading fusion explosions.

Voyager was somewhere up there, arcing through the absolute stillness of interstellar space, bombarded by dust and cosmic rays, its equipment long dead, but its precious cargo still intact, humanity's first offering to the greater universe. How many shepherdesses had lain on grass just like this over the centuries, stared at the stars, and sung of better days to come? How many daughters of the diaspora were looking up right now, humming *Izlel je Delyo Hagdutin* and remembering their grandmothers? This pale-blue dot was too small for small thinking. *Let's keep this Golden Record spinning*.

Diana awoke with a start.

Her feed was back, messages and notifications and data flooding in, threatening to overwhelm her. The morning sun was hot on her face. Dew-wet grass scratched at her neck. The sky above was pale blue and blank as a Zen mind. But Diana's mind was filled with cobwebs, the sticky tendrils of receding dream.

A call was coming in from Dag. She accepted it.

"You're alive." The relief in his voice melted something inside her. "What happened? Where are you? We're still here at Analog. Rachel's about to make the announcement."

"Thank heaven Helen wasn't able to track you down during the night," she said. "I'm here. I got in to see Lopez. He knows what's going on, and I don't think he'll fight it."

"Holy shit," said Dag. "I need to tell Hsu. He's already on a call with Taipei."

"Do it," said Diana. "I'll fill you in on the details later."

"I—" said Dag. "I'm just so glad you're all right."

"Me too."

After they signed off, Rachel began her announcement, the live stream sweeping across the entire global feed like wildfire. Press kits had been distributed, and journalists, pundits, and politicians were desperately trying to catch up and synthesize hot takes. The storm had begun in earnest and wouldn't end anytime soon.

Diana silenced the feed and sat up, rubbing the sleep from her eyes.

The White House. She was sitting in the middle of the Kennedy Garden right in front of the White House. But where last night the building had been infused with a kind of sacred power, this morning it had shed its symbolic gravitas. It was just a house filled with scared, manic people doing their best to guide a world that was impossible to tame.

And then the second call came, just as Diana had known it would.

"Good morning, Helen," she said, injecting a kick of jauntiness into her tone. "Beautiful day to be alive, wouldn't you say?"

"I don't know what the fuck you did, Maria." Helen's voice was a drawn blade. "But I get it. We both know how this works. There are players and there are pawns. The only way to be a player is to be dangerous, so dangerous that other players can't ignore or outmaneuver you. You've made your point. You're dangerous. So what exactly is it that you want?"

"Wow," said Diana. "No small talk? Not even a smidgen? I must say, I thought you'd fall from grace with more grace."

"What do you want?"

Diana rolled the question around in her mind like a marble.

"I'm not sure," said Diana, plucking a leaf from behind her ear. "But I'm looking forward to finding out."

CHAPTER 43

Diana turned over soil with her trowel. She relished the ache in her knees, the dirt smeared across her face, and the sweaty feeling of her hands inside the garden gloves. It had been a month since the "disruption," as the media had dubbed it, and there was more work to do than could ever be done.

Lopez had called off the raid, had quietly initiated an investigation on Helen, and had enlisted Kendrick's help in attempting a firm but moderate engagement with Commonwealth as it took its place on the world stage. Wall Street was up in arms over the forced buyback, and lawsuits were multiplying like litigious rabbits. Although governments were issuing dystopian pronouncements, Hsu's influence had solidified enough support in exchange for favors that at least they'd have a chance of making good on the gambit. Knowing that without the feed their countries would grind to a halt, most world leaders were playing ball. For now, at least.

Commonwealth had already elevated their Taipei, Paris, Singapore, Colombo, Addis Ababa, Santiago, Tokyo, Kumasi, Vancouver, and Amsterdam offices to the status of coequal headquarters and begun to shuffle key staff between them. Five locations had been granted embassy status. Frantic negotiations were underway at the UN. At the same time, Commonwealth started to roll out direct benefits, each algorithmically targeted at the level of individual feed users and funded by a portion of global profits. If you were diagnosed with cancer and your community failed to provide adequate public health care, your feed might automatically deliver a personal stipend for a private clinic. If your child was struggling with geometry, your feed could supply a plethora of teaching materials optimized for their learning style. If your home was swept away in a monsoon flood, your feed would direct you to a relief center where you would be provided with food and shelter. Overseen by Javier, these preliminary efforts had already earned friendly media coverage that helped to offset the flood of rhetoric from establishment politicians and financiers.

Diana still had no idea if any of it would work, or even what it "working" meant. But she had her hands more than full in the meantime. Ever since that fateful meeting in Analog, she had been acting as Commonwealth's chief intelligence officer, and Rachel had soon made the de facto designation a real title. They all had titles now, one way or another. Diana, Haruki, and Dag had all been roped into this all-consuming effort and had been sleeping at Analog or in the Commonwealth offices in whatever time they could snatch.

This was the first day Diana had been able to sneak away, and she knew precisely how she wanted to spend the few precious hours. She had gone straight to the nursery. Now she was kneeling in the dirt, replanting her barren greenhouse.

She twitched, nearly crushing the fragile root system of the fern in her hand, as she heard the door to the cottage open behind her. She pivoted on her heels, tightening her grip on the trowel. It wasn't sharp, but it was the closest thing to a weapon within reach.

"Hey," said Dag, somewhat sheepishly. "I didn't realize you were here. I just—I hadn't been back since, and I don't know, I figured—"

She remembered Dag coming out of the kitchen balancing plates of pancakes and grinning like a maniac, the smell of frying bacon wafting down, the lush greenery around them, the intimacy of the little table, her surgically deployed sexual innuendo. She had tuned him out so quickly in that conversation, retreating into the virtual universe of the feed, resenting the pressure of his affection and his inescapable presence in their home, seeking solace in finding a mission, a goal more worthy of her attention than the people closest to her.

Leeches and ghosts. Ghosts and leeches. *Whenever there's a chance to get real, you run for your life. I guess it must be easier to cling to God and country or whatever it is that makes spies tick.* She had kept the gates to her soul locked up tight, forgetting they were made of glass. Dag had seen the ugliness at her core from the beginning. Now he was probably here to collect his things and move out.

Diana dropped the trowel and snatched up the bag from the nursery. She needed to try. It might be hopeless, but she wouldn't be able to live with herself if she didn't at least try.

"Hey," she said, walking up to him, trying to wipe the dirt from her forehead but succeeding only in smearing it further. "Want to help? I could really use a hand." Reaching into the bag, she pulled out a second pair of gloves and a trowel. "I got you these." She smiled tentatively. "I'm on the market for an assistant, someone to coach in the magical arts of horticulture. I can't very well replant this greenhouse on my own. And, well, I hoped your offer might still be open?"

Dag looked down at the gloves, up at her, down at the gloves, up at her.

"Sure," he said at last, pulling them on, and a burst of light filled Diana, so bright that she swore it must be shining from her eyes. "But I'm warning you, no green thumbs on these hands."

Diana had to swallow away the lump in her throat before responding.

"Don't worry," she said. "There's no such thing as a green thumb. Gardening is all about learning how plants think, how they feel, what they need. It's about loving them for who they are, not who you wish they were. It's about trusting them." She shrugged apologetically. "I've been trying for years, and I can't say I'm very good at it."

"And here I was hoping it was just a lot of digging."

Even though it wasn't that funny, she couldn't suppress the laugh bubbling up from deep inside her. Dag grinned. She led him down and showed him how to dig a hole and plant a seedling, how soft the soil should be, how to loosen the root bundle and moisten the waiting earth. She shared her philosophy of gardening, how to envision the ways the garden would change as plants reached maturity, the differences between perennials and annuals, the personalities exhibited by various subspecies of mushroom, and how Darwin had become obsessed with orchids toward the end of his life, believing them to be the perfect botanical example of evolution. Finally she explained what gardening meant to her, how it was a sacred refuge, this greenhouse chapel, a bulwark against the chaos of the outside world. She came here to feel safe, to connect with something older and larger and more profound than herself, to kindle a sense of wonder and feed her soul. And in halting sentences, she told him how rare that feeling of safety was in the life she'd lived, the life she'd chosen, how precious these fleeting moments were to her, and how easily she could overreact if she imagined they were under threat, holding them so tight, they might shatter.

"I feel the same way about drawing," said Dag. "It's this door I can open inside myself. I go there when I can't go anywhere else. Only sometimes, I can't get out."

Diana looked at him, so intently focused as he gently placed a small fern into the hole he'd prepared. And she was suddenly overwhelmed by a shapeless emotion that crashed through her like storm swell. While she was out on missions these past few years, Dag had been holed up in the cottage, drawing. Diana had always imagined it almost like some kind of retirement. That after the carbon-tax affair, Dag had thought he deserved to just do something he enjoyed for the sake of it. That seemed fair enough to her after what he'd been through. But he hadn't been happily immersing himself in a favorite hobby. She recalled the violence, the horror, the tragedy woven through his illustration of postapocalyptic La Jolla. For Dag, drawing was an act of self-recrimination, an apology for sins he could never fully redeem, an expression of guilt so deep, it curdled any attempt at true happiness. Every stroke of his pencil was a razor laid prospectively on the wrist. Here was a man who hated himself almost as much as she hated herself. But he didn't deserve it. If there was one thing she was sure of, it was that he didn't deserve it.

Diana squeezed her eyes shut. Maybe she didn't deserve it either. But in order to change her destiny, she had to reclaim her past.

"Let's play two truths, one lie," she said, silent tears streaming down her face.

"Ahh, okay," said Dag.

"All right. I'll go first," she said. "I've killed a US president, I lost my virginity to an Olympic swimmer, and my real name is Maria."

"An Olympic swimmer?"

"I cheated, they're all true."

"No shit, did he have a nice bod?"

"Who?"

"The swimmer."

She giggled. "Huge pecks, small pecker."

"Eeesh, that must have been disappointing."

"Only in retrospect. At the time I didn't have anything to compare it with."

Her giggle morphed into a choked sob and then back into a giggle. Dag placed a steadying hand on her shoulder. Maybe in learning to hate themselves a little less, they could learn to love each other a little better. *Love if you can't help it. But trust? Never.* That was dead wrong, like so many of Helen's manipulative maxims. Lopez wouldn't have thrown off Helen's yoke if Diana hadn't confided in him. Nell wouldn't have offered up her treasured P-38 if she didn't truly care for Diana. Rachel wouldn't have changed Commonwealth's direction if Diana hadn't shared her deeper motivations. Kendrick wouldn't have warned them of the impending attack if they hadn't built a real friendship over the years. Dag wouldn't have helped develop the desperate plan on their flight from the Arctic if Diana hadn't finally told him what was really going on.

Espionage might require sacrifice, but trust was the currency of life. Spies were humans just like everyone else. They were just humans who loved chasing secrets. Secrets. Those gems of privileged intel that she had dedicated so much energy to collecting, whose possession made her feel special. But the superiority of omniscience was an empty sort of pleasure. It was a way to detach herself from the life she was too scared to live. Diana had spent long enough living by Helen's rules. Time to start figuring out some of her own.

"So, Maria," said Dag as he patted the soil around the newly planted fern. "How's this little guy looking?"

Diana removed her gloves and ran a finger up the stem of the plant and all the way along the edge of an exquisitely delicate frond.

"Beautiful," she said. "Just beautiful."

The future was wound up in the fiddlehead, ready to unfurl.

AFTERWORD

Unlike any other book I've written, *Borderless* had a title before I sat down to draft chapter 1. The dismantling of borders is a powerful theme in my life, and I began to recognize it beneath the surface of the headlines. The characters, plot, and world gravitated around this core idea before falling into place as I made my way through the manuscript.

I am a child of immigrants.

My father is from Amsterdam. My Jewish paternal grandfather was one of the only members of his family to survive World War II. He hid in a secret compartment while Nazi patrols searched their cramped apartment. Meanwhile, my paternal grandmother, a Protestant, became a secret agent of the Dutch resistance, ferrying information, supplies, and people out of the camps, even as she raised and protected her family. They fled to the United States when they worried that the Cold War might devolve into a third world war.

My mother is from Vancouver. Her family immigrated to Canada from the Orkney Islands north of Scotland, and for them, British Columbia must have felt tropical. I have many fond memories of scrambling over rocks and sneaking through forests on Vancouver Island with my cousins. And, of course, huddling around the monitor's glow to play *Final Fantasy VII* while our parents shook their heads in bewilderment.

My wife is from Colombia, and her family escaped the drug violence that plagued Cali by moving to Connecticut. Just before I embarked on *Borderless*, we volunteered with a local resettlement agency to host a Ugandan refugee in our home in Oakland. The initial commitment was for three months, but Marvin ended up staying for nine months and became a dear friend. We've learned an enormous amount from each other, and he continues to find it quite odd that my "job" is writing books.

As I prepared to write this particular book, I couldn't help but notice how different our world today is from the one my grandparents inhabited. Baby pictures from friends living in a far-off Austrian village greet me when I go online after my morning coffee. A momentary uptick in Sri Lankan tea prices zips through global markets at the impossible speed of high-frequency trading. We can fly halfway around the world only to board an on-demand car service and stay in a stranger's apartment complete with an unfamiliar toilet and a friendly list of local tips taped to the fridge.

While I worked my way through the rough draft, more modern oddities presented themselves. I used Google Maps to track the trajectory of Diana's flight to and from the Arctic. I played around with a research tool that projects the impacts of sea-level rise on specific urban areas. I discovered the beautiful true story of the Golden Record via Maria Popova's peerless blog, *Brainpickings*. Just for fun, I backed a Swedish artist's Kickstarter project and began a collaboration with a designer living in Argentina and an illustrator living in New Zealand. My grandfather spoke Esperanto, but he would never have recognized this weird dimension we insist on calling "reality."

Cars, telegrams, planes, phones, trains, broadcast media, and container ships made the world smaller. Now the internet is stitching the strange, scary, and wonderful pieces together into a single civilization.

Unfortunately the results aren't always pretty. As I write this, authoritarian populism is rearing its ugly head, hate-mongers dominate the news cycle, and a country of immigrants is beginning to turn away people like Marvin. This is something my grandparents would recognize in a heartbeat.

Fear at an uncertain future is all too understandable. Technology isn't just making our national borders more porous, it's shifting the borders of the twentieth-century social contract and causing a lot of people a lot of suffering. But letting fear get in the way of reason leads to ruin. Civilization is more delicate than it seems, and unlike previous civilizations that were geographically limited, this is the only one we've got.

Progress is painful. We use technology to do work we would prefer to avoid and then need to make up new jobs for ourselves. We enjoy the cheap prices made possible by offshore manufacturing and then realize we can't enforce social or environmental regulations across the supply chain. We download entire libraries of pirated music and then discover we must support artists if we want more of what we love.

Problems beget solutions beget new problems. The snake eats its tail, and we go round and round again. But that doesn't mean things don't get better. Child mortality, infectious disease, poverty, and violent death are at all-time lows. Literacy, longevity, and scientific knowledge are at all-time highs. There isn't a time in all of history I'd rather live in than the present, and there's nothing more important than doing our part to build a better future.

By the time I finally reached the end of the rough draft, Diana had become a close friend. As a quirky and dangerously competent spy, she was enormous fun to write. Chapter by chapter, she developed a stronger and stronger sense of agency until I felt like I was documenting her adventures rather than inventing them. Diana proved herself to be the kind of person who doesn't shy away from hard truths, who confronts and overcomes her own flaws, who aspires to serve rather than rule others, and who fights through all the madness and pain that life throws her way in order to do what she feels is right.

I have a lot to learn from her. Perhaps we all do.

Thank you for reading. I put my heart and soul into this story, and if you're still with me, I can only hope that it resonated with you. As in so many other arenas of life, the borders delineating the publishing industry are changing fast. But there's at least one thing that's as true as ever: writers write manuscripts, but books succeed thanks to the support and enthusiasm of readers. If you enjoyed *Borderless*, please leave a review and tell your friends about it. It may feel insignificant, but nothing is more powerful than word of mouth.

Onward and upward.

Cheers,

Eliot

FURTHER READING

People often ask about the writing process, but I find the reading process much more interesting. Reading is a superpower that we too often take for granted. It is telepathy. It is a time machine. It is a magic door into countless new worlds, hearts, and minds.

I am a reader first and a writer second.

Ever since I can remember, I've loved books. When my parents read me stories as a child, I would stare into the middle distance and lose myself in them indefinitely. Growing up, I would hide among the dusty library stacks until closing time. When high school English teachers passed out assignments, I ignored the curriculum and ventured off on my own. Curiosity is my drug of choice.

Sometimes reading a book stokes my enthusiasm so much that I simply can't wait to dive into a new story. My dearest hope is that *Borderless* did that for you. There are so many incredible books out there, fiction and nonfiction, that can entertain, inform, and transform us. Read. Read. Read some more. Oh, and please share your favorites so we can benefit from your discoveries.

After finishing a great book, I often wish I could ask the author what they are reading. What books touch their very core? Where do they find inspiration? Where does their enthusiasm lead them? I've found many of my favorite books thanks to recommendations from my favorite authors.

I'm sure you've realized it by now, but I'm a little crazy. Obsessed, even. But if you just happen to be a little crazy too, then I've got a secret for you.

Every once in a while, I send a simple personal email sharing books that have changed my life. Because reading is such an integral part of my creative process, I often find gems in unlikely places. The goal of the newsletter is to recommend books that crackle and fizz with big ideas, keep us turning pages deep into the night, and help us find meaning in a changing world.

I also share writing updates and respond to every single note from folks on the mailing list, so joining is the best way to get or stay in touch with me. There's nothing I love more than hearing from readers.

Oh, and if you decide to join our little gang, promise me this: when you come across a story that moves you, pay it forward and pass it on.

Sign up here: www.eliotpeper.com.

ACKNOWLEDGMENTS

Our culture unfairly privileges the author's role. Books are collaborative efforts from inspiration all the way to distribution.

Adrienne Procaccinni, Paul Morrissey, Courtney Miller, Colleen Lindsay, Brittany Russell, Kristin King, and the rockstar team at Amazon Publishing turned the raw manuscript into a book and shared it with the world.

DongWon Song, my indefatigable agent, provided wise counsel and necessary course corrections.

Tegan Tigani was a fabulous editor and whipped the manuscript into shape. Any surviving errors are mine alone.

Josh Anon, Lucas Carlson, and Tim Erickson contributed invaluable notes that helped make the story the best it could be.

Kevin Barrett Kane and Emma Hall designed the breathtaking cover.

Craig Lauer, Carl Franzen, Danny Crichton, Cyrus Farivar, Josh Elman, Tim Chang, Brad Feld, Malka Older, Micah Baldwin, Berit Anderson, Brett Horvath, Nick Farmer, Cory Doctorow, Katie Moran, William Gibson, Ramez Naam, Hugh Howey, Craig Mod, Patrick Tanguay, Meg Howre, Ben Casnocha, Omar El Akkad, Barry Eisler, Kevin Kelly, Elizabeth Bear, Rick Klau, Janis Williamson, Klint Finley, Warren Ellis, Zeynep Tufekci, Laurie Acheson, Azeem Azhar, Janet Morse, Chris Anderson, Becky Thomas, Eric Holthaus, Max Gladstone,

Tim Ferriss, George Eiskamp, Edith Howe-Byrne, Mike Masnick, Eric Raab, Nick Harkaway, Feliz Ventura, Dan Ancona, Jake Chapman, Carlos Hernandez, James Zhang, Jorge Luis Borges, Om Malik, Daniel Suarez, Haje Jan Kamps, Tim O'Reilly, Ken Davenport, Bryan Walsh, Ryan Holiday, Kevin Bankston, Maria Popova, Nick Greene, Franco Faraudo, Seth Godin, Andrew Chamberlain, Ev Williams, and Ada Palmer were deep, powerful, and generous sources of ideas and inspiration.

Karen and Erik Peper, my wonderful parents, taught me to follow my curiosity.

Andrea Castillo, my brilliant and beautiful wife, was a patient, insightful, and exceptional creative partner. Our dog, Claire, kept me company as I wrote.

Finally, you read *Borderless*. In doing so, you brought Diana and her world to life, and hopefully she will stay with you as you brave your own adventures.

To all, a thousand thanks.

ABOUT THE AUTHOR

Photo © 2014 Russell Edwards

Eliot Peper is the author of *Cumulus*, *True Blue*, *Neon Fever Dream*, The Uncommon Series, and *Bandwidth*, the first novel in the Analog Series. His near-future thrillers have been praised by *The Verge*, *Popular Science*, *Businessweek*, *io9*, and *Ars Technica*. Eliot is an editor at *Scout* and an adviser to entrepreneurs and investors. He has helped build various technology businesses, survived dengue fever, translated Virgil's *Aeneid* from the original Latin, worked as an entrepreneur-in-residence at a venture capital firm, and explored the ancient Himalayan kingdom of Mustang. His writing has appeared in *Harvard Business Review*, *TechCrunch*, and the *Chicago Review of Books*; and he has been a speaker at Google, Qualcomm, Future in Review, and the Conference on World Affairs.

Visit www.eliotpeper.com to learn more—and to sign up for his reading recommendation newsletter.